Darkly Dreaming

Book 1 of the Darkly Vampire Trilogy

Chloe Hammond

Darkly Dreaming
Book 1 in the Darkly Vampire Trilogy
by
Chloe Hammond

Copyright © Chloe Hammond
2nd edition 2016
Published by Reeves Publishing

<u>Dedication</u>

This book is for Mrs Kath Nicholas,
my English teacher at Glan-y-Mor.
Your belief that I would, allowed me to believe
that I could. Thank you.

Acknowledgements

I have so many people to thank. I want to start with my friends and family who have supported me through a very tough time, and gave me the love and help I needed to write my first novel. Especially huge thanks go to Chris Linley, Dee Williams, and Abigail Rose, who read, and read, and brainstormed, and read some more as I wrote and rewrote Darkly Dreaming until it read like I'd dreamt it.

I also want to thank everyone who has received my openness about my own anxiety diagnosis with details of their own quiet struggles. And even better, those who have let me know that watching me strive towards my life's dream, has given them the inspiration to try to do the things they had always wanted.

I also want to thank my friends in the Cake and Quill writing group who have offered me ears to rant to, invaluable advice, support when my spirits ebbed, and most of all laughs, lots of laughs. Special mention goes to Angelika Rust for her attention to detail and kindness in helping with the final, essential polishes, which have allowed Darkly Dreaming to shine like I hoped.

I cannot thank Catherine Lenderi enough for her wise editing, advice, and formatting. I'm so glad I found you. Artist Owen Claxton took my garbled ramblings about how I envisioned my cover and created the artwork I adore.

And last, but definitely not least, thank you to my husband, Garry Rowe, who never doubted that I could, and so I did. I love you too.

Prologue
Suzannah

Suzannah felt the penis in her mouth twitch as she twirled her tongue around the tip. At last. She was getting neck-ache, and the handbrake was digging into her ribs. Deft and practised, she sped up her sucking, and was relieved to hear the grunt of release from above her. She discretely spat his pleasure into the tissue she had been holding in her left hand ready. She took a swig of the travel-sized bottle of mouthwash in her handbag, swilled her mouth out, and opened the passenger door to spit neatly besides the car. She wiped her fingers on a perfumed wet-wipe, and pulled the passenger mirror down to repair her subtle nude lipstick, finishing with a blot of gloss in the centre. She cast her eyes critically over the rest of her face, and then used a shellacked nail in Parisian Pink to remove the slight smudge of eye make-up under one eye.

Suzannah didn't use cheap makeup, or exert herself, so she rarely suffered smudges, but kept a close eye just in case. She used small regular doses of Botox between her brows and at the sides of her eyes and nose as a preventative, and had miniscule amounts of filler injected into her lower lip to make her pretty mouth that much more kissable. She took care to ensure that while her face may have difficulty scowling, a tantalizing smile or sultry pout was only enhanced. She had neat HD brows, stuck in place, and although she would never wear anything as crass as false eyelashes, she had a few semi-permanent flairs accenting the corner of each eye, adding a catlike tilt to her naturally, rather bland brown eyes. Suzannah worried that dates might be mistaken into reading softness in her muddy brown eyes so she usually wore discrete icy blue contacts that more accurately reflected her calculating nature. Tonight she hadn't been able to wear them because she had a slight irritation in one eye, so she'd carefully adapted her makeup to make them look as rich as possible. Her appearance was cultivated to look fresh and pretty in a way that only very rich women could afford; it took a lot of time and very expensive products to look so dewy and natural.

Suzannah only had one ambition in life. To get married. To someone very, very rich. It was what she felt, she deserved. Her mother had skilfully married her rich stepfather, and then been able to send her to expensive boarding schools, so she could learn how to entice and entrap such a man for herself. Her future contained sun-kissed beaches, champagne-soaked skiing holidays, and two perfect children raised by nannies and private schools. She just needed the perfect husband to finish the picture. He had to be handsome, ambitious, dim, and completely in thrall to her. This man she had just sucked off was not him. He had, however, treated her to a perfectly lovely evening and so she had known that payment would be expected. Suzannah prided herself in her ability to judge a situation and know how to handle the men she dated. She would leave them pleasantly satisfied with her company, but under no illusions that she wanted to see them again.

She knew exactly the type of man she would marry, and at twenty-six was only just feeling the first stirrings of concern that her job in P.R had not brought her into contact with the perfect candidate, yet. Tonight's date was not interested enough in her; he had hardly bothered bragging at all. He had continually talked about the benevolent fund his father had entrusted to his care. They had met when he hired her to promote a fundraising event, but she had assumed it was a time-filler until he could take over the reins from his father. When she realised his enthusiasm was earnest, and not just an affectation, she had lost interest as quickly as dowsing a candle flame. Ethical concerns are very dangerous to a decent income and lifestyle. She had remained coolly charming, and after dinner, once they were in his Landrover, which she now realised he drove for necessity, rather than just rugged effect, she had suggested a slight detour to the local beauty spot.

Once they had pulled over, she had removed her essentials from her handbag in preparation, then reached over and unzipped his trousers. The fact he still wasn't fully erect as she'd taken him into her mouth had been further reassurance that he was only Mr Right Now, nothing more. An efficient blowjob would leave him satisfied and prevent him badgering

6

her for anything else. Suzannah withheld full intercourse until the ninth or tenth date; consequently, she'd only ever actually gone all the way with two men, both of whom had bitterly disappointed her by exposing weaknesses, one for gambling, and the other for cocaine. Luckily, their addictions had revealed themselves before she had actually married either of the Fiancés.

And so the hunt continued. A friend had recently suggested she should become a high class escort and earn her own fortune since she expressed no desire to feel love in return. Suzannah had scoffed at the suggestion, and discretely removed the girl from her contact list. Suzannah's friends were just opportunities to socialise and meet appropriate men. She did not share intimacies, although she collected those which could come in handy later and stored them like trinkets to use as careful currency to her own advantage. An escort has a shelf life in the way a wife doesn't. As long as she was the mother of his children, even if her husband eventually traded her in for a younger model, he would still be financially responsible for her. An escort could never marry into her social circles, everyone knew each other, and her past would soon be exposed.

Her polite blowjobs were expected payment to a man who had bought her oysters and champagne and tickets to the Opera, but full intercourse, although pursued, would lead to the loss of all respect, and this disintegration of reputation would spread. She had had to affect to be utterly distraught following the end of her two engagements, thus ensuring everyone knew she was the wronged party, and hence lessening the devaluing effect of two failed attempts.

After a final squirt of Dior on her throat to cover up the slightly too musky scent that had transferred from him to her, she looked over at her date with a bright smile that did not reach her eyes.

'Ok, out you get,' he said.

'What?' Suzannah blinked at him, owlish in her surprise.

'You can walk from here.'

'I, I…' Suzannah was dumbfounded; she had never misjudged a situation this badly before. Normally, her dates were so happy she had given them a blowjob they hadn't had to beg for, they were more than happy to run her home afterwards, while she chattered brightly about something inconsequential. She collected useless snippets to pepper and ease any silence.

She was wearing her Louboutins and they would be destroyed if she had to walk any distance in them. She looked at her date in disbelief; this was the height of bad manners on his part. He met her startled gaze with calm defiance. He was laughing at her, and the realisation made hot fury flood through her. Without another word, she flung his car door open and strode out, slamming the door without a backward glance. She stalked across the carpark as he wheel-spun away with an unnecessary bout of engine revving.

'What a dick,' she muttered. Once he had driven off, she realised it was very dark. The parking area was not lit, and although it was a clear night with a bright three-quarter moon, there were tall trees around three sides. This is why she chose to bring men here when she wanted to dispatch her obligation quickly. She felt vulnerable and alone. She burrowed in her Mulberry for her i-phone; the light from the screen was reassuring, but the lack of a reception bar filled her anew with rage. Her heels were four inches high and the tarmac was pot-holed and strewn with gravel and pebbles. Tottering carefully along with the screen light on her phone offering enough of a glow to avoid the worst of the rubble on the road, she picked her way across the carpark towards the main road.

'Can I help?' The woman had appeared silently at her shoulder, making Suzannah squeak with fright. Despite the darkness, Suzannah found she could see her quite clearly; the woman seemed luminescent in the phone's feeble glow.

'Oh,' she said, forgetting why she needed help. 'Ah,' she gasped, gazing at the stranger's beautiful face. Suzannah had never dallied with other teenage girls at school, she couldn't see the point. She never got girl crushes or appreciated the curve of another woman's breast. Her relationship with other women was either fiercely competitive if they were attractive, or utterly dismissive if they weren't. Now, though she was entranced, she felt wrapped in warmth, every limb languid and relaxed; she wasn't aware enough to realise she had stopped thinking and instead was just feeling, feeling bliss.

The other woman smiled and her plump lips curled back to reveal small spiked teeth, which lengthened as Suzannah gazed at her. Somewhere, very deep within, a small primitive part of Suzannah recognised a predator and set up a tattoo of alarm. But clouds of pleasure and relaxation quickly smothered the alarm before it did more than raise her heart rate for a beat or two. The beautiful brunette reached out and stroked a finger down Suzannah's cheek, and she was too enthralled to notice the hooked finger nail extending into a talon. Suzannah leant forward into the other woman's embrace. She was too lost to be aware as the bewitching beauty neatly slit the artery in her throat and nuzzled into her neck to feed.

Chapter 1
Rae

Plumereau Square, in the old town of Tours, looks magical. Lights are strung across between the ancient buildings and the whole central space is packed with rows of benches and tables, covered with white cotton tablecloths, jars of candles and scented jasmine. Music plays in the background; I hope there won't be too much Johnny Hallyday and U2 later, but for the moment chilled-out Blues classics are wafting through the gentle spring air: 'Summertime….' Billie croons softly. Staff from the different bars around the edges of the Square bustle back and forth, taking orders and delivering drinks, wearing white shirts, black trousers and the very French long aprons that come to the ankle.

Townspeople and tourists, students and farmers are happily seated together drinking, eating, and smoking. Arms are waved, shoulders shrugged and there are lots of Gallic "Ehs", "Boufs" and "Biens" mixing with raucous laughter, which gets louder as the evening progresses. My friends and I arrived early to make sure we got seats together, but even at six o'clock the Square was noisy and full. Our group has ended up having to split into two; I am sitting with Layla, Nicky and Maddy at the end of one table in the far corner of the Square, while Louise, Sam, Lizzie and Melanie are on the end of the next table but one down the square, next to an unlit narrow alley running between two medieval taverns.

Layla is my best friend, and has been since we met on our first day at University. I was an awkward teenager, I found social politics difficult. I'd changed schools and cultures frequently throughout my childhood, moving around the world following my academic parents' university tenures. The main thing I'd learnt was to avoid causing offence or becoming the butt of too many jokes by keeping my mouth shut.

Standing outside my personal tutor's room, waiting for the first meeting of my new university life, I was insecure and scared and trying terribly hard not to show it. I noticed the impish girl queuing behind me, but didn't dare speak to her.

Luckily, Layla was made of tougher stuff and proceeded to chat away to me through our induction, and then all the way to the union bar, and throughout Freshers' week. She was as insuppressible as a Labrador puppy, and by the time our lectures started we were inseparable, our names rolled into one- 'Raenlayla'. Throughout university our dreams and ambitions and adventurous plans were all shared and shaped to fit the two of us. Innocently, they hadn't included anyone else.

After graduation, careers and marriages dragged us apart from each other. Our attempts to maintain our happily-ever-afters had made us miserable and ill, individually. Layla and I had turned away from each other, and the other old friends who could see behind the deceitful smiles and question us into questioning ourselves. We were completely self-absorbed, struggling to keep our youthful dreams from shattering around our ears. We were always so busy, there was no time, too many things to do. We sent cheery messages on Facebook, the odd text saying 'Hi, I'm fine'.

Despite our attempts, Layla's marriage collapsed just before mine did, but while Layla's ended as quickly and cleanly as a razor slice, mine is dragging and limping out its death throes. At least her divorce meant she was able to rent me a room when I left James, so we've somewhat sheepishly picked the remnants of our friendship back up, after neglecting it for two decades, and we're trying to pretend everything is as it always was. I don't think we've forgiven each other yet, though, for not being whom we thought we were.

***

In the Square, the fete is in full swing, people are becoming more expansive, and mingling has started. Men tuck themselves in next to pretty girls, and women waylay handsome men as they make their way to the bar. By this time I am really quite sozzled, I'm sitting in a shadowy corner and I've blown out the candles closest to me so I can relax and people watch. I sway gently, humming along to the music, with my chin resting on my hands and a silly smile on my face as my half-mast eyes scan the crowd. I chuckle happily to myself as I watch a rather scary 'lady of a certain age' get knocked back by a good-looking young man who's been sat with a smiley girl all evening, but she has left his side now and the cougar has taken her chance to pounce. She is not gracious about the rejection and I am sure she would be scowling as she walks away if she wasn't botoxed smooth. The most she can do is stick out one rigid lip and flounce off, tossing her candy floss hair.

It makes me grin to sit at the party, mellow in the golden evening light, and think about how we all ended up here. Finally, we're getting our much promised weekend escape together, after almost twenty years of saying we would get away next year. To think, it's all a happy accident, and almost didn't happen.

On a Saturday evening, a few weeks ago, Layla had knocked on my bedroom door and trotted in carrying pint glasses of vodka and Diet Coke, with a carrier bag of takeaway swinging on her wrist, making her grip on the drink even more precarious. Her tongue was clamped between her teeth as she tried, unsuccessfully, not to slosh too much coke over her lovely, but completely impractical, new cream carpets. I jumped up and grabbed my drink, so she could concentrate on getting hers across the room without any more spills. As she reached my bed, she handed me her glass as well, while she plonked herself on the foot end, snuggling under the duvet, before reaching back for her drink.

'Singapore chowmein?' she tinkled.

My heart sank, she was being far too cheerful; she had an agenda.

She passed me a boiling hot tinfoil box of spicy noodles which burnt my fingers and made my stomach gurgle in anticipation. I dropped it quickly onto my bedside cabinet and then scrabbled in my bookcase for the two signed hardback Terry Pratchetts we use as tables. She never remembers trays.

'Good God,' I spluttered as I took a swig of my drink. 'That's almost all vodka.'

'Saves traipsing up and down for refills,' she told me smugly.

'Could have brought the bottles?' I suggested, still trying to catch my breath.

'Haven't got enough hands,' she pointed out.

12

I conceded this was true and took another swig. Once I knew what to expect, it slid down quite nicely, the warmth of the spirit spreading through my veins and relaxing me.

'This can't carry on,' she said firmly, apropos of nothing.

'What?' I feigned innocence.

'James,' she stated. I nodded, my heartbeat quickening. I knew what she meant.

We've developed a routine since I moved into Layla's spare room. Friday night is date night; Layla gets dressed up while I lie on her bed chatting and helping her choose what to wear. Layla loves to date; as soon as she was officially single, she signed up to every site she could find and started on a continual conveyer belt of first dates. Although she never sees anyone a second time, she collects an array of hilarious first-date stories that keep us whooping over our Saturday vodka nights. After we'd had a few drinks together, and I've confirmed she looks fabulous, she's off, flittering out, like a sparkly bird of paradise.

Home alone, I'll have a little bit more wine and listen to every heart-wrenchingly sad song I can find on Spotify so I can have a good cry while in peace. I really let rip with snot bubbles, and caterwauling along to the cheesy lyrics. I cry for how lost I am, how much time I've wasted trying to please other people, and how much I've hurt James without even feeling any happier myself. I thought that I could leave and everything would magically be better, but it's not like that.

Usually, I've reached a place of hollowed-out acceptance by the time James rings me, drunk and bewildered. I numbly listen to his beseeching and then tell him to sleep it off. But a few times he's caught me still howling; still lost in pain and guilt, and he's called a taxi to come and get me and take me to him. Then the next morning, I have to break his heart all over again, but with a hangover.

'You aren't being fair going back and forth like this,' Layla said sternly. I nodded again. 'Come on Rae, talk to me. You're not supposed to just agree with everything I say, you're supposed to argue back. You're supposed to tell me your side of the story. I make observations, and you get cross and let

13

some of the pain out, shouting at me. Come on, make me understand.'

'I will tell you, Layla. I promise. I just can't, yet,' I said, begging her with my eyes to understand. 'Hey, guess what I dreamed about earlier,' I shamelessly distracted her. She looked at me for a few loaded seconds, then decided to let me off.

'What?'

'France. I dreamt we were there again. We had found this little house down a lane, and we were going to buy it. We kept finding new rooms.' She smiled dreamily, and I was relieved I'd successfully diverted her. Somehow, as the vodka kicked in, I found myself suggesting we get a last-minute ferry crossing and retracing the path we'd hitched down France after university. Layla pounced on the idea immediately, and the next thing I knew she had booked it online in an alcohol-fuelled frenzy. We talked ourselves up, imagining re-finding ourselves, our young selves, as we went. As though we could unfurl those feisty, undamaged selves from the musty rucksacks with our camping gear.

Morning brought sore heads and a creeping horror at what we'd done. Too much too soon, living together in Cardiff we have other friends and our jobs, which take the pressure off each other. On holiday it will be just us. Neither of us wanted to admit we didn't want to go. I hoped my last-minute annual leave request would be refused, but my manager was worryingly enthusiastic, encouraging me to take two weeks, not just one. Layla is the department manager, so she had no excuse not to authorise two weeks as well. It's the first leave she's taken since she started her new job, and I think her team were starting to worry that she's Super Woman, always a better colleague in theory than practice. We both became quieter and quieter as the week passed.

I woke up in my customary lurch of anxiety gruesomely early the following Saturday morning. My mind immediately set up its usual churning around its well-worn tracks. What had I done? What was I going to do? Why couldn't I ever be satisfied? Why did I have to bloody mention bloody France? How the hell was I going to pay the stupid trip off my new credit card? I don't want to wipe out my tiny clutch of savings already. And then a genius brainwave sidled into my mind, the way the very best ideas do, while you are distracted by something else.

We could invite the others to come to France with us. We'd spent our final year of University living with the three other pairs of our friends. After graduation we'd eventually recovered from the realities of living with each other instead of the idealist hopes we'd had for a household of eight girls. We've all stayed in touch, meeting up every September to share news and gossip; we'd been promising ourselves a proper weekend away together for years.

Layla and I posted the suggestion on Facebook, tagging our friends into the post. We proposed that she and I would leave on the earlier ferry crossing we've already booked. We would spend the first week travelling slowly down France by train, since neither of us fancied trying to drive on the wrong side of the road. We could stop off at familiar towns on the way and get to see the bits we missed last time. We'd stay in hotels instead of campsites and eat in restaurants rather than heating tins of cassoulet over a camp fire. We would meet up with the others in Tours, the town Layla and I lived in when we were there. We could all spend our long-promised weekend away reliving our youth in the beautiful Loire Valley. Layla and I planned to show the girls our old haunts, assuming any of them still existed. Neither of us has been back to Tours since we headed home almost two decades ago.

'How has so much time gone by that we can fit such large numbers between us then and us now?' Layla asked me incredulously after we've posted our suggestion.

'Why does it feel that every step I've taken has been stumbling further into uncertainty, away from that shining surety of youth? Why, when I've been me for so much longer now, do I feel like I know myself less? How did I compromise so much of myself away?' I asked rhetorically, lubricated by relief and vodka into waxing lyrical about the complexities of getting older.

We must have accidently had our finger on the zeitgeist pulse. We often did when we were younger. We'd hoped a couple of the others would be able to make it at such

15

short notice, but five of them leapt at the chance, immediately responding enthusiastically to our post.

We waited with baited breath over the next few days as husbands were convinced, and flights were booked. I'd already checked the airlines and found a flight to Tours from London Stanstead airport on a Friday afternoon. They all live in London, so they only needed to book the Friday afternoon off work. Finally, we got confirmation that everyone other than Hannah could come, so Lizzie would bring her new best friend, Melanie. Lizzie promised us that Melanie's great fun and very easy-going, and it's those two who have to share a hotel room. Lizzie would have been the one who had to pay for a room by herself, and Nicky, Louise, Maddy and Sam weren't worried so Layla and I kept our concerns to ourselves.

Our trip was supposed to be just us, the 'house', but now there was going to be a stranger in our midst. We knew it would mean we would have to be on best behaviour, and make sure she didn't get bored or left out. We'd have to let her have a turn to tell her own stories about people we've never met. I felt surly and sulky, and perfectly entitled to be slit-eyed scowling selfish for a change; it had all been my idea after all.

***

Stepping out of the grand station in Tours on Thursday afternoon, we'd been bowled over by how familiar the beautiful tree-lined square in front of the station looked. We rushed to check into the Ibis Hotel we'd booked for ourselves and the other girls in advance. It's a bit basic, but it's close to the station, cheap and central. Once we'd dumped our bags in our twin room, we galloped back outside to adventure around and see how much of what we can remember still existed. The town was shockingly the same, and shockingly different at the same time. We wandered around and found our favourite Chinese restaurant, still in the same place, then we headed into town, and in the direction of the river until we could orientate ourselves with the breathtaking Cathedral. We found the theatre was still there, and so was the book shop where we frittered our limited money on precious English language novels.

16

As the day drew to a close, we chose a little bistro in the old quarter for our evening meal and sat outside enjoying the balmy evening, the good food and a chilled bottle of Vouvray, my favourite wine. We reminisced, and wondered, and ordered more wine. After dinner we realised we were gently tiddly, so we linked arms and meandered hotel-wards, only slightly unsteady on the cobbles.

Layla blamed me for the tottering, and I blamed the cobbles. Neither of us mentioned the wine. I noticed that we kept passing the same colourful poster in shop windows and taped to lampposts. Eventually, I stopped to get a better look; after squinting at it for a moment, I managed to make it out.

'Oo, look,' I called to Layla. 'Theresh a fete on Saturdsay in de Squarrrrre, the Frenches lovesh a good party. We can bring the othersh.' Knowing there is no way we'd remember what the sign said the next day, I took a photo with my mobile.

'I loves new technoloshy, Rae,' Layla said happily. 'In the old days we's a had t' steal dat poster.'

'Liberwate,' I corrected. 'Wees only ever liberwated.'

***

Sitting at the party now, I watch as the pairing-off becomes more definite. More and more people are moving into the corners, and candles are being blown out as newly met couples start to explore each other. My eyes drift around the Square and are caught by the group of British men, sat a couple of tables over from us. We'd chatted to them earlier, they are a slightly earnest woolly-jumpered group, cycling from Calais to the Loire Valley over a long weekend for the last bachelor of the group's stag do. The rest are married, and happily, I'd have thought, from talking to them earlier, but several of them are deeply engrossed with some women who have joined their table and are now sat on laps and kissing necks. Others of the group are sprawled drunkenly over the table with their red wine spilt and soaking into the table clothes.

'Well!' I slur to myself. 'Not so Mr Muesli after all.' Not my place to judge. Strangely, the men go both up and down in my estimation at the same time.

I giggle again as I notice that Melanie is one of the people who has pulled. She is sat with her back to me leaning into a blond man who has his arm around her and seems to be whispering sweet nothings into her ear. I frown slightly as I realise he is the man Lizzie was flirting with earlier. Indeed she'd been all over him, snuggling in as he nuzzled her neck, flinging her head back in utter abandon, but she is slumped over the table now, a sorry case of 'married Mum let loose' overindulgence, I think to myself. I hope this won't cause an argument later. On the one hand, Melanie has made a move on Lizzie's man, on the other hand, Lizzie is married, while Melanie isn't.

Oh well, none of my business I suppose, but at least it shows Melanie isn't the Little Miss Perfect she's been making herself out to be: pawing a stranger in public like that. All that cheek sucking and looking down her nose at Layla and me as we recounted exploits past and present with our friends. She really is starting to hack me off. Her voice has this shrill edge and she seems to feel that she can sit in judgement of people she hardly knows. It doesn't help that she looks like an annoyed hamster, with her fine mousy brown hair, chubby cheeks and non-existent chin. Layla and I have caught each other's eye several times throughout the evening meal as her strident tones overbore whatever the rest of us were trying to talk about.

The worst thing is that, just like we'd feared, all her stories are either work-related or about people we don't know, and even if you did care about assessing house insurance claims, or knew her friends, I still doubt they'd be funny. There was quite a scuffle when it came to splitting in the two groups this evening, and there was a definite feeling of triumph as we four had contemplated an evening without her. Indeed a large amount of the evening's hilarity in our group has been at her expense, but we feel she deserves it.

As I watch Melanie's shenanigans, a tall, distinctive man steps out of the alley and grabs his friend's shoulder. They seem to be arguing in hissing tones as Melanie lolls between them. Then the blond man stands, pushing her off him onto the table where she sprawls next to Lizzie. In an instant they are joined by the women from the stag group's table, and all five disappear back down the alley. "Hmm," I mutter to myself. 'Looks like they're a working group. I bet there's going to be some empty pockets in the morning.'

I go to nudge Layla and share my suspicions, but she is engrossed in a Frenglish conversation with the woman sitting next to her, and has, true to form, reached the point where she tells the stranger how wonderful she is and how much she loves her. With this in mind, and considering that Melanie and Lizzie are going to need to be borne back between us to the hotel, I wave over to where Maddy, Nicky, Sam and Louise are dancing with the other more energetic revellers in the brightly lit aisle between the two rows of tables. Eventually, I catch their attention and they meander back to us laughing and sweaty. Their smiles fade as they see the state Melanie and Lizzie are in.

Maddie and I hoist Lizzie between us, and Louise and Sam haul Melanie up. Nicky tucks her arm firmly through Layla's to stop her ricocheting off in pursuit of something shiny. It takes a long time to get back to the hotel. Melanie and Lizzie are dead weights and we have to stop for frequent rests, during which Layla tries to totter off and has to be caught by Nicky again. I expected Melanie and Lizzie to start to sober up as we walk them back, but they are still floppy and heavy, and we have to lug them, an arm each over our shoulders, their heads lolling. I, on the other hand, am sobering up quickly and starting to feel really annoyed at how inconsiderate they've been. What if the hotel won't let them in until they've sobered up? Who is going to sit outside with them?

I decide it's not going to be me; I'm not being nice at my own expense anymore. Luckily, when we get to the hotel, the night porter just rolls his eyes and shakes his head in disgust, pouffing his lips crossly as we stagger past carrying our shoes and fallen friends.

'Sorry, sorry, desolee,' I mutter. He doesn't offer to help us get them upstairs and as I look at the mirrored back wall in the lift I'm not surprised. Dehydrated, with smudged make-up and sweaty hair, we all look like sad forty-year-old trollops. I turn my back on the mirror in horror and promise myself it is just the harsh lighting; I don't really look like that.

We unceremoniously dump Lizzie and Melanie on their sides on their beds, turning the bathroom light on so they will be able to stagger in there in the night if they need to puke. After making sure they have a bottle of water each on their bedside tables, we leave them to it. Apparently, none of us feels like being nice anymore. The nights of sitting up stroking hair seem to be behind us. Unless we've all only done it for our closest 'pair'? I am too tired to figure it out, or even really care. My feet throb from walking home barefoot, my head is already pounding as my hangover kicks in and my stomach feels acidy and sickly.

When I get to our room, Layla is having a chat with God on the big white telephone. I take her a pillow and duvet, as I suspect she'll be there a while, hand her a large bottle of water from the bag of them I had the foresight to buy earlier in the day, and pat her on the head before closing the bathroom door. I neck half a bottle of water with some super strength painkillers, and munch some antacids as I collapse onto my bed fully dressed. I look forward to the morning, when we can look back and laugh.

All too soon my alarm goes off. I press snooze again and again, until I only have ten minutes left until breakfast finishes. Finally, I pull last night's dress off and drag on some trackies and a t-shirt - clothes I'd brought to be nightwear, but I can't bear the thought of anything more structured. I pat my hair as flat as possible and squirt some perfume into the air and step into the scented mist, holding my breath as my stomach clenches at the smell. I stick a piece of chewing gum in my mouth and stag towards the door.

At which moment Layla's bedding moves.

'Wait for me,' she rasps, sitting up. She doesn't even bother with my basic niceties, trotting alongside me in yesterday's clothes, her hair in a shaggy halo around her head. We get to the dining room with five minutes to spare. Nicky, Maddie, Louise and Sam are already there, keeping us a seat

20

and stockpiling coffee and croissants for us while the waiting-staff scowl. The girls howl with mirth when they see the state of us.

'Just like old times,' Maddie smirks as she passes me a coffee and the sugar bowl. 'Bleurgh!' is the most articulate reply I can muster for her.

We aren't allowed to take coffee up to Lizzie and Melanie, but we do manage to smuggle out some rolls and we take those up to their rooms. They are both still lying on their sides as we left them the night before. They are very pale, and in the strange light cast from the bathroom, they seem to almost glow. They are breathing so shallowly that for a horrible, heart-stopping second I think they are dead, but then Melanie rasps a snore and I snigger at how unladylike she is this morning.

Now I've been awake for a while, and eaten some lovely French carbs washed down with a couple of buckets of caffeine, I am starting to feel a bit better. After a long hot shower and scrubbing my teeth, I feel human enough to put on some make-up and face the world. Layla has also bounced back to her bubbly self, happily telling me she puked all the alcohol up last night, drank the water I'd given her and then slept the sleep of the dead.

Layla, Maddie, Nicky, Louise, Sam and I head out for a bit of delicate sightseeing and shopping, and more eating, and rather a lot of coffee drinking. We try ringing Lizzie's and Melanie's mobiles a couple of times but don't get an answer, so we buy them some juice and a baguette au jambon each and head back to the hotel in the early afternoon. The others need to leave to catch their plane home at three and so the bustle of packing and triple-checking passports begins. Layla and I are staying another night so we try to organise Lizzie and Melanie.

In their room we open the curtains and the windows and shout at them; we pack their scattered belongings as best we can, guessing whose clothes were whose. We pull the duvets off them and turn the telly on full volume to some bad French quiz show that seems to include a disproportionate amount of naked flesh. Nothing works. Lizzie gasps faintly, and Melanie snarls, but neither make any attempt to get up.

'Cheeky bitch,' Layla grumbles as the others come to see what's happening. 'She just growled at me, after I spent half an hour doing her sodding packing. Well, fuck her.' So the decision is made to leave them to it. They will just have to pay the extra to get the train back with Layla and I the next morning. We plan to stop in Paris, and then visit some of the regions we'd missed on our first visit for our second week, but they can catch the Eurostar home.

It's decided that Maddie will phone Lizzie's husband and let him know what has happened when she is at the airport waiting to board. Melanie lives alone, so we don't need to worry that anyone will panic if she doesn't get home when expected. We leave their bedding thrown back, windows open and tellies on, but turned down a bit for the sake of the other residents, in the hope it might rouse them. Or at least annoy them. By this time the others are running late for their flight. Layla and I decide to go to the airport with them to see them off, and then look for a nice spot for a picnic before having an early night. Just as we are leaving, I relent and scribble a quick note telling Lizzie and Melanie they've missed their flights, but Layla and I will see them home safe tomorrow, and not to panic because Maddie is phoning home for Lizzie.

When I go into their room to put the note on the bedside cabinet, I can't help but notice that Lizzie, who is closest to the window, looks worryingly white to the point of being translucent. I put my hand on her arm and feel that she's freezing, so I pull their duvets back over them, feeling bad. Layla had zealously pushed the window open to its widest point. As I stretch out to grab the handle, I look down and see the distinctive-looking man I'd seen the night before. The one who I'd thought was the pimp to the group of sleek blond men and women who had been mingling with the drunken revellers so thoroughly that I'd suspected them of picking pockets, or soliciting. The pimp is with a strange dark-haired woman.

They have a surreal, feral look about them and seem to rotate, looking up at me like cats beneath a canary cage, their eyes strangely large and luminous in their faces, so that I know it is definitely me they were looking at, rather than their eyes just being caught by movement. I only catch a glance of them

22

as I pull the window closed, but their image stays with me, demanding my attention. They seem malevolent somehow, and yet enticing. They make my mouth dry. I shake my head to dispel their image, telling myself to stop being daft. Why would they possibly have any feelings about me at all, never mind negative ones? It suddenly dawns on me that we must have upset them when we were trying to wake the sleeping beauties. God, I hope they don't have the room next door; we will have wrecked their siesta. The last thing I want is a pissed-off pimp having it in for me. I hurry downstairs to see if I can find them to apologise, but when I get outside there is no sign of them.

Chapter 2
Rae

Layla and I buy some delicious nibbles and settle by the river for a balmy evening picnic. We are happily retelling last night's adventures, filling each other in on the bits we missed, weaving our story of the party from the colourful strands of the night's events.

'You were never meant to marry him, you know,' Layla says as I reach for some of the fruit spread out on the borrowed hotel blanket between us. I freeze with a mouth full of strawberries.

'What?' I am baffled, and a bit horrified by what I think she's saying. 'What are you on about?'

'James. You were supposed to use him for a confidence boost. I knew he would adore you, but you were never right for each other, he's just too straight-laced.'

I blink. She watches me patiently as I swallow the suddenly tasteless strawberries and take a glug of water to force them down. I have been lounging back on my elbows, head tilted back, enjoying the sun's warmth on my throat, but now I sit upright, with my legs crossed. Layla mirrors me and we sit facing each other, while I fiddle with the strawberry husks in my lap, and only glance at her through my eyelashes. It looks like we're having the conversation now, and I've run out of excuses not to.

'You introduced us. He was your friend,' I protest.

Once we got back to Cardiff after hitch-hiking in France, Layla had struggled. She hated the boring, poorly-paid jobs she was offered through the agency she'd signed up to. She didn't tell me she was applying for the job in Swansea, and looked guilty but beseeching as she sat me down to explain she had been offered her ideal job helping to set up a rape support scheme there. I knew I would miss her like crazy, I could already feel my centre of gravity shifting as she told me; but I had seen her suffer with the jobs she hated for almost a year by then. Even as she enchanted her colleagues and made a wide circle of adoring new friends, I had seen her light dimming.

24

Friday nights out had taken on a slightly manic edge as she strove to escape the monotony of her nine to five existence. How could I let her know how devastated I was? I cheered her on, told her how excited I was for her, being offered such an impressive position. I knew she was going to a role where she could do so much good; and I was proud. I just wished the post had been in Cardiff.

I went up to Swansea with Layla to help her choose a flat, and she tried to persuade me to move with her, but although I had a vague browse through the job pages in the Western Mail like she asked, my heart wasn't in it. I belonged in Cardiff, and although she found a lovely flat right by the seafront, I just couldn't picture myself there. It broke my heart, but I couldn't live my life through her, and I had to let her go.

At her leaving party Layla led James over to meet me. She had beguiled James in her first job. He was one of many men of differing ages at the pub that evening who were following her every effervescent move with kicked puppy eyes. I wanted a man to look at me like that. James and I drowned our sorrows over Layla moving away that night, and woke up together the next morning. Hand in hand we waved Layla off, and I hid from my loneliness at losing her in exciting dates. James had grown up in affluent Cowbridge with his comfortable parents, and had studied accountancy in Bristol. He worked hard, but played hard too; Saturday afternoons watching football with the boys, followed by a skinful, were sacrosanct. James was a different kind of man from those I'd dated before. He was happy, open and straightforward; uncomplicated. If he said he was going to phone, he phoned.

Without my pivot, I needed his steadiness as I tried to find my own way in the world. I rarely saw Layla after she had moved to Swansea. We were both working so hard, establishing ourselves in our careers, then she had married a man she met there a couple of years after I married James. Although they would come to us for a night sometimes, and we'd go up to them a few months later, we were all busy with our new lives. James and I didn't really like Layla's husband, Mike, very much. He had a slightly abrasive edge, and seemed to feel the need to get one up on amiable James, so the gaps between the visits became longer and longer.

I try to explain this to Layla now, carefully skirting around my hurt at her leaving. I don't want her to feel guilty.

'Ok,' she says eventually. 'So he made you feel safe and loved. So you married him. But why did you become Rach?'

James had always called me Rach. When we first started dating, he had just ignored the fact everyone else, including me, had called me Rae. I hated it, but throughout our relationship he called me Rach so persistently that I stopped correcting him, and the new friends we acquired copied him, until eventually everyone called me Rach. Even me.

'I've been trying to figure it out too,' I admit to her. 'Where it went wrong, why, how much was my fault, you know, me being greedy, wanting more than anyone gets.' Layla frowns, starts to open her mouth, then thinks better of it and just nods for me to continue. She is going to let me explain this in my own way. I relax a little. 'I tried to work out when it started going wrong. I think the first warning signs were at the wedding. I wanted a laid back little wedding, but Marie was more traditional.' Layla frowns slightly again.

'I don't see how what your mother-in-law wanted has anything to do with your marriage?' Layla seems confused. I laugh softly; Mike's mother had emigrated soon after they'd met, and they rarely saw her so she'd had little impact on Layla's marriage. My wedding had been the start of Marie smothering my marriage with a particularly aggressive style of love.

'I accidentally let her takeover because I longed to be accepted into their family,' I mutter, ashamed of myself. 'I wanted a low-key celebration, a night in the pub with our friends after a quick ceremony, and then a honeymoon somewhere delicious, but Marie was horrified. I'd really disappointed her by utterly refusing to get married in a church. So it seemed churlish to refuse the marquee in their gorgeous garden too. James is their only child,' I attempt to explain to Layla, who pulls a scrunched-up so-what face.

'Our wedding was her only chance to organise one. You know my Mum isn't a weddingy woman, and she didn't really approve of us rushing into matrimony, so that left Marie. To begin with, we had great fun trawling through all the wedding magazines she kept buying, and I was quite happy to let her choose the colours of the flowers and napkins and things, even if she did pick lilac. You know I hate lilac, almost as much as pink, but none of those details mattered to me, not like they did to her. It was such a little thing to agree to, to make her so much happier.'

'I did wonder how the hell I ended up in a puce dress,' Layla scowls at the memory.

'Yeah, sorry about that. I don't think she liked you very much. Didn't consider you a good influence. You should have seen what she wanted you in, originally. At least the one you wore didn't have frills.'

'Frills? Ugh!' Layla shudders.

'I just wanted everyone to have fun. None of the faffy details really mattered, I was marrying the man I loved, and everything else was just trimmings.'

'Is that how you ended up in white then?' she asks. I nod.

'It meant a lot to Marie, and she was paying for most of it,' I shrug, not really able to explain how unanchored I had felt at that age, how unable to hold my own against the love bulldozer Marie had proved to be. Especially not to Layla, who always seems sure of herself. I wasn't sure I would be able to find the words to get her to understand what it was like. But I had to try.

'Do you remember how it had rained all of the week leading up to the wedding?' And it rained even more on the day. I refused to think of the snug function room at the pub, instead I gamely abandoned the white satin court shoes with the sensible heel that Marie had chosen, and put my wellies on.

'Marie was so horrified when we just laughed and hoicked up my dress, and clipped it above my knees with bulldog clips. And then when I slipped in the mud so I had a muddy bum all day I thought she would actually implode'. Layla grins at the memory. We had laughed and laughed,

James, Layla and I. We'd had a lovely day, and I steadfastly refused to see Marie's tear-stained face and horrified expression.

'That is the last time I can remember really, really laughing,' I confess to Layla now. 'But at the time, fitting in seemed to work for me. First, I got married and got myself the stable family I had always envied, and then I secured a place on the Probation training course. I was so excited when I got a job within the Cardiff team, and James was so proud of me. I loved working there, and I was good at it.'

'Somehow, after I'd handed over control of my wedding, it was impossible to ever get Marie back out of our marriage without a huge row. Everything was always done for my best, just not always what I had thought I wanted. I was young and eager to please James and be loved by his parents. Rae asked awkward questions and caused arguments and got into trouble at work for not being suitably subordinate. She upset James's parents by disagreeing heatedly with something they'd read in The Daily Mail. Rae caused nothing but trouble and I needed to be who people wanted me to be. I needed them to like me, and I believed that I needed to be like everyone else for that to happen. I slipped the Rae who'd hopped and skipped along, slightly out of step with the rest of the world, further and further into a dark corner of my psyche. I became stable, and practical, and useful. I became Rach.'

James and I had made new friends as a couple. We had them round to dinner on a Friday night, and James joined a wine club so we could serve good wine with the Jamie Oliver meals I cooked. I'd ignored Layla's voice in my head jeering as he held court, quoting what the accompanying pamphlet said about each bottle, as if he was saying something new and original.

These friends would help me clear the dishes away, and tell me what a great couple James and I were, reaffirming that my life was going well. Even while we struggled through losing his business, and almost losing the house we were like swans- smiling and smooth on the surface, while we paddled like hell underneath. I was annoyed by old friends like Layla, who looked a little closer to see where Rae had gone.

'I stopped drinking because alcohol let 'Rae' out and I needed to be Rach. I couldn't bear waking up to the anxiety attacks the next morning, while I tried to remember what I'd said to whom, and how much of myself I'd allowed to leak out. You know how much I hate being vulnerable.' Layla bobbed her head again, her eyes large, absorbing my pain with me. She was walking back through my life with me, as only a best friend will, looking at the ugly and shameful with me, and not loving me any less for it.

'Letting too much of myself show usually leads to being misunderstood and hurt, or taken advantage of and hurt, or worse being pitied and you know how much I detest being pitied.' Layla nods sympathetically. She can understand that, she hates being pitied too.

'Our new friends had only ever met this utterly sensible, upstanding member of the community with an important job, lovely home and nice husband. They wouldn't have guessed at the inner struggle to make the transition complete. I talked less and less about myself and my feelings because I realised that people preferred me when I listened to them. It was so much safer. I wouldn't accidentally expose a point of a view that caused offense or ended up obliviously boring people when I felt strongly about something and talked about it for too long.'

'I can't really blame James for this loss of self; you know how I've spent my whole life trying to fit in and he is so loud and sure of himself. He has never doubted himself, or how much other people like him. So they love him. I basked in the glow of his popularity. He drew all the attention, so I could relax and let him shine.' I glance at Layla again; I am exposing my underbelly, and after years of keeping my own counsel, this is hard. She meets my gaze. 'I became lazy and didn't push at my own shyness to step out from his shadow. In the seventeen years we were together I was just as complicit in what James wanted taking priority over my desires. I became passive and pleasing, you see, I hadn't realised that by pushing forward my rational self at the expense of emotional, irrational me, I would muffle my feelings and make them harder to identify. I didn't know I wouldn't get rid of them and all their inconvenience.' I take a sip of water, bracing myself for my confession.

'In hindsight, I can see that I mistook my emptiness for hunger. I sedated myself with sugar, swallowed words with sweets and crammed myself so full of chocolate that I could lose myself in overeater's self-hatred. And that's a hatred that's so strong it could distract me from anything else I might have started to worry about.' Layla and I had never discussed my gradually increasing weight over the years, but I had seen her seeing when I disappeared to do something important whenever the camera came out at social events, and I'd noticed her noticing when I wouldn't try clothes on during shopping trips anymore.

'I didn't really realise what I had done until our thirteenth wedding anniversary. We celebrated at Marie's, can you believe that? She was making his favourite meal, so I wouldn't have to worry about getting it right. She always insists she's a better cook than I am. She just puts shit loads of salt into everything. Anyway, that night I was stood there in their horrible apricot and mint kitchen, all ruffles and primp.' Layla snorts. 'And Marie was clucking and fussing over immigrants taking all our jobs and houses or some other such nonsense.' I grimace, just remembering that night makes me tense.

'That was when it suddenly dawned on me that I had made a rod for my own back. All the times I had bitten my tongue when they started spouting this bullshit had given everyone the wrong idea. I never wanted to start an argument with them, and Granny Reeves always told me that if I didn't have anything nice to say, I shouldn't say anything at all; but my silence had been taken as agreement. They actually thought I agreed with them.'

Layla guffaws.

'And that wasn't all- in my moment of epiphany I looked across their fussy kitchen at James. He was standing on the other side of the room swirling and sniffing a brandy, and laughing with his father, and I realised that James has slowly reverted to type. Without me even seeing it happen. He's become a little more right-wing with each birthday, he isn't racist or homophobic or anything definite like that, which I could argue with.' I look at Layla to see if she recognises what I'm talking about; her wry smile tells me she does.

'He just developed this slightly smug demeanour, which implied that he, the white middle class male, was that teensy little bit better than anyone who wasn't the same.' I grit my teeth; the memory of his priggishness is pissing me off. I wish I could keep hold of this feeling; when I'm angry with him, it's easy to walk away.

'I scoffed at him for it, and he denied it, but it was there subconsciously in everything he said and did. Even losing his business just made him worse; instead of looking at the greed and corruption of the bankers and big businesses, James and his family pointed their finger at the poor and sick, so they cheered cuts to benefits and front line services.'

'He'd already stopped doing all the little things that made me feel special: I held my own door open by this time, and if I started shouting at the news presenter, he would laugh and pat me on the head and tell me to shush because he was trying to listen. If at any time I tried to talk about feelings or the things I was interested in, he would just nod his head at whatever he was watching on the telly and tell me to wait until his programme was finished.' Layla flinches at his obtuseness, shaking her head.

'I was changing too. As I got older, and more tired, my fuse got shorter, my desire to please others waned. I was reverting to type too.' I chuff a dry little laugh. 'Maybe my self-confidence was growing at last or maybe I was just too damn exhausted to be on best behaviour anymore, but I'd stopped being so *nice* all the time,' I continue. 'I stopped answering my phone to freshly dumped friends after eight in the evening. I stopped giving up all my free time to listen to their woes. It had finally dawned on me that I wasn't getting back out of my life as much as I was putting in. I don't remember a flash of revelation, I just found myself taking better care of myself. So I didn't have as much time to run around trying to please everyone else. I found myself not caring so much whether or not they liked me. To my amazement there were no arguments. Some people did drift away, but I found I didn't miss any of them.'

31

'That night, as James was standing there, mirroring his father's gestures with his snifter, I realised I completely despised him.'

'That long ago?' Layla asks. I nod glumly.

'Once the immediate crises of losing the business, almost losing the house and the restructure throughout my department had passed, there was a calm patch. That was when I noticed the ennui and frustration creeping in. I did try talking to James to begin with, explaining that I needed more spontaneity and romance, but I just baffled him. I tried tears and tantrums and then careful step by step directions; which he'd followed, precisely. He didn't understand that I needed something bigger, a life of grand ideas and world-changing ideals; if I let myself think about it, his small safe life of little details made me feel claustrophobic, tethered and desperate. There was no point complaining, though; I was just confusing him.'

'But I was a coward, even as I looked at him in their kitchen, and knew I couldn't stand him anymore, I quivered inside. The thought of trying to extract myself from my marriage was beyond me.'

'I still don't understand why you didn't leave him? Why did you stay after you'd realised you couldn't stand him anymore?' Layla asks, stretching stiffly and moving onto her side, with her head propped on her hand.

I take a gulp of water; it's warmed up nastily in the evening sun. I lie on my opposite side to Layla, so that we are curved on the blanket like Yin and Yang. I meet Layla's worried eyes. I hate letting her see my weakness, I know she will understand everything I have told her so far, but the thought of explaining why I had stayed in my marriage for two more years after that my epiphany moment galls. I can't even explain to myself satisfactorily, I will have to admit what a coward I have been.

'James was my shelter. Without him I would be exposed and alone, like a snail without its shell,' I explain. Layla flinches. 'He's not a bad man, he's often unreservedly kind, and he loves me. Or a version of me at least. I was worried I was being greedy, wanting more than anyone gets. I

32

still worry about that. And in terms of practicalities, it all felt completely overwhelming. It would be impossible for either of us to buy the other out of the house, so it would have to be sold, and there was no equity, so all of our hard work would have been for nothing. James would be heartbroken, and I couldn't bear to be yet another thing going wrong in his life. I still loved him in a fond, sisterly way. I didn't know what on earth to do. I couldn't bear to leave him, and I couldn't bear to stay.'

'I found a solution. Over the next few weeks I realised I could slip back into daydreaming, the escape from boring school days. I was delighted; I smiled serenely on the surface but inside half my mind would have slipped off into my torrid daydream world. It was a delicious world of ravishing, passion and dangerous excitement. It became like a drug no one could tell I was using, and I wasn't doing anyone any harm, was I?' I look at Layla, checking for judgement, but see only understanding.

'I could be a hard-working employee, an uncomplaining wife and all the while I was pursuing ecstasy and adventure in my head. I daydreamed more and more, and when that wasn't enough, I night-dreamed more. I developed the ability to wake up in the middle of a juicy dream and instead of it drifting away, I could keep it in my mind, stroking the feelings, wrapping them back around myself in soft enticing strands so I could slip back into sleep and back into the dream. Even when I was supposed to be awake, I'd be half-dreaming, picking up the threads at any opportunity and snuggling back into them.'

One night I'd dreamt I was sitting in the back of an open topped car somewhere warm. The sun was shining and we were travelling along a long flat road in the country. I wasn't paying attention to where we were or where we were going. The driver was in the front of the car, to my right with their back to me, but I wasn't paying any attention to him either. I was sitting sideways in the left side of the back seat. My right leg was along the width of the leather seat and my right arm was laid across the hot metal on the back of the car. My left leg was bent and my foot was in the foot-well. My left arm was slung around the man slouching languidly into the cradle I'd made of my body. He wasn't wearing a top, his shoulder was level with my face and I kissed him, gliding the tender inside of my lower lip lightly over the fine golden down that traced the line where his neck met his broad tanned shoulder. He tasted of sunshine and salt.

My left hand was lightly stroking his stomach, using only the very tips of my nails to skim feather soft over the skin where his low-slung waist band sat; touching so gently his muscles jumped like fish under my fingers and his breath caught and hitched as I moved inwards from his hip. I was feigning innocence, pretending outwardly that we were just sitting there. Pretending to him that I had no idea what I was doing to him and just sat there fidgeting while I looked out at the scenery, minding my own business. But I knew.

I knew he was rock hard. I couldn't see, but I could feel his arousal vibrating through him, catching my own. I knew I was about to follow up the casually licked kiss on his neck by gently sucking the skin between my teeth, scraping them against his flesh just hard enough to centre all his sensation there, while my fingertips were going to dip under the waistband of his worn soft jeans where the waistband was tented up, so I could hear his hitching breath catch into a moan that he'd swallow into silence. I woke up then, soaking wet and resentful that it was morning and I had to get up.

I spent the whole day slipping back to that point, dreamy and distracted. Uninterested in what was going on around me, smiling my fangy smile so no one would notice, because I knew no one would look close enough to see. How could reality compete?

I feel myself blush now as I remember, while Layla looks at me knowingly. I sit back up again and shake out my shoulders to dispel the memories.

'I could be exactly who others wanted and needed me to be, and live a contented blameless everyday life, while in my mind I had filthy adventure after filthy adventure. I daydreamed through meetings at work and through evenings with James's parents. I was cowardly: I killed poor James off in a myriad of different ways; or I had him run away with another woman, any other woman. Anything so that even in my dreams I could be blameless. Then I would set out on exciting exploits in my mind, unburdened and free to travel the world and find passionate love.'

'The truth will out, though,' I smile ruefully. 'I always thought that was bollocks. I believed that if I just denied my feelings completely enough, to the point where I could deny denying anything and believe myself, then there wouldn't be anything left to deny.' Layla quirks her eyebrow at my convoluted explanation, but I ignore her, I'm on a roll.

'I spent my teens and early twenties being angsty but now that was boring and it was time to grow up. I was sure the feelings would wither away from lack of light and attention. In polite society this is called 'pulling yourself together', 'not making a fuss' and 'not being silly'. However therapists, and wiser women than me, would call it dangerous. The feelings didn't go away. They stagnated and mutated and became hard to recognise.'

'Then, we had that conversation about you leaving Mike. Do you remember?'

Layla nodded.

'It was the first time for a long time I had felt that the world was properly in focus, because you needed me.' It was the day Layla learned her final attempt at IVF had been unsuccessful.

'You rocked my world that day. Not because you were leaving Mike, you know I always thought he was an arsehole. I was sad you were sad, but I hoped this would be your chance to find someone who knew how lucky he was to have you. I was shocked to the core you had been through all this without telling me how bad things were, but when I thought about how decisively you acted to remedy what was wrong in your life, I was blown away.'

I have never wanted children myself, I find them exhausting and irritating, but Layla had always longed for them. Seeing her acceptance that she wouldn't be having them with Mike, and that leaving him would probably mean she couldn't have them at all, was a revelation. This wasn't a subject we really talked about, so I looked at her carefully before I continued.

'Knowing you were willing to sacrifice your chance to be a mother to escape an unhappy relationship, that avoiding a life of denial inspired you to walk away from something you yearned for, burst my crystalline bubble of self-deception. I remained sitting in the beer garden after you left with it shattered around me and the bright light of reality made me feel exposed, scared, stupid and sad. I couldn't bear it. I wouldn't bear it.'

'That night when I got home I told James what you were going through and he was so sad for you and worried about how you would get through everything. I didn't even know he was sending you that big bouquet of peonies, and the open invitation to come to stay with us until you rang to thank us. How could I leave a man who was so kind? It wasn't James's fault I wasn't happy. I was being unrealistic and greedy. I didn't have to leave him.' Layla drew a breath ready to speak, but I ploughed on.

'I made a deal with myself. I would stop daydreaming and live life fully again. I'd do all the things I wanted to do. I'd break each task into bite-size pieces so I wouldn't feel overwhelmed. I'd conserve my energy for myself and not squander it on others. I'd be authentic and autonomous, and all those other words self-help books say you need to be to live well. I'd lose the weight I hated, and in the meantime I'd stop using it as my 'I'll do that when…' excuse. I'd sort out the rest of my life and live more truly. I wouldn't need to leave James, though. And so I hoisted the biggest shard of my denial bubble and tried to live exuberantly under it.'

'Of course it didn't work. James was baffled when I suddenly became argumentative and put my foot down over the strangest things. To get the energy together to make these big changes, I had needed to utilise the anger and resentment that I'd swallowed for years. They made me heavy-handed and over the top in my reactions. James couldn't take it. I'd thrown a hand grenade into our life and he was the biggest casualty. I hadn't wanted to deal with hurting him by telling him I didn't love him anymore and so I ended up completely confusing him

36

as he begged me to go back to being my old self, the woman he had fallen in love with.' I rub my face with my hands and reach for my water, but it is empty. Wordlessly Layla hands me her bottle and I take a swig. It's fizzy, which makes me wrinkle my nose. I only like still. She shakes her head when I offer it back to her, so I hold it in my lap, fidgeting it up and down as I continue.

'Despite these horrible wake-up calls, I kept up my denial. I explored every other area of my life, but not my relationship. James had no interest in what I was discovering about myself as I explored my inner child on what he called my hippy-dippy courses. He was jealous when I lost some weight and I started to walk tall again. I looked up and noticed who was noticing me, I rediscovered my flirty side, when he'd always been the one to charm the birds from the trees. He was frustrated when I made new friends and didn't really want to spend time with our old friends anymore. I was bored by them and he was threatened by the more exciting people I wanted him to meet now. We started to argue, and I wouldn't shut up for the sake of peace anymore. I was determined to be more genuine and that meant expressing what something made me feel, even when it was inconvenient for him that I felt that way. It was hard; I had to steel myself continually not to revert to my default setting of peace maker- diffusing situations, making everyone happy, and smoothing everything over.'

'Throughout our marriage James had brushed off the times I tried to talk to him about as a bit of lady melodrama or PMT, and when I'd let things lie after a row for the sake of harmony, he thought I'd forgotten them because they weren't very important. But really I was seething inside, and now all that frustration came out. He couldn't accept the change in me; he was convinced I was having a nervous breakdown or an early mid-life crisis. He thought I would wake up one morning with my head screwed back on straight and go back to being the Rach he'd married.'

'Meanwhile, I started putting my belongings that I didn't use on eBay, but I found myself selling everything. James was even more convinced I was going mad, but suddenly I realised all the material things I'd unwittingly bought to pad myself against life felt like lead weights holding me down. So I sold, sold, sold. Then I did a couple of car-boot sales and a charity shop trip, until all I had left was one wardrobe of clothes and a box of shoes, and my wedding dress. The dry cleaners hadn't been able to get the mud out of the back properly, so it was no good to anyone else, but I couldn't quite bear to throw it away. I really didn't know what to do with it, so I hung it at the back of my wardrobe and ignored it.'

While James and I were caught up in this turmoil, Layla's divorce had been finalised and she'd moved back to Cardiff. Helping her set up home had been my lifeline, sitting together on the bare floor of her brand new home on the afternoon we'd picked up the keys, she told me how fighting so hard not to show her grief over her failed pregnancies had exhausted her and distanced her. She'd put an invisible wall around herself, and one day she'd realised that she didn't feel desperate, bereft, angry, or devastated anymore; she didn't feel anything. Just tired, always, always, tired. On the day her divorce came through, so did her feelings. She felt, then, big raw, snotty, ugly feelings, and thank God this time she let them out, reaching out to me just as I needed her too. We spoke on the phone more often, and I had helped her hunt for cheap furniture for her new home. I was so pleased she had moved back to Cardiff after being offered a promotion in the Cardiff Sexual Assault Referral Centre, known locally as SARC.

'I thought I was managing. I thought I'd compromised and we were bumbling along ok, James and I, but it was all just simmering under the surface. Do you remember that Saturday afternoon we spent in B&Q choosing the colours for your second bedroom?' I ask her. Layla thinks for a moment, then nods.

Layla had asked me what I thought of a tin of a gorgeous dusty green paint, for the feature wall in her spare bedroom, the rest the same soft cream she was using everywhere else. I loved it. I longed for such colours, but James had wanted everything in white and cream. The closest things we ever got to colour where 'biscuit' and 'pale taupe'. She saw me look at the tin dreamily, and reach out to stroke it with one finger. 'It'll be your room,' she'd told me. I looked at her quickly in surprise. 'For when you stay over after nights out, no need to trek all the way back to Whitchurch then.'

'Well, that night I endured another hideous meal at James's parents' house,' I tell her now. 'We were celebrating his surprise promotion to head of his department.'

I describe to Layla how I'd grabbed a big glass of sweet rosé wine as I walked into the kitchen, and then drank it too quickly while Marie screeched. I'd recently started having the odd glass of wine again with Layla after our shopping trips, and I had enjoyed them, so I hadn't thought twice about accepting my mother-in-law's offer. She always offered; throughout all the years I didn't drink, she'd always offered me a glass of wine when I came into her home, or when we went out to a restaurant together. She always acted slightly flustered when I said no and made a show of offering me a tea or coffee, although I always just asked for a glass of tap water.

'Oh! Hitting the bottle are you, Rach?' she'd commented as I took that first glass from her.

'Rae,' I said.

I explain to Layla how I had tried not to notice her surprise when I accepted her routine offer. How I tried to ignore the way it betrayed she had always known I would want water, while acting like she had forgotten, and I was putting her out, every single time we saw them. I describe the way I swigged back my first glass of wine and the warm flood of 'I don't cares' had encouraged me to grab another. That disappeared just as quickly while we chatted in the kitchen before dinner, and his parents started scaremongering over the anonymous 'Them' again, Marie clucking and cackling like a scolded hen over an article she'd read in the Mail on Sunday about hordes of Eastern Europeans descending like locusts to strip Britain bare. I realised I couldn't do this anymore.'

'Gosh Rach, you really are knocking it back tonight, aren't you?' Marie had commented as I poured my third glass. I realised that my pouring hand was a bit unsteady, and the 'don't cares' had become the 'do care very muches', and I might not be able to hold my tongue much longer. In a moment of exhausted clarity I realised I hated them, and I hated the way James had become more and more like them. I put the glass of wine down and filled a tumbler with water. I ate my meal in silence, not even listening to what the other three were chuntering on about. I had finished my second glass of water, and somehow, without me even meaning to, I found myself sipping the wine again. I was starting to feel headachy and fractious.'

'Yeah Rach, I know you feel the same, don't you?' Marie asked.

'Hmm?' I hadn't been listening.

'That replacing benefits with food vouchers is the right thing to do. Why should people who won't work get to buy anything other than the essentials? Aren't you listening, Rach?'

I started to change the subject like I always had, but then I remembered I wasn't supposed to be complicit anymore. I thought of all the arguments against what she had just said. I took a breath and started to answer her, but then I imagined trying to explain to her how the benefit system kept people paralyzed, how there was so little help to make the move back into the kind of lowly paid job that people with a limited skill set could expect. I thought about trying to explain the horrors of zero-hour contracts and trying to patch together a living. I couldn't be bothered; she was too ignorant to begin to understand the complicated system I would need to explain.

'What about when James was unemployed?' I asked instead. 'Do you think he should have just had food vouchers?' James looked up from his meal, alerted by my tone of voice. He'd sensed this conversation was not going the way these conversations usually did. He knew how I felt about them, I ranted to him often enough. He'd laugh and tell me you couldn't teach old dogs new tricks. He looked at me in concern, and saw the high spots of colour on my cheeks, which he was learning to recognise meant trouble. He reached out and patted my hand anxiously.

'Oh no, not people like James, Rach, don't be silly. I mean the ones who won't work.' Marie hadn't learned to see the warning signs yet.

40

'Where are all these people?' I asked. 'Have you ever met any of them? Or do you just read about these imaginary hordes in that vile rag and take it as gospel. Your own bigotry is contradictory- one second you are complaining about all the foreigners coming over here taking all the jobs, then you're saying no one wants them anyway. Meanwhile you've never done a day's work in your life!' I was shouting by now.

'Oh Rach...' Marie started, looking horrified.

'Rae! Rae! My fucking name is Rae!' I screamed as I pushed back my chair and bolted out of the door.

'So I stormed off home,' I explain to Layla. 'I strode through the drizzle, my head buzzing with imaginary eloquent arguments, you know how you do, in hindsight?' Layla grins and nods. 'When I pictured explaining myself to James's furious face, which would be waiting for me at home, I swung between standing up for myself and making excuses for what I had done. I had to walk around the block an extra time, my anger hadn't abated and I seemed to have decided I was leaving him, so I wanted to do another circuit to make certain I was sure before I told him.'

'James wasn't at home when I got there, though, so I bundled myself quickly into bed and pretended to be asleep when he did get home. He didn't investigate, and climbed in quietly beside me. I lay awake besides him all night worrying at my decision like a terrier, trying to scare myself out of it, but I couldn't; some switch had flicked in my head. He was snoring lightly as he slept contentedly, ignorantly, beside me, and it alternately made me want to suffocate him in all his smug complacency, and then two seconds later filled me with gut-churning guilt.'

'At first light, I turned my mobile to silent and started texting you to see if you fancied having a lodger. By the time James woke up, my plan was in place.'

Even a man as inattentive to the detail of others as James couldn't miss my grey sleep-deprived face and swollen eyes, blackened from hours of crying, as he came back from the bathroom. He stopped stock still in the doorway, and stood there silently as I told him I was leaving. He sat on the end of our bed with his shoulders slumped in defeat and his

41

clasped hands hanging between his spread knees as I packed.'

'When I had fitted the majority of the belongings I had left after my Ebaying into two suitcases, I acknowledged that even while I had been lying to myself that I could stay, I had subconsciously prepared for my escape.'

I avoided looking at James's shocked, grey face as I came back for my second case. He didn't help me, but he didn't hinder me either; as I closed the bedroom door behind me and walked downstairs, I did my best not to listen to his choking, gasping sobs.'

'During the night I'd decided I couldn't bring myself to turn him out of his home too; he loved it in a way I never had. I had told him we could sign over the mortgage into just his name and he could get a lodger in to help him with the mortgage, but his recent promotion should mean he could just about manage it as long as he was careful, and I knew his parents could afford to help him.' I blink back my own tears as my throat closes with guilt and misery in the telling. I wipe my runny nose on the back of my hand. Layla pulls a handful of toilet roll out of her pocket and hands it to me as she scoots across the blanket to sit beside me. She puts her arm around me, and pats my back as I cry myself out, crooning softly that everything will be ok. And I allow myself to begin to believe her.

Layla

Rae has never talked about what happened that night before. She's never talked about any of this before. She just said she'd left him and looked utterly bereft, so I set about trying to cheer her up. I haven't seen her cry like that since we were students. As I let her cry herself out, I mull over what she's told me today. I knew the conversation she mentioned immediately, because it was a turning point in my life too. I'd felt that Rae and I had drifted so far apart that I would be going through my divorce alone. She surprised me, though, by taking my side like

42

the ferocious tigress she always had been in my life, and I knew without her saying that I wouldn't be alone.

We were in a pub beer garden, tucked in a corner of the beer garden after we had been to my hospital appointment. I had needed to discuss my latest failed attempt at IVF with the consultant. He had scanned my womb and confirmed that my body had naturally passed everything after my miscarriage at eleven weeks; I wouldn't need a D&C. Rae had taken the day off work and come with me because Mike wouldn't; understandably, she had thought he couldn't, but as she realised he wouldn't, I saw her jaw set and her eyes narrow. In the past I would have changed tack, talked about all the exciting things we did together, rather than one of the things he wasn't so good at. I've got to be honest, though; I hadn't realised she thought he was an arsehole. Indeed, at one time I thought she was jealous because Mike was so much more dazzling than James. Just goes to show.

'Mike says I have to stop making such a fuss,' I told Rae that afternoon. I was fed up of covering over Mike's deficiencies, and all too ready to have Rae rip him apart with me. 'He told me it wasn't a real baby, just a bunch of cells,' I sobbed. Rae stared at me with her mouth open. She flapped her hand to shoo away the waitress who had been approaching behind me, to see if we wanted to order yet. The whole point of coming to a pub for lunch was that we would be left in peace and could order when I was calmer. I had been close to breaking point while we were still in the hospital, and Rae had driven to the pub holding my hand in her lap, glancing at me anxiously and chattering about mundane things. Helped me to keep myself together until we were somewhere safe. Unfortunately, it was a beautiful day, and there were a lot of people wanting to sit out in the beer garden, so the pressure to eat and leave was strong. 'Let's just leave Rae,' I muttered. I was in no condition to be hassled.

'Hah, fuck them,' she growled imperviously. 'Let them try.' I considered standing up, threading my way through the crowed seating area, and then trying to talk to Rae properly in the stuffy car, and I knew I couldn't. Rae had me tucked in the corner, protecting my privacy as best she could.

'Mike said I shouldn't have been stupid enough to tell anyone I was pregnant until after the twelve week scan,' I continued, the cork was out of the bottle now, and the words spewed out of me involuntarily. I hadn't realised how desperately lonely I had been. I couldn't remember why I had decided not to talk about this with anyone, something about pride and looking stupid, I seemed to remember. Rae saw me glance up as the hapless waitress wandered back over clutching her notepad. Glancing over her shoulder, she sent the bewildered girl such an icy green-eyed glare that she scuttled over to a neighbouring table instead. As I started sobbing loudly, I saw her flick the startled girl a quick eyebrows raised look to indicate 'See?'. The girl left us alone after that. She's good like that Rae, even while you can feel you have her full attention and sympathy, she will be scanning the vicinity, heading off any disturbances, fiercely protecting you while you're vulnerable.

'He said that if I hadn't told anyone, then no one would have known I was pregnant, and I wouldn't have to keep telling everyone I'd lost it, huh huh huh, and then I would be over it by now, huh huh huh, and I wouldn't keep making such a fuss. I am not making a fuss, huh huh huh. Am I?' I was really howling now, choking and sobbing. Rae waited until I looked back up at her, then held her gaze and shook my head.

'No, Layla. No. You are not making a fuss. It's only been four fucking weeks. Tell him to go get fucked, and come and stay with me.'

I couldn't take up her offer, I needed the routine of work, and I knew there was a position coming up in Cardiff I wanted to apply for; it was a promotion, and would be my chance to leave Mike. I didn't want any recent sick leave to ruin my chances. Anyway, letting it all out with Rae was already making me feel better. Rae might have thought I was all very organised, but actually it was only while we talked that afternoon that my decision to leave Mike crystallised and became reality.

Rae made a half-hearted suggestion that we should try some counselling, but I explained that the trauma of the four IVF treatments and devastation each time they failed had

44

destroyed everything we had had together. Mike's sparkle had faded. Instead of looking at me with delighted lust, he flinched away from me. Injections and disappointment had robbed our relationship of all its mystery. This was the first time I had become pregnant, my first miscarriage, but I had been almost as upset as each period that proved I wouldn't become a mother arrived.

'I can't,' I explained. 'We've moved so far apart. I found myself daydreaming all the time, whole swathes of my life just gone,' I added.

She blinked at me in astonishment. At the time I thought it was because I had said I was leaving Mike. I still thought she envied my luck marrying a man like Mike. Now of course I realise that her shock was because I had been dreaming too. Until then she must have thought she was the only one who could slide away from life's harsher realities into delicious escapist fantasies.

'I tried speaking to Mike about counselling, but he just screamed at me that I want too much, that I'm after his very soul,' I explained.

'Fucking bastard!' She was outraged.

'Now that I know that this round of IVF has failed too, and the consultant thinks my body needs a rest before I even think of trying again, I'll be going home to tell him I'm moving out. He won't be bothered; I think he's been lining up his secretary to replace me for a while. I've been in the spare room for months now, once we didn't have to bother with the ovulation shag anymore.'

'Fucking clichéd fucking bastard,' she growled. 'Younger model?'

'Yeah, you guessed.' I felt exhausted and devastated, but also relieved. Lighter somehow. 'I don't know how the hell I managed to marry my bloody father!'

'I knew what the doctor was going to say today, in my heart. I'll get the estate agent to come around tomorrow to put the house on the market. Once it's sold and the money's split fifty-fifty, we won't have any reason to see each other again,' I sighed. I refused her offer of a lift home, preferring to walk back home, letting the rhythm of my steps soothe me so I could organise my thoughts ready to confront Mike that night.

Our conversation was quick and cold. I asked for a divorce, he agreed. I told him the house was going on the market the next day. He said good, packed a bag and moved in with his girlfriend. I was lucky; the second couple who looked around it, bought the house. They were young and full of life and plans. I hoped my smile wasn't a rictus as I nodded along to their plans to open through the kitchen and dining room into a family room. I excelled in my interview with the SARC, and the job was mine. As soon as the sale went through, I was able to relocate lock, stock and barrel back to Cardiff.

I stretched my budget as far as possible, taking out a massive mortgage so I could just about afford a little two-bedroomed stone terrace in Splott. I planned to get a lodger to help with the mortgage, but never seemed to get round to advertising anywhere. Then I received that early morning SOS text, and realised that I had been waiting for her to come. I had decorated the room for her, and all my dreams and plans for a single life had featured the two of us grinning together again.

She wasn't grinning when she arrived, though. She was grey, and drawn and deathly quiet. I was so pleased to see her, I had to restrain myself. I was expecting Rae to bounce back, as resilient as usual. I couldn't understand why she'd allowed it to drag on for so long, why she was torturing the two of them so much. Now we've talked, I can understand why better. She made a promise of forever, and she doesn't break her promises. It's guilt that keeps dragging her back. I don't think she feels like she has the right to be happy and move on with her life, while he is unhappy.

I still can't really understand why she married James in the first place. He's a lovely guy, but he's one of life's plodders, and there's nothing wrong with that, it's just sometimes you can actually see the cogs going round when he's trying to follow a conversation between me and Rae. And when she stops what we're saying to explain things to him, I actually feel claustrophobic, like he's absorbing all the air. Mike and I used to laugh about him after we'd spent the weekend with them in Cardiff. Mike just didn't have the patience for him, and he'd snap at James. It would be hard not to laugh, because I knew what Mike meant. But Rae would look so hurt and I'd just want to shout at her, to ask her why she married him when he's such a knob? I couldn't though, I tried once when she first told me she was marrying him, and she got quite vicious. She told me she'd met someone who really loved her and would never leave her, and since I'd moved to Swansea and left her in Cardiff I couldn't really argue. Could I?

Rae is different, she's sort of ethereal. It's like she has one foot in a different plane, and she doesn't communicate herself very well. Once you really know her, you realise she is painfully shy, and will go to the ends of the earth to help you. But she is also utterly fair, so if you're in the wrong, she won't automatically take your side just because you're her friend. And she's a stickler for rules, breaking them really stresses her out, so people think she's boring. She might hold you responsible for your own fuck-ups, but she just wants you to learn from mistakes. And she'd still love you even if you do something really terrible, if you had a good reason for doing it.

A lot of people don't bother getting to know her properly, they take that air she has of always being slightly distracted- as if someone from another place is whispering in her ear- as arrogance. And because she always listens really intensely, and wants to hear both sides of a story before she makes her mind up, people think she's stuck up, because she doesn't always jump in and join in gossip. Mike never understood why we were friends, said she was like a dollop of cold custard, while I was like champagne, all fizzy and delicious. It's sad, because once you get to know her, she's utterly loyal and loving and just about the funniest person I know. Once she's relaxed with you, she lets her silly side out. At university we would just laugh and laugh, and when people asked what we were laughing at, we wouldn't be able to say, and would make us laugh even harder so they'd either just shake their heads and walk away, or start laughing with us, caught up in the contagion of our giggles. Those people became our friends.

I hope that this holiday, and especially this gruelling conversation will have set us in the right direction, though. I hope we've cleared the air, and we can start to move into the future now. Rae must see she can't go back to him. It would kill her.

Chapter 3
Rae

It is dark by the time we get back to the hotel. The night porter pouffs, but otherwise ignores us, so we scuttle guiltily past, aware that the days of being able to charm middle-aged foreign men with our drunken antics seem to be over. Before I go to our room, I pop in to check on Melanie and Liz one last time. I guiltily notice that in my rush to get downstairs to apologise to the freaky people outside earlier, I hadn't locked their door. Their lights are off so there is only the light from the hallway behind me to illuminate the room as I walk towards Lizzie. I quickly scan the room to see if anything has been moved while we were out, looking for evidence that either of them has been up and about. The curtains have been drawn, but not properly, so I can see the window is still open a crack. Liz's covers are off her again, and she is lying on her back. At first I take this as a good sign, but there is something slack about her face that causes my heart to tug and stomach to freeze, even before my conscious mind has absorbed the information that she is dead.

I know most people would scream now, but I don't scream when I'm really scared; I freeze. My hand covers my mouth and my eyes feel like they were popping out of my head. My other arm wraps around my waist, holding myself together. Layla is standing behind me in the doorway. Seeing me freeze, she kicks the door closed and flicks the light on.

'What?' she hisses. She has the same instinct to secrecy as me, until we've assessed a crisis and decided on our action, we go quiet. As the fluorescent light hums and flickers and finally snaps on, Melanie, face twisted beyond all recognition, rises shrieking from her bed and flies at Layla, latching onto her and burying her face into Layla's neck. For an instant I think that she's been terrified by whatever has happened to Lizzie, but Layla is screaming and gurgling and stumbling around trying to push her off. I realise she is tearing at the side of Layla's throat with her teeth.

49

For an agonising moment I am transfixed in horror and terror until, in slow motion, I power myself across the room as my friend falls to her knees. I seem to grow as I move, as the decision for fight not flight fills me. I grab Melanie's hair at the scruff of the neck and wrap it around my wrist, with my other hand I grip her face under the chin and rip it away from Layla's neck. She slides her chin, slippery with Layla's blood, lower in my grip and sinks her teeth into the pad of flesh at the base of my thumb, as I spin her up and away from Layla.

I smash the side of her face into the wall and then smear it across, over to the window, pulling my hand away from her mouth and throwing my weight into her back so I am behind her and pushing as she reaches the window frame. The window flies further open under our weight and her top half tips out. I almost topple with her, but I pull back in time. Without even thinking, I jerk back and down, snatch up her feet and flip her up and out of the window, turning my back quickly so I won't have to watch her fall.

Bent double and panting, my eyes lock with Layla's where she lies on the floor. Wordlessly I stand, close the window, and help her up. Slipping my arm under her shoulder, I support her out of the room, pulling the door closed behind me.

'What the fuck do we do now?' I gasp as I drag her into our room. She is staggering, barely able to walk. I am speaking to myself; I don't expect an answer. All I can think is: *I've just killed someone. I've just killed someone,* round and round in my head. The vision of Melanie's feet flipping out through the window is all I can think about. I know Layla is injured and I need to get her help, but I seem stuck and disconnected, like I am watching myself play a role in a drama from a thousand miles away. Picking up the phone is beyond me.

'Nothing. You do nothing,' says a voice from behind me. I look over my shoulder and see the sinister man from earlier. He has come into the room behind us and stands in front of the closed door with his arms folded. He makes no attempt to help me. 'Your friend is fine, a little fall like that won't hurt her now. Elaine has taken her to safety. It is a shame the other one didn't make it, but some people don't. It cannot be helped. We will make it look like an accident. You don't have to worry about anything now, you are about to pass out, and we need to make sure no one comes near you.' As he speaks, he moves to stand in front of us.

I realise my hand is throbbing unreasonably where Melanie has bitten me. It feels like fire is moving slowly up my arm, my legs are like jelly, and my eyes have become unbearably heavy. I heft Layla over her bed, and drop her onto it.

'She needs a doctor,' I slur, swaying. 'I think Melanie had rabies.' It is the only thing I can think of that would make sense of her behaviour, and pets need rabies jabs to come from France to the UK, so it must be a problem, or so my soggy thought process insists.

'No,' the creepy man says firmly. 'You can't go anywhere for twenty-four hours. You are about to metamorphose, like a butterfly. Once that is over, we will take you away. You need to sleep now. Everything will be different when you wake up. Sleep now.' I want to get Layla help. I want to alert someone that Lizzie is dead. Who is this man, in our room, telling me to sleep while my friend is so ill and I've just killed someone? But I have no choice: my body gives up and I sleep a black, dark sleep.

*****

My eyes open and I stare into darkness. For a moment everything seems normal, apart from the noise. Slowly, I realise that the loudness that woke me is just the normal sounds of the hotel, but it seems like someone has turned up the volume; the lift sounds like an express train. Laughter in the street four floors below sounds like someone is shrieking in my ear. I become aware that the room is pitch black. There is no light edging the door or window, but I can still see quite clearly, like I'm in a black and white film: everything clear, but no colour. My skin feels like someone has taken the top layer off. The cheap polyester sheet over me feels like lots of thick, itchy wool blankets. It's odd, my feet seem further down the bed than usual.

51

'What the fuck did I drink last night? Did some Bastard spike me?' I turn my head towards Layla whose face is turned towards me on her pillow, her eyes are wide open staring straight into mine. My stomach freezes and a hand clamps icy fingers around my heart as I gaze into the eyes screaming opposite me, then she blinks and slowly focuses on me.

'What have you done to your eyes?' Her voice is silky and fluid like warm melted butter.

'What have I done? Yours are freaky as hell.' I shoot back, only my voice is buttery too so it comes out sounding like a caress.

'What's with the Cadbury Bunny voice?' Layla asks. 'Hmm. We must have been spiked. I feel really odd.' I reach over to the lamp on the bedside table between our twin beds and flick the light on. Pain ricochets through me. My eyes feel like they are burning. I clamp my hands over my face and screw my eyes closed. After a couple of seconds the pain abates and I slowly unscrunch my eyes, then allow the light to sift in through gaps between my fingers. My eyes adjust, and at last I feel it's safe to take my hands from my face. I look over at Layla, she's still squinting through her fingers. She lowers her hands slowly and I stare hard at her face. She looks like a cartoonish overly perfect version of herself.

'Your eyes look like mosaics,' I tell her, 'like the most exquisite blue mosaic at the bottom of a pool.'

'Yours look like a lioness's, like sunlight on water,' she sighs, leaning in closer. 'You look like you've been airbrushed.' She blinks and sits back, staring at my face dreamily. 'And turned into an avatar of you. It's freaky. I don't know what they gave us, but it's some crazy shit, man.' She may have been trying to frown and appear horrified, but she just seems girlishly perturbed with only the faintest line forming between her brows and her plump, pink, pillowy lips puckering prettily into a little pout.

'God yeah, that's exactly what you look like.' I'm entranced, gazing at her.

'Ah, you're awake.' The sinister man sidles back into our room. His voice sounds like velvet, but his presence brings my memories from last night flooding back, sickening me. 'So,' he says quietly, with a slight frown, 'you're Pretty Ones'. He contemplates us for a moment.

'What have you given us, you fucking freaky bastard?' Layla coos.

'You never know how the process will affect,' he continues as if Layla hasn't spoken. 'That friend of yours, Melanie? She's an ugly vicious little bitch. Elaine's had a terrible time with her. Is she always so vile?' I just stare at him. One part of me is trying to comprehend what he is saying. Process? Affect? Melanie's still alive? The other part is entranced by him. How could I have ever thought he was creepy? He is beautiful, gilded bronze, like Icarius, as he flew so close to the sun.

'What have you done to us?' Layla repeats.

'Come on,' he says brusquely, 'you've had time to adapt to the worse of the sensory overloads now. We need to get you out of here while it's dark.' As he says it, I realise he's right, the background noises that had seemed so loud just minutes before have faded. I realise I can still hear each separate sound just as clearly, but they don't feel so overwhelming anymore.

'We need to make sure no one sees the change.' He continues as if he's discussing holiday travel plans. 'Your belongings are gone, and Simon has paid your bill. You need to walk out of here looking happy so if anyone checks the CCTV, they'll see you leaving of your own accord with new friends. Do not touch anything or anyone. There's a lot you don't know yet. You are incredibly dangerous now and unless you want a massacre on your hands, you'll do as you're told.'

'But…' I start.

'No discussion, there isn't time. I will explain once we are safe.' He stares at me, his eyes are the bright, hard green of a perfect emerald. His look brooks no questions and no disagreement. I stand up and wobble as if I am teetering on towering stiletto heels. I am a lot taller than I used to be, and my whole centre of gravity has shifted. I take a step and it feels like my legs are stretching forever. The man makes no attempt to steady me as I totter and wobble.

'What have you done to us?' Layla hasn't budged, and is staring at me in appalled horror.

'What are we?' I whisper. I know this isn't something we've taken now. I instantly wish I hadn't asked. I suddenly know with total clarity that I don't want to be told. I don't want this to be real. He looks at me coldly, beautifully, with his glittering eyes.

'Vampires,' he says simply.

***

I should think he's crazy. I should think the drugs have made me trip out. But I know with utter certainty he's telling the truth. I can feel it in my newly elongated bones.

Somehow we get out of the hotel. Whenever Layla and I move closer together as we stagger, uncoordinated and stumbling, down the hotel's dazzlingly bright and seemingly never ending corridors, he snaps at us not to touch each other. The hotel seems unrecognisable; there are so many details I hadn't even seen before and so many more colours. It would be easy to lose myself by drifting into a trance as I stare around me, but the man chides us along. The air has been infused with the most delicious scent, under the chemical stench of bleach and air freshener, perfumes and shampoos. It's irresistible and stirs a ravenous hunger within the depths of me, and draws me towards bedroom doors inhaling deeply.

'Out!' he hisses. 'Now.'

We are ushered into the back of the car by the beautiful man, who then slides into the front passenger seat. Another dark-haired man is already in the driving seat, his gloved hands clasping the steering wheel.

'I am Guillaume,' the golden man tells us, as the car pulls away from the front of the hotel. As he speaks, I realise he is speaking French, and that I have no problem understanding him. My mind is processing what he says far more quickly than my usual schoolgirl French would have allowed. I can understand him as well as if he were speaking English. He does not turn around to look at us as he continues in a low voice, which forces us to lean forward and listen closely to make sure we catch every word. I am sitting behind

54

the driver, so I can see Guillaume's cold and impassive profile, but he makes no attempt to turn his head to make eye contact with me.

'This is Simon,' he indicates the driver with his head. 'I am the head of this Pride of vampires,' he explains. 'I can only apologise for what has happened. We usually do not spread. Indeed, there is a rule within the Pride that we do not. However, one of the females, Patrice, felt she knew better and let one change, a female named Suzannah. Then Patrice let Suzanne hunt alone, and the next thing we knew we had a group of new ones. I told her they were her responsibility to keep under control,' he sighs.

'I should have known better,' he coughs a little and rubs his fingers over his chin and throat. I realise that although he appears calm to the point of disinterest on the surface, he is feeling something else. Whether it is guilt or anger, I am not sure.

'Anyway, they slipped away from her last night, and by the time she told me what had happened, they had wrought havoc. We would normally have come for you sooner, but we had several bodies to dispose of, a rumour of bad drugs to start, officials to bribe, and some new ones to take to a safe place for the metamorphosis. We weren't sure how many, if any, of you had been infected. It took us a while to find you, and then your friend gave us quite a chase.'

'She's not our friend,' I mutter, irritatingly silkily, and in French, spoken without effort. I want to be bad-tempered and ungracious, but I no longer seem to be able to be anything other than voluptuously appealing. Guillaume continues as if I haven't spoken.

'It is a shame we didn't find her a little sooner, we could have ended all this before you became involved, but we've caught her now and she's on her way to the farm too.' His blasé dismissal of our nightmarish new existence stuns me. 'Once we are all there, I can decide what to do about you all.' He turns and mutters to Simon, speaking too quickly for me to catch what he says. I lean back in my seat, narrow-eyed and contemplating.

'What has happened to us?' I ask. I've been reeling, and now it's just dawned on me that we are in a car with two sinister men we don't know, in a country we don't know. I'm feeling weirder than I've ever felt in my life; all this nutter Guillaume has done is chunter on about some sort of gothic shit and take us away from the hotel, where our two dead friends are. Ok, I'll give him that, it's a good idea to get away from the hotel. No one is going to believe us that Mel murdered Lizzie, then tried to chew my throat out, so Rae chucked her out of the window. I don't care what he says, there's no way she survived that. Oh, and then we lay down and had a little snooze. Oh God, it's all such a mess, and my head is whirling. I can't think straight at all.

'I have told you, you are vampires now,' Guillaume speaks patiently, as if explaining to an idiot that the shop is closed now, but will be open tomorrow.

'Bollocks!' I want to snarl, but it comes out as a simper. 'You've drugged us. What have you given us, you fucker? What are you? Some kind of drug lord? A human trafficker? What do you want with us?' He ignores me, as if I'm a pesky child.

'Oh my God! Answer me!' I kick the back of his seat. 'Stop the car. We're getting out.' Guillaume half turns in his seat to look over his shoulder at me.

'We can't let you out of the car. There is a very good chance you would go into a blood frenzy, and leave the same kind of mess as I've just spent two days clearing up. It's too dangerous. Simon, could you oblige please, while I explain to the ladies what it means to be a vampire? We need to get them back without further incident.'

I wonder what help he was asking Simon for, but then decide I don't really care as the effect of whatever I have been spiked with changes, and I start to feel whoozy and floaty. His words drift over me.

'But what does that mean?' Rae asks. It's no good, despite myself, I listen. Now I'm feeling calmer, I find I'm interested to hear what sort of story he is going to spin.

'When a human's skin is broken and has contact with a vampire's mouth a virus is passed into their system. A vampire emits a wave of calming influence, which Compels a human to do as the vampire wishes, like a rabbit with a weasel, if you will. When the human is sedated, the vampire can feed in peace. Usually we aim to drink the human dry so their heart stops,' he explains.

'Sometimes when a vampire is young and inexperienced, or overexcited like a fox in a hen house,' his tone conveys the contempt that his face fails to show, 'they fail to completely drain the human. It is the rule of our Pride that we only feed on transients, people who won't be missed, and only far from our home region of Lyon. We always kill. We never spread.' Guillaume is silent for a moment, tapping his fingers on his leg, then he continues.

'If the human infected with the virus is not killed, they quickly slip into a coma, and the metamorphosis starts. I compare it to a butterfly because the changes that occur are on the same scale. Inside you are completely different now. Often the human does not survive the transition, and they die during the process. If they survive and awaken, they are a vampire. The vampire is taller, leaner, stronger and faster. The body and brain both perform better than a human's possibly can.' I am listening, and thinking about how it felt to wake up in the hotel, how the sounds and smells were so overwhelming, and how much the light hurt my eyes.

'The new vampire sees further, hears better and smells as well as a dog. All of these senses are overwhelming to begin with, but you'll learn to filter. Your skin is tougher; you have lost all the fat in your bodies and are far more muscular than any human.' He waits a beat for that to sink in.

'You think quicker, and learn faster now. See how you are already thinking and speaking in French with no difficulty, when before you could barely put together a coherent sentence.' I scowl at his casual insult, but realise with mounting horror that he's right. I hadn't even realised that he and I were both speaking in French. I sit upright and look at Rae, ready to scream at her, and shake her out of her complacency, but then another wave of calmness hits me, and

57

I find I just don't care. I sink back in my seat and stare out of the window as Simon drives with reckless speed through the night. The lights we pass blur together with the raindrops on the windows, like the information Guillaume is showering us with.

Rae

'You will heal quickly and are immune to all the diseases and illnesses humans suffer from. Although if someone you feed from is very ill, their blood will taste unpleasant,' Guillaume continues. 'You will not age. You will not die of old age, but you are not invincible. You are a lot more resilient than a human, but to kill you, someone only needs to separate your head and heart.' He takes a breath and leans his head back with his eyes closed before he continues to relay his list of changes we need to understand about our new existence.

'You can ignore the silly stories and films. You can be photographed, and will see your reflection in a mirror,' he continues. 'You can go out in the day light, but I recommend you don't because you look very different now, and the only hope we have of remaining a legend is if the humans who see us up close die immediately. They must not be allowed to acquire photographic evidence. You are not 'undead' or 'supernatural'. You have just been infected by a virus that has caused a physical transformation.'

'You need to remember that when you do kill someone, you have to dispose of a blood-drained body. There isn't a helpful vampire organisation that comes and clears up your mess for you like there is in the films either.' He talks about killing and disposing of bodies so blithely that it takes my breath away.

'You can go into people's homes without being invited. Although, of course, it's polite to wait until you are,' he smiles sardonically at his own joke. 'Any other myth you need me to dispel?' he asks. Considering that he has told us that he doesn't turn people into vampires, his spiel sounds very practised, but then I suppose if he's been busy for the last few days tidying up after these maverick new vampires, he has probably done it quite a few times recently.

'Will we lose control of our senses and get overwhelmed by blood lust and be unable to resist murdering any human we meet?' I purr.

'There is a risk of that when you are newly changed. New ones are learning to control all their new senses and desires and gifts.'

'Gifts?' asks Layla softly. She has been quiet since her last outburst but now she pipes up charmingly. She is speaking in elegant French as well. Before being infected, Layla's French had been worse than mine. I had studied it to G.C.S.E level, whereas she'd dropped the subject at the first opportunity. I don't know how much more evidence she could want to convince her that this isn't all just some horrible drug-induced trance.

'The virus affects all vampires differently. It seems that something about who they were when human affects how they turn out. No one knows for sure how it works exactly, and there is no way of knowing in advance which traits will have which effects. Indeed, a vampire can go years and suddenly discover a gift they did not know they had.'

'Ah, let's see, where was I? Oh yes, you will only be able to ingest blood; anything else will pass quickly and painfully through you, but it is the only thing that will appeal to you now anyway. Your tears will be red from now on; we don't know why, some side effect of the changes you've gone through.'

'You will not need to hide in a coffin, or spend daylight hours in a helpless coma.' Guillaume continues his monologue, questions obviously aren't really encouraged. 'You will still need to sleep, and I recommend a nice comfortable bed for that,' he says drily. 'However, you won't dream.' I stare at him in horror. How am I supposed to escape now? Out of all the earth-shattering revelations of the past forty-eight hours this, bizarrely, feels the hardest to accept. I have always escaped whatever life throws at me by slipping into dreams.

When I consider, though, my entire life is now one surreal dream I can never wake up from. I am stuck, forever darkly dreaming.

***

It is already daylight when we finally reach Guillaume's farm, set deep in the countryside. We sit and absorb the beauty of our new home for a moment, before Layla climbs out of the car and dutifully trots after Simon and Guillaume who are already striding towards the big old Longere with our bags. I open my door and unfurl into fresh air and immediately the fuzzy headedness of the journey clears, and I'm mesmerized by the colours and smells enfolding me. The feeling of the breeze on my skin is delicious, tickling and fresh. I look around, slowly absorbing the jewel hues of the countryside and farm gardens, entranced by the play of light over the fluttering leaves of a silver birch against the denim blue of the sky. I gulp in a lungful of the scent of moist earth, sap, garden roses and mown grass laced with delicate green smells I can't identify.

Several vampires have stopped their incongruously domestic tasks in the garden and are standing watching me. I could happily pause by the car here for hours, enthralled by my new senses, but the other vampires staring at me is unsettling. I can understand why Guillaume told us not to let humans see us in the daylight, their limbs are freakishly elongated and pale, and their eyes are huge. A group of three females stand together and whisper out of the sides of their mouths to each other without taking their eyes off me. Intimidated, I scuttle after Guillaume and Simon who are waiting at the threshold of the house, gesturing at me impatiently to hurry up.

We are shown to a small room each in the attic which, Simon tells us, Elaine has prepared for our arrival.

'It's a good job you have such a big house, my friend,' Simon laughs to Guillaume, who just nods curtly.

My room is small and sparsely furnished with a small double walnut bed and an armoire that has a foxed oval mirror in the door. There is a low window under the eaves with a little white cotton blind, and besides that there's a high-backed chair with a cushion, and blanket folded over the back. The floor

60

boards are bare, with a small rug next to the bed. The bed is pleasantly soft with old linen bedding, smooth as silk from decades of washing and careful care. I put my few belongings away, and slide my empty case under my bed. As I stand upright again, still a little unsteady as I learn to co-ordinate my newly extended body, I catch sight of myself in the mirror. I check the blind is down on the window, and the door is firmly closed, then I slowly undress and stand naked in front of the armoire and gaze at the transformation.

My brown hair tumbles past my waist in thick, shining pre-Raphaelite curls the colour of conkers. My eyes are huge and instead of their usual muddy hazel colour, they are the shocking yellow green of peridot crystal, and my eyelashes and eyebrows are thick, dark and long. My high colouring, wrinkles and freckles are gone and instead I have the perfect pink and white complexion of a Victorian doll. My lips, blushed a gothic burgundy, are curved in a perfect cupid's bow, and look like I am about to smile when actually I want to scream. My teeth are new, smaller, whiter and sharper than I had before. I look ageless, inhuman, a beautiful freak.

My neck is long and creamy, my shoulders broad with elegant collar bones leading to long strong arms. My breasts are big and high and round with small pink nipples. I am still an hourglass shape, but my short waist and heavy hips are replaced by a long waist and the delicious curves of a belly dancer. My body is completely hair free.

'Yay, no more shaving!' pipes up the relentlessly optimistic little voice that waits in my core for absolute crises. I turn and look at my arse over my shoulder: it is high and heart-shaped between my back that bows and swells like a cello, and muscular dancer's legs, which go on and on. My skin is pale and luminous so I appear to almost glow, and it's smooth and tight-looking with no veins or scars. I poke my thigh inquisitively: it is firm and cold and the skin feels tightly bound to the muscle underneath. I realise queasily that I feel like the dolphin I swam with on my Honeymoon. My toes look like I've had a neat manicure in shiny aubergine. I compare my fingers: smooth, long, tapering fingers tipped with pointy matching aubergine nails, but while my toe nails are short and

61

neat, my finger nails are long with a ridge down the centre of their length, from the bed to the tip, as they curve slightly so they look like dark amethyst claws.

I don't like them at all, so I pull on some knickers and a dress from the armoire and go downstairs, determinedly ignoring the fact that my new height has made my perfectly decent tea dress into a mini dress that is straining at the bust and my bras don't fit my new bigger breasts, so I've just had to do without.

Downstairs I find a female vampire in the kitchen unloading some bedding from the washing machine. I look at her hands and confirm she has the same nails as me. The more vampires I see, the more I realise that some features are universal- like the nails, dolphin skin and big eyes- and others are specific to the individual like Layla's beauty, and my own. I'm pretty sure Guillaume has the same gift as us- he is a Pretty One too- but I'm not sure about the others yet. I wonder if it is polite to just ask someone outright the first time you meet them, like you would ask a human what job they did, or is that considered the height of bad manners, like asking the person how much they earn?

'It's rude to stare,' the female says as she squats in front of the washing machine and reaches in to get the last pillowcases out of the back of the drum. She doesn't sound especially friendly, but isn't particularly hostile either. I think of the overwhelming tide of questions I have and the potential offense I could cause by saying the wrong thing. I take a big breath, open my mouth, and then let the air hiss out as I decide to play it safe.

'I don't like my nails like this,' I tell her holding my hands out towards her. 'Can I cut them?' She takes a step back from me but looks at my nails.

'Yes, you can,' she says. I feel a little spark of optimism. 'But you'll need to use an angle grinder, and they'll grow back within ten minutes. There's one in the tool-shed if you want it.' She laughs and walks around me and out of the kitchen. I decide I may as well go and sit outside too. I leave enough time so it won't look like I am following the rude cow and then I go out of the back door. I catch a glimpse of her to

62

my left and promptly stick my nose in the air and turn to my right, affecting not to have seen her. I walk through a gateway and into a large protected yard with barns surrounding three sides and the high garden wall I've just come through completing the square. To my left, on the other side of the yard, there is a five-bar gate set into the wall allowing access to the fields beyond.

The gate is propped open and as I wander through, I see the farm lands opening out before me: fields of produce and crops where the Pride grows the fruit and vegetables to sell. Beyond these, rolling to the horizon, are the hay fields and grazing land for the dairy and beef cows. I stand there completely overawed by the subtle variations of shades in each colour, the intricate layers of the countryside smells, the soaring songs of the birds and breezes.

Lost in the beauty of my surroundings, I am startled when a hideously ugly female approaches from my left, where there is a gate into the fields from the gardens. She is heavy-jawed and browed; her forehead seems to have developed an extra plate of bone, so she bears an overwhelming resemblance to a gothic gargoyle. She isn't here to chase any evil spirits away, though; she is the evil spirit. Despite the distortions to her face, as soon as she speaks, I recognise Melanie.

'I heard you'd come out. Admiring the scenery, are you? You two are causing quite a stir. I see why. Pretty Ones, huh? Some bitches get all the fucking luck, I tell you. Well, this is the farm.' For a second I am completely thrown by her complete change of subject after opening hostilities, but then she continues. 'The pigs are kept away from the house. They stink and vampires have sensitive noses. They're good meat to sell, and they're useful when we need to dispose of the bodies. Pigs will eat anything.' She chuckles nastily as I walk away from her in disgust, trying to keep my thoughts off from the sickening images she has inspired. 'Don't think I've forgotten mind,' she calls after me. 'I owe you for throwing me out of that window, you stupid whore.' I whip around to face her again.

'And Layla and I owe you for turning us, you mad bitch!' I scream at her. She laughs, and I notice several other

63

vampires have sidled out of the gate to stand along the wall watching, grinning and giggling, like hyenas.

'It wasn't my fault! It hurt my eyes when you turned the light on. I didn't know, did I? I didn't have a knight in shining armour there to hold my hand through the transition, did I?' she whines. Melanie's account of how things happened is so far removed from the reality of my experience that I can't be bothered answering her. She has obviously decided to paint herself as the martyr. As I glare at her, she scuttles back to join her audience of the other new ones, and from there she obviously feels emboldened to push her luck even further.

'You might have the looks, Rachel, but this time I'm the one with the friends,' she grins and nudges the vampire next to her. He leans slightly away from her, but otherwise ignores her while his eyes hungrily range over me from top to toe and he licks his lips. I am left feeling like a piece of meat in a butcher's shop window. I turn and storm off down the path between the fields. Mel runs after me goading me further, but I ignore her, and she soon gives up and turns back towards the farm.

Layla

Once I am alone in my room, the strange detached acceptance of our situation evaporates. I spin about wildly, looking for a way to escape, but my eye is caught by the mirror on the wardrobe door. I am transfixed, staring in terror at what I have become. I look like a cartoonish version of a fifties screen siren with a tiny nipped in waist and a curvy compact body. I'm taller than I was, but not much. My hair is a golden halo, and my eyes are immense tranquil pools, completely belying my fear. I have plump pink cheeks, and my pink mouth sits in a moue of vacant anticipation, as if I am waiting for a gentleman to tell me a jolly jape. I try to look as traumatised as I feel, but I only acquire an air of delicious distraction.

My clothes are straining around my new proportions, and there's a large dried blood stain down my side from where Mel savaged me. I notice there's a pile of clean clothes on the bed, so I grab a t-shirt and swop my top quickly, without looking in the mirror. Once I have put the clean top on, I peek myself again. I still look like a tousle-headed moppet, but no longer like one that is the next victim in a horror film. I grab my denim jacket out of my case and pull that on to cover up my strumpet's curves; it's tighter than it was, but the boxy shape dilutes the Jessica Rabbitness of my look a little.

I wander over to the window, trying to decide what to do. My mind is spinning, and my heart pounding. As I gaze distractedly over the gardens, I notice Rae swaying away from the house, through the gate and down the field. I start to tap the window, but then realise that with all my heart and soul I want to walk outside too, so I whirl around and scamper down the stairs and out of the house after her.

As I reach the gate to the field I saw Rae go through, a group of vampires push through it, coming towards me. I cower backwards, terrified of their smooth skin and striking crystal-coloured eyes. They are giggling and bantering between themselves, until they notice me huddled behind the gate they are walking past. Then they drop silent and nudge each other pointedly, smirking and ogling me. I drop my eyes and ignore them until they have walked away from me.

I skitter quickly around the gate and away from the confident pack of vampires, and see another vampire, a lumpen ugly thing marching lopsidedly towards me. 'Guys, wait for me, Guys,' it calls after the rest of the herd. As it draws close to me, I realise it is Mel, twisted and distorted out of all proportion. I cannot deny it any more. I am a vampire. And it's all her fault. I feel fury boil through me, and I lunge at her shrieking my fury, bowling her backwards into the field.

65

Rae

I can hear running water and follow the sound down into a sheltered river valley. By the time I reach the broad flood plain, I am so entranced with the natural beauty around me that I have dismissed Melanie and her nasty little friends from my mind. I walk through a copse of young hazel and come out onto a pretty sunny clearing on the river bank. I am about to sit down by a tree so I can absorb the dancing play of sunlight over the river water, when I realise that there is someone sitting beside the river already.

As he turns to face me, I realise it's the stag from the stag group, although I only really recognise him from his jumper and cords ensemble, because he is smooth, pale and taller with the big vampiric eyes now. He does not look much like his happier, scruffier, slightly worthy human self. I struggle to remember his name from when we'd chatted at the Festival in Tours; it may have only been a couple of nights ago, but it feels like a different era. Layla and I renamed him Mr Muesli so quickly that I have trouble not calling him that now. Brian! That's it. His name is Brian.

'Hi Brian,' I say, lowering myself beside him and dangling my bare feet into the river. 'They got you too, did they? I saw you and your friends with some dodgy-looking ladies that night, but I thought you were just making the most of your last night of freedom. I'm sorry.'

'Who are you?' he asks, showing no signs of remembering me.

'It's me, Rae, remember? I was with Layla and my other friends in Tours the night of the Festival, we chatted about you and your mates riding down from Calais. You laughed at me because I can't ride a bike.' Brian is staring at me.

'Rae? But you were … and now you're…'

'Yes, I was a dumpy, dowdy forty-year-old then, and now I look like some sort of perverted Victorian doll. Apparently, I'm a 'Pretty One', I've been told that other vampires get useful gifts like making people forget, or making everyone listen, but I just look good. I mean, I've always wanted to, all my life, but this feels like cheating, like it doesn't count. What about you? What's your gift?' Brian looks more puzzled as I explain, rather than less.

'What do you mean, a gift? I don't know what you're talking about.'

I tell him what Guillaume has told Layla and me about the metamorphosis.

'It's an ancient virus we are infected with; we were contaminated when a vampire's mouth had contact with our blood. Have you been told you can only eat blood now?' He nods glumly. 'But it's not like in the legends; you're fine with garlic, and crosses and stuff. Oh, and you can still die if your head is cut off, or you're stabbed in the heart. You won't die of old age, but you aren't immortal.'

'How do you know all this? It's all been such a whirl. It was the woman called Elaine who brought us here. She didn't talk much.' I think Brian is trying to scowl, but only the faintest line appears between his eyebrows.

Elaine collected Brian and his friends from the party. He explains that he doesn't remember any of the evening in Tours after a spectacular-looking woman turned from talking to his friend and started to talk to him. Elaine described to him how vampires can Compel humans. Brian tells me that she explained that they soothe and entrance humans so they will willingly let them feed. Once the female turned her attention on him, he had been spellbound as she drank, and then he'd slipped into the coma as the virus spread through his system. The other party goers hadn't noticed anything amiss with Brian and his friends, they would have just thought they were drunk, as I had.

Elaine told him afterwards that she and Simon carried them to a car and, while Simon returned to help Guillaume find us, Elaine drove them through the night to the safety of the farm. Two of his friends were killed as the vampires drank, a third died in the car to the farm, and a fourth didn't survive the final stage of transformation and died, like Lizzie, without waking up. She didn't tell him much about being a vampire once he woke up, so he is transfixed as I tell him all that I know.

67

His friend, David, survived the transition with him and is up at the house. Brian admits they haven't really spoken since the change. I think about how since arriving at the farm in the early morning, Layla and I have stayed in our separate rooms until I ventured outside. Not avoiding each other as such, I reassure myself, it's just that her denial of what's happened has made me uncomfortable; I don't want to have to be the one who makes her accept our horrible new reality. It's harder to admit that I hate seeing the change in her, I hate the stark reminder of how much I have changed too, and I just don't know what to say to her right now. We are too close, and this was too big for platitudes. I am too overwhelmed to talk about how I am really feeling yet.

Brian becomes upset and sheds red tears as he talks about being unable to return home, about how his fiancée, Meg, will be destroyed when he doesn't return for their wedding; it is only two weeks before their wedding, which they had saved very hard for. He tells me how he was a late bloomer, more interested in devising ways to make recycling more efficient within his role in his local council, and cycling at the weekends to really worry about not meeting anyone. Then five years ago a friend of a friend introduced him to Meg and they had been inseparable since. Until now.

He's deeply traumatised by the deaths of his friends too. Elaine has told him that it's been made to look like he and his friends took some bad Ecstasy, which killed his friends. CCTV footage will show him callously leaving his stag do with his friends and another woman. He's been told unequivocally that he can never return to Meg. I let Brian talk, there is nothing else I can do to soothe his pain.

We spend the afternoon side by side by the river and as he talks about all their plans together, and how upset everyone will be, I realise I have not really considered the future, I have been too caught up in the moment. It's different for Brian- he's had a life he loves whereas I have been trying to escape mine anyway; be careful what you wish for, my Granny Reeves used to say.

During the car journey here, Guillaume told me that there is a High Council of five of the oldest vampires in

68

existence. They monitor all the chatter online. They specifically infected a computer expert with the vampire virus once they realised the new technology was here to stay. If anything shows up online that is too specific, not just part of the romanticised gothic vampire fan generalities, it is investigated and dealt with. 'Dealt with', I'd flinched at all that phrase contained. Any vampire found responsible for risking the secrecy of the virus would meet the same fate. If they live in a Pride, the head of that Pride would be held responsible for that vampire's actions. No vampire can risk humans finding out we are real, Guillaume had explained in his sombre, unflappable voice. Vampires may be stronger, but there are more humans and they would annihilate the vampires, after they experimented on us, and learned how to steal the vampire's gifts to use in war and business.

Somehow, I haven't really considered that this means I will never be able to see my parents or sister again; if they see how I have changed, I would have to either kill or change them. If they found out and told anyone, one of the other vampires would kill them. I don't see my family often, we communicate mainly by email and phone. Our relationships aren't that close: my parents are glamorous academics, travelling the world by research grants. They are exciting people with heads full of concepts and ideas. They adore each other, and us girls, but we were raised to be independent and self-sufficient. They had remained oblivious to the fact that I am neither.

As a child I had longed for food at mealtimes, stories at bedtime, and a best friend. My childhood was spent settling into school after school. My grandparents had suggested that I might be sent to a boarding school so I could have some stability, but my parents had been aghast at the suggestion; they loved me, they just forgot that I needed feeding before ten o'clock at night sometimes. So I spent my childhood, until I was fifteen, moving from school to school every couple of years.

My sister, Santana, was a happy accident, conceived in rural Mexico. She was eight years younger than me, and had benefitted from my parents finally settling down so I could concentrate on my G.C.S.Es. She didn't start school until she was five, and then only moved once, back to the UK when she was seven. By the time I had finished my A levels and was leaving home for university, my father had been made head of his department, so they remained settled throughout her education. They only spent their summers on exciting explorations of locations so far off the beaten track that most people had never heard of them. I had always longed for family holidays by the beach in the Algarve so I could explain where I had been to my friends without them glazing over in confusion, but Santana thrived on these far-flung adventures and kept her schoolmates enthralled with her descriptions of digging her own toilet in the Serengeti.

It was no surprise to anyone when she decided to follow her university girlfriend over to New York within three years of graduating. There they set up and successfully run an edgy art gallery together, which somehow survived the recession, and even thrived. Santana and I aren't like sisters. We are hardly like acquaintances really, she is confident and worldly in a way I'm just not. We exchange pithy emails frequently, and I enjoy seeing her online blog about her shows, but we don't really have anything meaningful to say to each other, and on the rare occasions she visits the U.K, we quickly run out of chat once we get beyond the initial enthusiasm of seeing each other.

She is tall and lean; glamorous in an understated white linen and good silver jewellery way, like our mother. The two of them always have things to talk about, leaning together over restaurant tables, heads and hands almost touching, as they dance out their stories to each other. As I approach them they draw back and turn to me, their lights seeming to dim as they welcome me; they make me feel fussy in comparison.

Not long after my sister emigrated, my mother had been diagnosed with skin cancer. Happily, her treatment was swift and efficient, and in less than eighteen months she was given the all-clear. It meant that she and my father received a large payment from the critical illness part of their life insurance.

Once they knew my mother was completely recovered, my parents handed in their notice for their jobs, sold their house and headed off into the sunset. Initially, I was anxious about them setting off to travel to bizarre and remote corners of the world when she had only just attended her one-year all-clear check-up. But we met up just before they set off, and once they started talking about their plans, I was completely swept along with their descriptions of where they were going to go. They were going to travel around the Seven Wonders of the World, and they were utterly delighted at this freedom to travel anywhere they wanted, purely for pleasure. They gave me pause for thought. My Mum was lit up from within, and my Dad couldn't take his eyes off of her.

She turned to me, as my father paid the bill, she was a bit tipsy, and giggled as she told me that the cancer was the best thing that had ever happened to her. She declared it gave her the reminder that life is too, too short, and the money to escape the daily grind. Her eyes were sparkling with excitement, but as they held mine, they clouded slightly with worry. I thought she started to say something, but seemed to think better of it and just patted my hand instead.

That was the last time I saw them. Since then my parents have seen the seven most wondrous sights the world had to offer and are now taking part in volunteering schemes all around the world. I receive excited emails, and the occasional crackly phone call bursting with their enthusiasm. Once they knew I had left James, I received repeated invites to go out to see them at each of their projects, but I wasn't feeling resilient enough for the brash advice of two academics who were lucky enough to marry the right person at the first attempt. Sitting by the river, my heart contracts as I think of them, and realise that not seeing them often is not the same as never seeing them again.

But I am a monster now, I remind myself, and the thought of the disgust, fear and repulsion on my family's faces if they ever saw me again, and learned what I have become, is too much to contemplate. Even without the strict rules I wouldn't want them to see me. Brian feels differently, though. He is sure that Meg would love him anyway, and that the

71

horror of losing him with no explanation will be far worse for her than the explanation. I envy him his certainty in her love, but I'm not sure I agree with him. I worry he is being overly optimistic about the strength of anyone's love in the face of what we've become.

'Are you hungry?' I ask, thinking it will gently remind him about what we have become without me having to say it out loud, but also because the more time is passing, the more the hunger is all I can think about. My stomach burns with it. Brian admits he is ravenous too. Elaine told him she was going with Guillaume to get our first feed, but that was ages ago, so we decide to head back to the house to see if they have returned yet. As I become aware of how much time has passed while I've sat talking with Brian, I realise I've left Layla alone for too long, and feel a stab of guilt and the urge to hurry back grows.

'Thank you for listening to me.' As we stand up, my mind is already back up at the house, on Layla. Brian casually reaches his hand to my shoulder and leans forward to give me a friendly peck on the cheek. As he touches me, everything changes in an instant.

My head falls back as my back arches, and his friendly grasp on my shoulder becomes molten. He slides his hand up and cups the back of my head while he is kissing, and licking, and nipping, down my cheek, lingering on my mouth and then down onto my throat. Then back up to bite and tug my earlobe, and back down to the dip where my collarbone meets my neck. At the same time his other hand slides around my waist and down onto my arse, pushing me hard against him. The need in me is as instant and furious as a gas flame; it becomes me. Only where he touches me is the need sweetened and slaked.

Within seconds we are naked enough for him to be inside me, filling me, our eyes locked in the intensity of the moment, as almost instantly I am rocked by my climax, which tips him into his bliss. We are gasping and grasping and... and then as quickly as it all started, I see the need wane from his eyes as quickly as my own vanishes and we are just two embarrassed vampires who don't know each other very well, stumbling around trying to put our clothes back on, hoping that no one can see us.

'Well,' I say sheepishly as I pull my clothes straight. 'That's new.'

***

'Don't touch anyone,' I say later, as Layla stalks into my room. I've been hiding, curled up in my bed, surfing the net on my laptop. Since I can't escape into deep, dreamy sleep anymore, I've resorted to looking for clips of cute cats to distract myself. I was wondering where Layla had got to, but was too unsure of her mood to look for her.

A bit of me is worried that she will blame me for what has happened: if I hadn't gone into Mel and Lizzie's room, if I'd been the one to turn the light on, if I'd pulled Mel off sooner. Hell, if I'd never suggested inviting our friends to France with us, or better yet, never mentioned France at all. I've been torturing myself with these if onlys, and have become increasingly convinced that this is why Layla had vanished when I got back to the house.

'I know!' she snaps, pulling off her jacket and throwing it and then herself onto the chair, studiously not looking at me. She pulls her knees up and wraps the blanket around herself so only her eyes peep over the top, her hands curling the blanket against her mouth. She stares obstinately out of the window.

'Ohhhh,' I say, as realisation dawns. 'Who?'

'That fucking bitch Melanie! I wanted to kill her, not fuck her. She got into my face and started having a go, so I went for her, and well, you know… ' she trails off.

'I didn't know you…' I start.

'I don't,' she says curtly. 'Didn't,' she amends. She looks at me from the corner of her eye. 'You?'

'Mr Muesli.'

'Mmph.'

'Mhum.' She is looking straight at me now, mirth twitching her lips, but I won't meet her eye. She sniggers.

'Mr Muesli? Brian?'

73

'Uh huh.' I feel the giggles start in my stomach, and then we are roaring with laughter, clutching our stomachs until blood red tears trickle down our cheeks like garnets on marble. Laughing together makes us feel a bit like us again, but we are careful not to look too closely at each other. Careful not to see there aren't any crinkles around our eyes, or dimples in our cheeks, just open mouths in smooth statue faces.

Chapter 4
Rae

After another two hours of sharing silly clips on the internet, we decide we've waited long enough to be fed, and set off to look for Guillaume or Elaine. As we reach the back door, it flies open and one of the new vampires I'd seen that afternoon, with Mel, bursts through. She is stocky with bright ginger hair, and I imagine that as a human she was freckly, but her vampire skin is as smooth and white as alabaster.

'There you are,' she grins into our startled faces. 'Come on, we've been waiting for you, dinner is here.' We quicken our step behind her as we follow her to one of the big barns. Inside it smells of sweet hay and horse and something else, something absolutely delicious, that I had last smelt at the hotel. I realise that all the other new vampires, including Brian and David, are stood around something. I recognise Suzannah and Patrice from their seduction of Brian and his friends in the Square. They are standing to one side smiling broadly.

'Ah, here you are, Georgette,' Patrice coos. 'Here's your meal. Enjoy.' I follow her eye line and realise that inside the semi-circle of vampires crowded around, there is a human male, dirty and scruffy and gibbering with fear. I can tell instantly that no one has bothered to Compel him. This man is not in the seductive trance I saw people at the festival in. I am confused and look up at Patrice.

'They taste better when they're scared,' Patrice says, as though she can read my thoughts. 'As you drink, your mind will be filled with images of all the important things in their lives. All the things they've done that have mattered to them. When they are scared, these images are much more vivid and enjoyable. When we are forced to take prey in a crowd, we use the Compelling so they don't scream and call attention to us. Then we can't risk becoming too engrossed in their memories and too inattentive to our surroundings.'

I look down at the man and I know I cannot feed on him. The hunger rips through me, Patrice is right, his terror adds an extra nuance to his scent, making him almost irresistible, but I swallow it down. Deep in the very core of who I was, I know I cannot kill this man who has done nothing to me. I can't save him, there are too many New Ones, and they are boiling and baying with desire, but I can make this easier for him. I push through the others who step back quickly out of my way avoiding any contact with me. I crouch in front of the terrified man and smile at him. I put my hand on his leg and tell him everything will be ok, he just needs to go to sleep now. I keep my voice low and soothing.

I have no idea if it will work, I haven't been taught to Compel prey yet. I worry it will have the same effect it had on Brian, but I set my intention, and it works. My voice is low and soothing, not seductive, and within two seconds his eyes roll back into his head and he is still, breathing deeply and calmly. Behind me the other New Ones mutter and bitch. I stand up and step back from them, meeting their angry jeering and hissing with fury.

'You see, Suzannah,' Patrice says haughtily. This is what I told you about. This is why we need to select the ones we turn so carefully. If they don't already show a taste for the voluptuous, the rich, the decadent, they can become very moral and dry. I watched you for weeks before I was sure that while you were a measured and careful human, you were also suitably self-preserving and would thrive on the freedom of being a vampire.'

'I know, but the blood just smells so good. They were supposed to die not turn. We were sloppy.'

'You are disgusting,' I breathe. 'All of you. Only days ago this was you. If you must kill, there is no need for your prey to suffer.' I step farther away from them even as my hunger surges. Layla steps back to join me, and a second later David and Brian join us. Suzannah and Patrice stand back and laugh as the young ones surge forward and latch onto the man like leaches. Georgette holds back for a moment looking at me, but then she's urged forward by Suzannah, and drops to her knees with the others to feed.

'All the more for the rest of us.' Patrice laughs.

Sickened, I turn to leave, and only then realise that Guillaume has come into the back of the barn and is standing

76

behind us holding hospital bags of blood. His handsome face is impassive. He leads us into the house and shoos the other vampires out of the kitchen. He sits us at the table and hands us a bag of blood each. It is cold, and thick, and does not smell delicious like the live human had, but I drink it, and my hunger is sated.

'I'm sorry for the delay,' is all that Guillaume says.

Layla

Gosh, that was intense. The man smelt so incredibly good, and the barn was filled with excitement and the joy of the kill. It is times like this I'm so glad that Rae is my friend. The way that scenario in the barn was presented, it was like it was the only option for us, now we are monsters, vampires. We have to feed, we can only eat blood, therefore we have to kill, and here is some poor dreg of humanity, whom no one will miss, to eat. The hunger was so strong; I was hunger, all of me burned with it. And, I hate to admit it, a part of me wanted to be accepted by the others, I wanted to fit in with the Pride.

I don't know where Rae found the strength, but she remembered who she is and in remembering, reminded me too. She didn't stop me, or even look at me, there would have been no judgement if I had fed once she had calmed him, but her actions freed me from the blood lust, and once we walked away, Brian and David could follow. And immediately, there was Guillaume with our other option, blood donated to a hospital. Thick and nasty and gluttonous, but filling. She's incredible, my friend. Why the hell that tosser Guillaume hadn't told us sooner that there was the option of bagged blood, I don't know. Dick. I can't imagine how I would be feeling now if we'd fed, and then turned around and seen him there, all sanctimonious with his sanitized bag of blood.

David, though. Oh my. I didn't really notice him as a human, but now he's vampire, I can't keep my eyes off of him.

77

As a human his features had been bland, his wholesomeness, and marriedness, had meant I hadn't taken any notice of him. Rae had struck up conversation with his group while we were waiting to be served at the party, but my eyes had ranged, looking for more exciting fare.

Becoming infected with the virus has caused him to grow taller and broader, so his shoulders are like a great sheltering oak, and his hands are sure and strong. His face is squarer, and more chiselled, so he looks almost laughably masculine, but his big grey eyes, with thick blond lashes, and his boyish mop of sandy hair mean he just looks faintly bewildered by his growth. And he carries himself with this calm manliness, it's like he knows that whatever life throws at him, he can handle it.

All his clothes are really tight on him now, so where he used to wear sloppy baggy clothes, now his chinos are really strained over his bum, and his worthy knitted jumper pulls skintight over his back and chest, but hangs loose around his waist, arching upwards to reveal a delicious slice of muscled back, where his top's too short for him now. Lickable.

He looks very serious, until he smiles, and then his face leaps alive with mirth. He's so tall now, with great long legs, that he towers over me; but as we walked back to the house from the barn, he slowed right down to walk besides me, bending slightly to talk to me. I trotted besides him simpering and giggling like a silly school girl, I couldn't help it. I have a total crush.

I have to keep reminding myself that this is not the time or the place to fall in love. I need to deal with what has happened to me, and support Rae as we find out what our future holds. But then David will catch my eye from across the room, and grin at me, a dimple like a finger print in cream in one cheek, and I'm lost all over again, gooey with longing. Luckily, Rae doesn't seem to have noticed yet. Little Miss Sensible seems to have had her own head turned by our enigmatic leader. Good luck there, Rae, I don't think Mr Perfect will be able to love anyone other than himself, but if he dares hurt my friend, he'll have me to answer to.

Rae

First thing the next morning Elaine tells us to email anyone who would be likely to worry about where we are. She asks us all to bring down our laptops, and then once we've got them, she takes us into the kitchen and sits us around the big pine dining table. Elaine is shorter than me and relatively bland-looking, for a vampire, although she is perfectly presented at all times, like any good French woman. She has a brusque manner about her, but does not seem unnecessarily cruel. She walks around Layla, David, Brian and me as we compose our messages, monitoring what we are writing, and editing as necessary. I send upbeat emails to everyone describing a whirlwind French romance that means I couldn't bear to return home. I resign from my job, and tell James that our life together is definitely over in the same jaunty manner.

I feel a deep swell of relief as I send that email. It's finally, properly, over. For his sake I have to stay away. I let go of the guilt I've been carrying and finally feel free. Buoyed by the surge of joy this release brings I set to tackling Maddie, Nicky, Louise and Sam. There are a storm of emails and Facebook messages from them begging to know if we are ok, demanding to know what happened to Lizzie, asking if Layla or I know where Mel has gone.

Layla, Elaine and I discuss our replies carefully, so we are coordinated in our blasé responses. I profess shock that Lizzie is dead, but no interest in her funeral arrangements and quickly skip onto details of my imaginary romance. I am deliberately annoying, and Maddie soon pops up on Facebook messages to ask what's going on. I construct an argument with her, leaving her baffled at my selfish heartlessness. Good, she will tell our other friends, and they will stop contacting me. Layla wades in, and picks up the row and exacerbates it. We resist the temptation to point the finger of blame towards Mel, to protect the Pride we have to protect her, so I feign ignorance to her whereabouts. I try hard, throughout these orchestrated arguments, to avoid thinking of Lizzie's still, pale face that last time I saw her.

The emails to Maddie and the others, and her job are the only ones Layla needs to send, she doesn't really have a blood family. Layla's father had left his wife and two teenage children for his younger, prettier secretary, and Layla was their unexpected child. Her mother had loved her very much, but her father had always been removed and disinterested. Layla and her Mum had been a little unit, always waiting for him to come home from work. When her mother had died suddenly of a brain haemorrhage in the middle of Layla's A levels, Layla had been knocked reeling. Her father had become even more distant, replacing Layla's mother with an even younger model with such haste it was impossible not to suspect she had already been on the scene. Layla's older half-siblings were completely disinterested in her and her loss. The blame they directed towards Layla and her mother for the breakdown of their own family, was implicit in all the conversations Layla could ever remember having with them.

She was left to her own devices for the next two years, during which time she flunked her first set of A Levels to see if anyone would notice. They didn't. So she re-sat them the following year and achieved the grades she needed to do the course that interested her, but not the grades required to do Law like her father had hoped. When I met her at University, she had been as desperate for someone to love as I was.

David and Brian are in a tougher situation today. Several of their friends have died, in what has been made to look like an out-of-character experimentation into recreational drugs gone horribly wrong. They both had lives they wanted to return to. Elaine advises them to say something about the drugs giving them a revelation, which meant they couldn't stay in such constricting lives, so they had decided to travel together, and not return. David gets his typed and sent as quickly as he can, then goes and sits alone in the garden with his head in his hands. Layla and I can see him through the window. After a couple of minutes Layla stands up and leaves the room. I watch through the window as she approaches David and sits beside him, carefully not touching anywhere on his body, but leaning slightly towards him as they fall into conversation.

Brian ignores me, but I sit in the kitchen with him in mute support for the hours he spends mulling over what to send. He starts to type repeatedly, and then deletes it all, with blood tears and cursing, while I look on, mutely sympathetic. Eventually, Elaine comes back and types a quick, harsh statement about a horror of commitment after his enlightening drug-fuelled experience and clicks send. He gasps in horror, and starts to type another message, but Elaine snarls at him that he has no choice; that he needs to just get it sent to whoever else needs to see it. Then she watches him closely until he sags, and does as he's told.

Layla

I watch David type his email to his family, telling them he is off on a journey of self- discovery, so they won't see him for a while. Despite the vampire smoothness of his features, his drawn brows and utter silence give away his distress. He types as quickly as possible, but his greater bulk and broader fingers mean he fumbles his keys. His frustration is quiet and self-contained, a sadness at prolonging his own agony, rather than the anger and aggression I've come to expect frustration to produce in men.

I watch him get up and leave without looking at anyone. I find I've stood up to watch him leave, and my eyes follow him across the garden to a secluded spot where a big old log has been laid beside a weeping willow to be used as a seat. He sits with his back to the house, and his massive shoulders slumped. Without even being aware I have decided to follow him, I am trotting across the lawn towards him. I cough daintily to attract his attention. I don't mean to cough daintily, but I cannot be anything other than beguiling now and my body finds a way to turn the most basic function into an

81

act of adorableness. Thankfully, vampires don't fart, otherwise I swear it really would be roses.

David looks over his shoulder at me, and his handsome face breaks into a massive grin. If I avoid noticing his jagged pointy teeth, he looks healthy and handsome, and pleased to see me. He pats the log next to him, and I hop over the log, and fold myself neatly besides him. I find my body arching towards him, ankles crossed, hands clasped, like a fifties screen siren coyly inviting a kiss. I pull myself together and shuffle back a couple of inches. Only then I find myself leaning back on my elbows, lower body angled towards him, hips tilted and one leg casually crossed over the other, foot swinging so it almost brushes his ankle, while I gaze at him poutily.

'Sorry, sorry,' I say, sitting up primly, clamping my knees together and ramming my hands between them. 'I can't help it. I just want to sit here and talk to you, but I can't seem to stop myself being a vamp. Oh, ah ha. Well, none of us can stop that now, can we? Aha ha. I mean, I've become a coquette. Oh, help me. I'm rambling.'

'I know what you mean,' David rumbles. 'I expect to just be me, and instead I've gone all Action Man. I feel like a right dick. I went to open my window this morning, and just pulled the latch right off, and everything I say sounds all deep and profound. It's awful. I look like Desperate Dan or something.' I beam at him in delight.

'Oh thank god for that. You understand. Well, please just ignore anything daft my body does, we can just have a natter.'

So that's what we do. We make our pact to ignore each other's extremes, and quickly relax and talk, telling each other about our lives. It turns out that David wasn't as happily married as I had thought. His wife sounds like a bit of a cold fish, always working late, never the right time to talk about children, sleeping in London three nights a week most weeks since she'd been promoted. David is wracked with guilt that he doesn't feel worse about never seeing her again, but admits that the sweet-natured, but hardworking girl he'd fallen for, had been absorbed into a driven career woman a long time ago.

Rae

After Brian's email is finally sent, we are called in to a meeting in the great hall. Layla, David, Brian and I stand on one side of the room against the wall. Brian still wouldn't look at me and stands examining his bare feet. None of us has shoes that fit us anymore and we are all barefoot. Patrice and Suzannah's New Ones are on the other side of the room, sprawled over all the sofas and armchairs they have dragged over there; laughing together, sliding us sly sideways looks. Melanie is with them. Laughing loudest, hideous face turned towards us as she points and whispers to her neighbour. I notice that she can touch the other vampires. I realise they are all casually touching each other as they speak, or move over for someone to sit beside them. I remember that they had been touching when they'd watched Melanie rile me in the garden. I mull over the meaning of this, and decide it must have something to do with being a Pretty One.

Patrice is sitting slightly to one side with Suzannah; they aren't laughing with their new Ones, but still regard us with an air of complacency. Patrice in particular reminds me of a mother cat whose kittens have killed a family pet; she knows there will be consequences, but she's proud of their prowess.

Guillaume strides into the room with Simon and two other males I have seen around the farm. They stand behind him, leaning slightly against the wall with their hands clasped loosely in front of them. They have adopted the casual attitude of bouncers; primed to leap into action but busily pretending they are relaxed enough to lounge, because their presence alone will be enough to keep the peace. I know there are more vampires living on the farm than those in the hall. I realise that Guillaume is expecting trouble, despite his cool demeanour,

83

and has picked his most reliable and trusted comrades to support him without risking bringing the others in. This can only mean that what he is about to say will be controversial. I wonder what this will mean for us. I remember his comment in the car about deciding what to do with us.

Guillaume stands at the front of the room waiting for silence with an air of command. A couple of Patrice's new vampires continue to mutter and giggle a little in a deliberately inflammatory manner. Guillaume clears his throat; Patrice laughs musically, then hushes them. Suzannah smirks. Guillaume looks at Patrice, blinks and then starts to speak.

'We have lived here for more than eighty years. No one bothers us. No one knows what we are. Our produce brings us money. We need this place. The only way we can maintain this life is if we feed on humans minimally and far away from here. I am the head of this Pride. My word is law. I own the land. I said no spreading. I said no New Ones and in two weeks we have ten. We cannot sustain this. Patrice, you disobeyed me when you turned Suzannah. You cannot control her. You will destroy her and the others she has turned, especially that ugly one you have with you. She is dangerous to everything we have strived for. They all are.' His voice is calm and measured as he delivers this death sentence, so it takes a second to sink in. I feel my eyes go wide, and I stare at him.

'Guillaume, darling, let's not be hasty. You don't want to do that. It really is unnecessary,' purrs Patrice. My head spins towards her and I can't believe my eyes. She is always haughtily elegant with brunette hair kept back in a dancer's chignon, long silk skirts, and soft cashmere tops in soft pinks and creams, but she is transformed now. She has shaken her hair loose, and her ankle length skirt has developed a thigh high slit and one achingly long and elegant leg has slipped and slid over the other bringing uncontrollable thoughts of them uncrossing and sliding open. Her cold blue eyes are now sparkling and hypnotic, her lips plump flushed pillows. She manages all this without looking cheap or obvious.

'Don't you dare turn that on me, Patrice,' Guillaume snarls. He has turned his back to her and speaks to the wall.

The other males with him have done the same. 'How many rules do you think you can break before I expel you?'

'Well, darling, let's be fair about this, if my babies have to die, then so do yours.' Patrice slinks up behind him, and raises one hand as if to touch his shoulder, but she stops and her hand flutters for a moment undecided, then drops back to her side as she thinks better of what she was about to do. I see Guillaume exhale as if released as she takes a step back from him, twisting her hair back up, and dimming her eyes back to icy grey. She turns towards us, smiling smugly.

'What?' I shout, stepping forwards. 'Hold on. We do as we are told. We have no desire to inflict this horror on anyone else, and have refused to kill. We have only fed on the blood from the hospital.' Suzannah and the other New Ones jeer and laugh at my indignation, howling in derision when I mention the bags of blood, Patrice's bubbling chortle joining in.

'Oh well, darling, if you're going to be a rude little upstart, you can die first.' Patrice's face lengthens and distorts as she moves towards me. Suddenly, Layla is beside me, but I hardly recognise her. Her face is long and her mouth gapes nightmarishly open. Her teeth have become long slender spikes protruding diagonally from her mouth and meshing viciously as she gnashes.

Her steps are rigid and awkward, and her shoulders are wider and have risen unevenly to her ears. Her hands claw in front of her, grasping towards Patrice. Her fingers have extended, the bones protruding from the flesh with her nails long and sharp inches beyond where the flesh ends. Her back has arched like an angry cat's and her ribs have dislocated so sharp bone spikes are sticking through her skin and clothes all down her sides. Her legs are longer, but not quite even, adding to her lopsided lurch as she lunges across the room towards Patrice, screaming an alien scream, like nothing I've ever heard before.

Patrice leaps backwards, hunching her own shoulders as Suzannah and the New Ones rush to her side. I feel my own mouth opening and pain ripping through my face and down into my spine, arms and legs. The agony spurs the fury and speeds up the transition. Tall normally, now I tower over the others as the unworldly shrieks tear from me. I am lost in a red sea of rage, filled with an overwhelming desire to rip and tear and destroy, and enjoy every second. Every worry, every hurt, every fear I have suffered over the last few years well up inside my and stoke the flames. It is pure and clean and red hot and liberating. So, so liberating. I shriek with delight and start to run towards the others. I want Melanie, I decide I am going to rip that evil bitch's face right off. I slobber in anticipation.

A hand grabs my sleeve and Guillaume is at my side pulling me around to face him. He is taller than usual, as tall as me, but isn't distorted like Layla and I are; his face is just a little longer and his shoulders a bit broader, with his chest puffed for confrontation. His emerald eyes meet mine and he holds my gaze, not letting me look away.

'Calm,' he commands. 'Calm,' he soothes, his words penetrate my haze and I slowly calm, retracting and returning to my usual form. Without the anger, the transition is bone-grating, flesh-tearing agony, but he holds my gaze throughout. Guillaume steps back as my change completes and lifts his hand from my arm, but his eyes continued to hold mine.

'What the hell have you been through? All vampires display when they are threatened or enraged, but if a vampire is turned while they are in a place of great pain emotionally, then they get the Rage.' At his unusually kind words I turn away, so he won't see the tears he's brought to my eyes.

'The Rage, as you have just experienced, is both a blessing and a curse. It makes you immune to the Gifts of others, but also blocks your own Gift from influencing others. Even while it empowers you, it weakens you,' Guillaume continues in his soothing tone, as if he is unaware of my emotional turmoil.

I look for Layla and see that David is doing the same for her as Guillaume has just done for me. Blood tears pour down her cheeks as the searing pains of transition tear through her.

David hadn't got to Layla in time though, and she has ripped through Melanie's face, tearing her ugly visage so one eye socket is empty and chunks of her cheek and lips hang

86

horribly off the bones. Blood and gore drip from her talons. Melanie is staggering around screaming and holding her face together as best she can while the others in her group stand back aghast, open mouths and raised hands the only sign of their horror.

'How Layla loves you,' Guillaume murmurs as he steps back, before turning and raising his arms. 'Quiet everyone,' he calls. All the vampires in the room turn to him, apart from me, I am gazing at my little friend and then I open my arms to her and she runs to me and flings herself into my embrace, hugging me tight and sobbing brokenly and we are ok. We are immune to each other, just like we are immune to Patrice.

'I think,' says Guillaume quietly, 'that maybe I have been a little hasty. We will see. There will be a trial of three months. Those who can comply and be useful to the group may live. Those who can't, will be destroyed.' He turns and strides back out of the room, his friends following him. Everyone else takes his lead and starts to file out of the room. Melanie walks alone, grimly silent now, her one remaining eye glaring balefully at Layla and me as she leaves. I can see that the flesh is already starting to knit back together, but her eyeball is gone and there is nothing to heal. As she passes, she is close enough for me to see the pale shine of scar tissue starting to fill in the socket. I see we have made a permanent enemy. I shudder.

'Hmm. Feisty,' says Patrice as she leaves, flicking her hair and eyeing me contemptuously, as though I am a gaudy fairground whore in a room of debutants. I can't help myself, I deflate. 'Don't turn your back, my pretty,' she croons softly, 'the Glamour doesn't work from behind.' She snickers and walks away, leaving Layla, David, Brian and me in a little huddle.

'Fuck!' David exclaims, 'I'm glad we're on your side.'

***

'Excuse me.'

As we leave the hall, a wispy blonde female approaches us timidly from the kitchen. I haven't noticed her before, she isn't one of the bitchy females that whisper and titter whenever we pass them, and she's not one of the haughty elders that speak earnestly with Elaine, Simon, and Guillaume, and treat all of the New Ones with disdainful indifference. We have not settled in well with the other vampires, which has thrown Layla; she is used to being popular. I stop to see what the little blonde wants.

'You do know you can exist on animal blood, don't you?' she speaks breathily, appearing shy, as if unsure of her welcome and anxious not to cause offense. We stare at her, mouths agape as she drops this latest bombshell. She twists her fingers nervously, shooting worried looks through her lashes over our shoulder, checking who is approaching us. There's a determined little jut to her chin which says that she's decided to have her say, even if it is awkward. Even if she's been told not to speak to us. When she sees we haven't brushed her off, she continues, 'That's why so many of us choose to live and work here on the farm. The animal blood doesn't smell or taste as good, but you can learn to ignore the cravings and get by, and you don't even need to kill the animals. You can just manage the blood-letting carefully.'

'Not for your first feed, you can't.' Guillaume is suddenly, smoothly behind us. 'You would cramp up and the last stages of internal transition would not complete, you would be weakened and left in permanent pain.' I turn on him eyes blazing, and he staggers back a step. The blonde girl spins away from our group and runs off with her hand over her mouth.

'Why didn't you tell us? Why didn't you tell us that in your sanctimonious spiel about the dos and don'ts of being a vampire?' I struggle to find the words to begin to voice the depth of the betrayal I feel.

'I needed to make sure you would drink the human blood first. There's plenty of time for all the other learning you still need to do.' His voice is firm and cool, but he won't look at me.

'But, but, if I'd known… Do you have any idea what these last few days have been like for me? How I've felt thinking that I have to commit murder and cannibalism to survive, and that I might not be able to resist ripping the throats out of innocent people; that I might start to enjoy it.' I gulp my rage back down and stand with my hands on my hips staring at him, demanding a reply. He looks up at me briefly and then back at his feet.

'Yes,' he answers bluntly, giving me a flash of insight into his own transition. 'Why do you think I bought the bags of blood?'

'But what about that man? The homeless man they killed in the barn?' I'm puzzled and cross.

'That had nothing to do with me. Patrice and Suzannah caught him and brought him back for their young ones while Elaine and I went to buy the blood from our contact at the hospital. It's not easy to get blood without answering a lot of questions. Elaine's gift makes memories fuzzy and vague, but there's only so much she can do. When we got back here, all of you were outside to eat. It was not up to me to stop you if you had wanted to. It is not up to me to judge how the other vampires wish to feed, as long as the rules are adhered to. I had never told you I would make you kill your first feed; it never occurred to me that you would think I would do such a thing. I told you that I was going to get you the blood you needed.

'Please remember, this is all new to me too. I have never turned anyone. No one in this group has, other than Patrice's recent exploits. We came together as a peaceful Pride of mature vampires. I only know my own experiences of being turned, and I was an accident, left to struggle alone. This is how I know not to drink animal blood first. I am in pain every minute of every day. I did not want that for you.'

I'm stunned. I would never have known that he is permanently in pain. He's always impressed me as being calm and in control. For a second I consider how magnificent he would have been if he had received the human blood for his first feed. Then the realisation dawns: Patrice had sent Georgette to get us on purpose. She knows Guillaume doesn't feed from humans, and wanted him to return home and find us all feeding. This would protect her young ones, there would be nothing separating the two groups when it came to time for Guillaume to make his decision about what to do with the new ones; and even if we didn't feed, watching us squirm was an evening's entertainment for her and her young ones.

Layla leads David away; Brian has already disappeared, but I have no idea where. Guillaume gestures with his head for me to follow him into his study. He chivalrously turns a chair away from the fire into the centre of the room for me to sit on. I haven't been into his study before. It is a beautiful, masculine room with mellow mahogany furniture, aged leather chairs, shelf upon shelf of books lining the walls and huge windows which let in lots of golden light. It smells richly of wood smoke, leather, and bees wax, and the musty bindings on the ancient books. After pulling out the chair for me, Guillaume moves to the window, and stands with his back to me, arms folded on the window sill so he is leaning his weight on them. At first I think he is more relaxed with me after his revelations, but then it dawns on me that the fight has exhausted him and he's struggling to stand. I'm moved to realise he is allowing me to see him this vulnerable, I feel my stomach flip, and heart contract with hope.

'You need to feed,' I say. He nods tiredly.

'Elaine has gone to get more blood. I don't often drink human, but when I am this tired I need to. It takes some of the pain away for a while.'

'Can I help?'

'No. Just listen while I tell you about Patrice. The more you know now, the better. She is dangerous, and you have made an enemy of her.' He sighs, and sags further forward across the window sill.

'Why don't you sit down?' I ask. 'You're struggling.'

'I can't,' he answers shortly. 'I can't look at you. You are almost impossible to resist when I am at my strongest. If I give in to you now, I will lose myself into the narcotic dream you offer. I wouldn't feel pain anymore, and you would have complete control over me.'

'Well, sit in a chair with its back to me then,' I reason practically. I tamp down the swell of joy that surges through me as he describes his desire for me. At least that explains why he won't ever look at me for more than the briefest glance. He isn't just being rude.

90

'That would be exceptionally bad-mannered of me.' He laughs a little and then sinks into the chair I've pushed up behind him.

'So, why are Layla, Patrice and I immune to each other?' I ask after he's been silent a few minutes, ignoring his confession of lust for me as casually as he'd confessed it.

'I don't know. I've only ever met the one Pretty One-Patrice. It's a rare Gift. Suzannah is not one, so we have only our experiences of how others react to Pretty Ones, we had no idea you would be immune to each other, although we should have guessed really. All the Gifts make you immune to that Gift in another vampire. It's just that the Pretty Gift has had such a negative impact on my life, I have erred on the side of caution'. His voice is hoarse.

'Look, let me start at my beginning, it will make more sense that way. I was young, unmarried, and I had just bought this farm. It was much smaller then, just the house and yard with a few acres, just enough for me to look for a wife and start a family. Since then I have created a company and bought any land that comes up for sale as soon as it comes on the market,' he explains. 'A few weeks after I had bought the farm, I was repairing the roof and needed more nails and some wood for shelves in the larder, so I went into the town for market day.' His voice has turned dreaming and he gazes out of the window, back in his youth, planning the improvements he would need to make so he could invite a young bride home.

'I remember starting the walk home as night fell, and then the next thing I knew, I was waking up in a ditch. Changed. I did not know what I had become, or why. I just knew I was different, and could not be around humans. I drank from my lifestock. Luckily, I was new to the community and not really known, so it was not difficult to become known as a recluse. It's much easier now with supermarkets. We never have to see anyone face to face when we sell our produce.'

'Anyway. A few years after I had become a vampire, I stumbled across Patrice at a market several towns over where I went to sell my produce. I went to a different market each time to avoid too much scrutiny. I knew as soon as I saw how she moved what she was, even before she lowered her hood and I saw her face. I watched her take a young man into an alley and kill him. She beckoned me over to feed with her, and I could not resist. I became completely spellbound by her. While I was with her, the pain I'd endured for the previous two years vanished. This was as addictive to me as her glamour. I became her willing plaything, and did as she bid me. I learned about the High Council from her, and the rules, and the gifts and learning to control and filter my vampire senses so I wasn't so overwhelmed.'

'I didn't know what my gift was, though. Patrice implied that I had been so damaged by having cattle blood for my first meal that I didn't have one. It was only five years later when three other vampires turned up at the farm that things changed. They had heard about us. Patrice was careless and foolhardy. She could control me, and so felt she could control anyone. The three who arrived were Simon, Elaine and Nicholas. They saved me. They pointed out that if they had heard of us, others would too, including the High Council.'

'Elaine taught me how to resist Patrice's control: stop her touching me, stop looking at her directly. She told me that Patrice could choose to turn her gift off, and so we set up this community and set our rules. I was going to banish Patrice, but she begged to be allowed to stay. She had hated living alone after her maker was killed, she hated being a vagrant drifting in the shadows, so she promised to live by our agreement.'

'We were called to the High Council to explain ourselves and given a final warning to comply with their rules. Since then we have all complied and Patrice is useful to the Pride; between her and Elaine we can usually avoid any trouble. And until last month she had obeyed the rules. I knew she chaffed against them, but for over ninety years she has managed to abide by them, just. Others who wanted to live peacefully have come to join us, some didn't like the rules, and they left again. Some of those who chose to stay suffer from having drunk animal blood first, like I do. Especially little Annie, she refuses to ever drink human blood, even from the hospital, so she never has any reprieve. She hasn't let the pain turn her bitter, though, she just keeps to herself and concentrates on her bees.'

'Aren't you immune to other Pretty Ones then? Layla and I are immune to each other, and Patrice, I thought you would be too,' I ask. Guillaume laughs. 'Is it called something else for men then?' I huff, annoyed he is laughing at me.

'No, I'm not a Pretty One. It was only when the others came, I found my gift. I can lead. I can get others to listen to me. This is why we agreed we would not use our gifts on each other. Patrice did not like it when I found I could control her as long as I did not look directly at her. Our living together has to be by mutual compliance. No one wants to be controlled by another.'

'What did Patrice mean when she told me not to turn my back? How does the glamour not work from behind?' I ask, remembering what she had jibbed at me as she passed me in the hall.

'Exactly that,' Guillaume replied. 'Your power only extends in front of you. You can persuade anyone to do anything you choose if you turn the full force of your charm onto them while you face them, especially if you touch them. Be careful when touching when you're newly changed, though, you won't always be able to control the results.'

'Yeah, I know.' It's my turn not to look at him.

'However,' he continues, 'you are vulnerable from behind; your gifts do not protect your back from vampires, and if someone attacks you from behind, they can quickly overpower you.'

Layla

Several uneasy days of truce follow. I spend my time with Rae, David and Brian down in the river field away from the other Young Ones. Rae and I head down there first thing in the morning, and David follows. Poor Brian is stuck tagging along. He doesn't want to be left alone with the others, but he hates being near Rae. He doesn't know that I know what happened, but he is so uncomfortable whenever Rae is near,

93

it's hard not to laugh. You would think she deliberately set out to seduce him the way he behaves, like he's this irresistible super stud. Bless him, despite being a vampire, he is still utterly forgettable. In fact, we do often forget he's there, and then realise with a start he's still sat next to David when he pipes up a comment in reply to something David or I say. He won't speak to Rae unless she deliberately goads him, asking a question he is forced to answer. She hasn't got a cruel bone in her body, but even she can't resist teasing him, finding that point where his manners outweigh his dislike of her.

Down here, by the river, we are exploring what it is to be a vampire together, experiencing running water on our new sensitive skin, crushing leaves to smell with our new noses. Watching birds fly between the branches, transfixed by the array of colours, shades we couldn't see as humans. We've found out that David's gift is, predictably, strength. He can easily lift Brian over his head, although they are about the same height. The strength seems to means that he has some immunity to Rae and me, either that or he just doesn't care about the risks of being in our vicinity. We are all careful not to test it too far by touching.

Rae has started borrowing books from Guillaume's office, since she has discovered he has shelves and shelves of them in there, or she downloads e-books; either way once she is bored by the new sensations we are exploring, she sprawls in the long, sweet, meadow grass and escapes into other worlds until drifting into sun-softened sleep.

While she is distracted, David and I talk, about ourselves, about the lives we have left behind, about the things that were important to us and how we felt about being wrenched away from them. We discover a shared love of the silliness of Monty Python, and Black Adder. He is impressed by my appreciation of all things geeky and sci-fi, but we disagree bitterly over the best Doctor Who, and whether replacing the whole Being Human cast worked or not.

During one of our rare moments alone, Rae asks me about our closeness, which is becoming all consuming. As soon as I wake up, he is the first thing I think of, and I fall asleep smiling about some funny shared quirk. I had no idea it is possible to feel like this about someone. Rae tried to pussyfoot around the subject, talking about all the extreme sensations we can feel now, and how much new stuff we are learning about being vampires. But I heard what she was saying, the warning she was sounding. I told her that he was the only good thing that has happened to me for years, but I'm not going to risk this incredible friendship with a re-enactment of what had happened with Melanie.

I think I accidentally hurt her feelings when I said that, I didn't mean to exclude her, I just don't class her as something that's happened in the last few years- we've been friends for over twenty years. She's my constant. But she turned a bit sharp then and snapped that it's a bit late, since it's obvious to everyone that I've fallen hook, line and sinker for him. This is a bit rich coming from her, given the way she gazes at Guillaume when she thinks no one's watching.

My feelings for David have made me think about me, and what was wrong with me as a human. None of the doctors could ever tell me exactly what that was, which is why I kept trying so long. I've been thinking about what we were told, about being affected by the virus, so we are not undead, not supernatural beings, but rather highly evolved creatures, with the best bits taken from each branch of our evolutionary journey, so we are vesting superior now to the humans we were, but we are still living. I've wondered if that meant I might be fertile now, if maybe, just maybe, David and I might have babies. I hardly dared to allow the thought to be fully formed in my own head, I certainly didn't speak it aloud to my friends. I decided to ask one of the older vampires, just as a theoretical question.

One afternoon when Elaine is showing me how to tell weeds from young bean shoots, before I ruined another crop, I ask her about it. She looks incredulous for a moment, and then shakes her head.

'Do you see any babies?' she snaps. 'No, the virus changes us, so we are no longer purely mammal, so our ovaries don't work anymore, and neither do the males testicles. We're barren.' She finishes grimly, then stomps back to the house, leaving me to finish weeding the vegetable bed. I'm glad to be alone, I hadn't admitted to myself that a heart full of hope had blossomed, but as it dies viciously, I feel each petal fade.

Chapter 5
Rae

In the evenings we sit in the lounge of the farm house playing board games, avoiding the other vampires who sit in the kitchen. Occasionally, Annie comes to join us, now she knows we are keen to only drink animal blood too. Simon, Elaine or Marcus, another of Guillaume's closest confidants, pop their heads around the door to check we are ok, before going back to work in the office. On several occasions we have steadfastly ignored the noises from the barn, which give away the times when Patrice or Suzannah bring back some poor individual to their death. We also ignore the hunger, and the desire for the chase that rips through us at the screams and scent of blood, avoiding each other's eyes, silently concentrating on our hand of cards while we wait for the surges to pass.

Two vampires called Christophe and Robert bring us glasses of warm, fresh pig blood. They are remarkably coarse and crude for vampires, and they leer at Layla and me in lewd appreciation. We do our best to ignore them, but we can't help wrinkling our noses as the stench from the pig shit on their boots assault our fresh new senses, until David loses patience with them, and snarls at them, and they swagger out, like bantam cockerels determined to save face, even while they beat a hasty retreat. The texture of the fresh, warm pig's blood is better than the chilled hospital bags, but the taste is rank and makes us gag. The first night we had the pig blood, Marcus, who had come into the lounge to see why David was snarling, laughed at our expressions as we drank and promised us that cow or horse blood is even worse, because they were herbivores and their blood was very bitter to a vampire.

'If an animal blood diet is the choice you want to make, then this is the reality you want to live with,' he had told us, shrugging before returning to the office. So we grit our teeth and swig it down; no matter how bad it tastes, it will never be as bad as the killing out in the barn.

After hiding out with Layla, David and Brian for eight days, I have decided that I have had enough of being a gooseberry. Layla and David have become inseparable, despite Layla's protestations they are just friends. My arse! Brian still won't look at me and only speaks to me if I directly ask him a question. So, when I get up the next morning, I decide to go to see if I could be any help on the farm. I'm not sure how the other vampires will accept me, but if this is to be my home, I need to start mingling. Hopefully, Annie will be around and she can teach me about her bees. As I head towards the back door, Elaine calls me to one side.

'We've got a problem. Your husband is in Tours,' Elaine never softens her words; she always bluntly gets straight to the point. 'We have someone there who has been paid to let us know if anyone came around asking too many questions. I thought you emailed him?' She scowls at me.

'I did!' I'm defensive. 'I sent everyone the email. I haven't checked for replies, though,' I concede. 'I suppose I should have. I never thought he'd care that much. We've been separated for months. Maybe I shouldn't have said I met someone. Maybe that raised the possessive beast in him. Shit. Now what will we do?'

'Well, if he disappears while he's out here, that's going to make far more questions.'

'What? I'm not going to kill him!' I'm shocked at the suggestion. Elaine shrugs.

'And you don't want to turn him?'

'Oh God, no!' I'm adamant. The only good thing about being infected is that I can walk away from James, feeling virtuous for not putting him at risk. Leaving isn't my choice anymore, so I don't have to feel guilty.

'Well, sort it out,' Elaine barks and then disappears into Guillaume's study. I ignore the rush of envy that sweeps through me as she squirrels herself away with him.

'Just the New One uncontrollables,' I reassure myself, ignoring the memory of him telling me how Elaine saved him from Patrice, which wants to stamp through my memory. 'Breathe through it.' I unscrew my eyes and unclench my fists to see Annie looking at me fearfully. I smile at her, and her scrawny little shoulders sag in relief and her face brightens into a sunny smile.

'Want to help me with the bees?' she asks. I'm not sure why she is going out of her way to be friendly to me - maybe my Glamour can soothe her pain a little, just from being near me -but I don't care. Any kindness at the moment is gratefully received, and I happily grab a basket of empty jars and follow her out into the garden. As I work alongside Annie through the afternoon, I try to think about what to do. I know James, and I know he is tenacious once he decides he wants something, and far too late he seems to have decided he wants me.

As my hands are kept busy collecting honey and checking the hives, my mind tosses possible solutions to and fro. I know what I need to do, though; the only thing that might work, even if it is dangerous. That evening I seek out Elaine and tell her I need to meet with James. It is the only way he will back off; when he hears that I've met someone else, from me directly. Initially, Elaine is adamant that this must not happen, that I will have to find another way to persuade him, but I am equally determined that there isn't another way. I don't want anything awful to happen to him, and I want him to restart his own life, not waste his time pining after me. I owe him that much.

I explain my idea to her. There are some spectacular waterfalls- Le Grand Saut on the Herisson river just the other side of Grenoble, not that far from where the farm sits in the countryside that surrounds Lyon, but far enough to be safe. James loves things like that. I can hire an open-top car, using that as an excuse to tie my newly lustrous hair back into a plait, cover my head with a scarf, and wear big sunglasses. Teamed with a roll-neck jumper, leather driving gloves, trousers and flat shoes, it could pass for a French chic look. Elaine cocks an unimpressed eyebrow at this; until I point out I only have to convince a Welshman that it is French chic, if he even notices what I am wearing. If I am already sat in a shady, gloomy area near the waterfall when James arrives, his eyes would be dim from the bright sunshine on the approach, and then he'd be distracted by the beauty of the waterfall behind me. I could be horrible, and he would storm off quickly, sorted. Elaine considers it for a few minutes, tapping her chin with her fingertips.

'It might work. I can teach you to control your Glamour better, and frankly I don't really see what other choice we have. I'll talk to Guillaume about it and let you know.'

An hour later Elaine taps my door, and opens it, sticking her head round.

'He doesn't like it,' she says as she comes in and perches on the end of my bed where I am watching a mind-numbingly stupid film on my laptop. 'But tough. I have told him it is the only way. He insists that Simon must go with you, though. The two of you can take his '63 Citroën Deesee coupe. Simon can drive you, and if James does not accept what you say, or looks too closely, Simon will be there to deal with him.'

'Deal with him?' I swallow.

'Yes, every one of us is at risk if he is not convinced; not just from the humans, but from the High Council too. We have worked too hard these last few weeks to keep this contained to fail now, for the sake of one human. If you want him left alive, it is up to you to keep him that way. Come, I need to teach you how to control your gifts.' She beckons me over to the mirror.

We spend the next couple hours in front of the oval pane while I attempt to learn how to turn my Gift down. Elaine advises me to picture it like a gas flame I can turn down. I scrunch up my face in concentration. She tells me to imagine walking into a bar as a human, one where I didn't want to draw attention to myself. It's years since I've drawn any attention when I walk into anywhere. I can see I am frustrating Elaine. Finally, exasperated, she suggests being in a classroom at school when the teacher asks for homework you haven't done. Ah yes, I can remember that. That feeling of trying to dip below radar, of hunching inside so the outside looks nonchalant and not guilty, but you've drawn in your 'look at me' vibes so the teacher's eyes are supposed to pass right over you.

As I think of this and remember what I used to do in the classroom, Elaine silently points my attention to the mirror. I look up at myself through my lashes. The result is remarkable. I am still there. I still look like ravishing, vampiric me, but somehow I am just less noticeable, duller. Elaine goes and digs out some clothes for me to wear. I am so tall that only Nicholas's trousers fit me, although they sit on my hips, not waist, which I've always hated. I have to wear some black brogues Brian had brought with him, which also annoys me because I had always liked my little feet but now they're big, and strong.

'All the better for running, my dear,' Elaine laughs at me as I lace up the brogues with a look of disgust on my face. We decide that the roll neck jumper draws too much attention to my breasts and a big untucked man's shirt with the head scarf tucked into the turned up collar works best. Finished off with the cream leather driving gloves and the biggest pair of Chanel sunglasses we could find I don't look too bad. Elaine shows me how to apply make-up badly to make the bits skin on my face that I can't hide look as human as possible. She warns me to apply it at the last possible moment and not to touch it once it is applied, because it won't adhere to my smooth, poreless, vampire skin, and will slide off my face as easily as it would a doll's.

The look will be finished with a generous squirt of Chanel No. 5 to cover up the fact that vampires are absolutely scentless to a human nose. While James might not notice this consciously, he would notice subconsciously and start looking for other flaws in my disguise. My usual perfume won't smell the same on me anymore, and a strong dose of a perfume I know he hates would be another way of keeping him at arm's length. I would just have to ignore the nausea the strong chemical scent aroused in me. Synthetic chemicals are all my vampire nose will smell of any perfume now.

Elaine leaves me practising how to turn the flame of attractiveness down in the mirror. I find that, like Elaine had said, I can picture a stove and imagine turning a knob on the hob while watching the flame on the burner dim, and this seems to work. With the flame simmering low I look at myself in the mirror and see that without the shine of the Glamour, I am not so unlike I had looked in my twenties when I was sparkling with happiness and enthusiasm for life. I can probably pass for someone who has had a lot of very good work done.

Before I go to bed, I finally open my emails. I delete the angry ones from my boss and friends, and read the slightly anxious ones from my parents and Santana with a tear in my eye. They just want me to be happy, and hope I can find joy with this mysterious Frenchman who has swept me off my feet, and they are glad Layla is with me, and look forward to seeing us soon. They're vague, though, I know there is no danger of them turning up here as well. Chatty emails will keep them happy and on their adventures. There are a lot of emails from James. They start off furious, become contrite and begging, and then stop after a final one that asks me to meet him in Tours. That one must have been sent once he had decided that he was coming over to look for me.

I type a reply telling him I'm not in Tours anymore, but not saying where I am. I am curt, and express my reluctance to waste his time as I don't have anything to say I haven't said in my last email, but if he is determined to waste both our time, I will meet him at the Grand Saut Falls. I let him know that there is a little hotel near the waterfall called Hotel Du Col De Machine where he can stay. I describe its rustic sweetness nestling by the road. I imply it is somewhere I have stayed, a romantic getaway, rather than somewhere I've just looked up on Trip Advisor.

When I try to sleep my mind keeps stubbornly circling back to the first time I got drunk and ended up back in bed with him. It was about four weeks after I had vacated our marriage, and the first time I'd seen him, although he'd continually phoned, texted, and emailed to ask me to meet him and talk about my decision since I'd left. This time I'd called him and told him I would be popping over briefly the next evening to pick up the last couple of bags of my belongings. I'd been wracked with anxiety about facing him all day. I was guilt-ridden and sure he'd either be incandescently angry with me, or weepy and begging me to move back home. I kept reminding myself that this had to be done, this was the full stop; after this final gruesome process, I could walk away and sort my life out with no more loose ends. The bright beacon of the full stop and walking into my own future kept me going through my discomfort and desire to run away from the horribleness of it all, leaving it until another day to sort out.

I knocked at the front door because it was his house now; despite his pleas to talk, he had wasted no time getting the solicitor and Mortgage Company's paperwork sorted out so the house would be in his name solely. As if he feared I would change my mind, but I'd signed all the paperwork and returned it immediately. This was his house, his debt, I felt lucky to be free of it. When he let me in, I was surprised he welcomed me warmly. He made no move to interfere as I collected my last belongings; indeed most of them were neatly wrapped and packed: there was just one painful pile we would need to discuss. He was kind and thoughtful; he offered me a coffee, then a glass of wine. We had things we needed to sort out, and we were being so adult and constructive. The first bottle slid down, then another.

The next morning I had been so relieved when I woke up, cuddled into his big strong back. The last four weeks had been so tough and terrifying and I had been anxious, doubting my decision to leave him after almost fifteen years of moderately happy marriage. Back in the marital bed I felt safe and relaxed, back where I belonged. We had ambled over to the local café to soak up some of the excess alcohol sloshing in our guts, with grease and caffeine. I sat enfolded in a dreamy rosy glow, gazing at him in the morning light beaming through the smeary window, thinking about how stupid I'd been to leave this man; he was so strong and sure. I was so lucky he'd waited for me.

"So, you think it's a good idea then?" I had asked, gazing at him happily over the cup of coffee I was clutching in my slightly shaky hands. I wanted to restart the conversation we'd begun the previous evening. We'd been getting on so well that I had forgotten myself and talked about my tentative plans to start my own business. It was a long time since we had got drunk together and shared our hopes and dreams with each other. I hadn't dared to tell him about my hopes while we were still together; we had had to work too damn hard to pay our mortgage to contemplate doing anything financially risky.

My Probation Officer wages weren't very high, but they were consistent. James was an accountant by training. Originally, he was ambitious; after he qualified, he had worked for someone else for a couple of years to gain experience and then, almost ten years ago, he opened his own practice. He needed a big lump of cash to set up on his own so he'd suggested we sell our dinky first home so he wouldn't have to take out a bank loan.

James had never loved our first home together like I had. It was a bijou flat in that part of Cardiff which estate agents call Roath, but everyone knows is really Splott. We were lucky enough to have bought it just before the housing boom. I had redecorated it to emphasise every drop of natural light, squeezing storage into every nook and cranny. It ended up being worth five times what we paid for it within the four years we lived there. James had set his heart on a thirties semi in Whitchurch, near his parents. I'd wanted to make him happy, so we had stretched our finances to their limit, used the cash from selling our flat to set up his business and then taken out a slightly less than honest self-cert mortgage to buy the house of his dreams.

It was one of those houses that had been gutted of all the awkward little rooms and opened up into a vast space. It had had all the imperfections and quirks ripped out, leaving a white expanse of sleek new kitchen and dining area where the glass dining table took pride of place; flowing on to become the lounge space, where the huge white leather corner sofa was positioned around a gas fire. A flick of the switch had flames dancing over smooth pebbles.

I had pointed out that the fire was slightly dwarfed by the huge flat-screen television fixed to the wall above it, but James was adamant it was necessary for watching football. The alcoves either side of the chimney breast had three floating shelves each, which held the tasteful ornaments James's parents bought us every Christmas, Birthday and Anniversary; and glossy coffee table books no one would ever want to actually read, but no real books. James's complaints about my tatty books had persuaded me to switch to an eReader as soon as they'd come out. I had to admit that it took up a lot less space, but I missed my higgledy piggledy piles of old friends, and I missed being able to share my favourites with my friends. It was a beautiful house, very beautiful but utterly soulless.

Initially, his business had gone from strength to strength. He had a good reputation and he quickly established a reliable client base. Then 2008 came along, and the next thing we knew, companies big and small were going bust left, right and centre. I supported his decision to remortgage the house when the trouble first hit. If we released the equity that had built up thanks to the crazy rate the house prices had risen in the seven years we had owned it, then he was sure he could save the business. The money had allowed James to struggle through the first year of the recession, convinced things would pick up soon, but they hadn't. It had been like watching dominoes fall, and despite fighting it as long as he could, he eventually had to admit defeat, and walk away, before we lost the house as well. He had felt lucky when he was offered a middle management job by a big insurance company a year later, but the mortgage on the house was so high by then that neither of us could take any financial risks.

For years I'd harboured a secret dream of setting up a little interior design business, giving previously loved furniture a new lease of life. I had fantasies of tootling around Britain and Europe in a van, picking up unappreciated treasures in auction houses, junk shops, and flea markets, then bringing them home to restore and sell to my discerning clients. I wasn't interested in making a fortune, I just wanted to be able to pay my own way doing something I loved.

I hadn't talked about my ideas with James while he concentrated on setting up his business because he wouldn't have understood that I was talking about 'one day'. I had just nursed my ambition like a secret pebble in my pocket, taking it out to turn over and look at every now and again, then slipping it back away without showing it to anyone else.

Just as our life had started to look stable enough for me to broach the subject of part-time hours at Probation, the financial bubble burst. We were caught up in battening down the hatches, doing everything in our power not to become homeless. Only an idiot would even think of throwing away the stability I had; so many people were scrabbling for security around me, it would have been churlish to resent my good fortune when I didn't lose my job.

So when I had drunkenly told James about my idea that fateful night, it had been his enthusiasm that had won me over, made me feel I had misjudged him, casting him as my boo man instead of acknowledging it was my own self-doubt that held me back. Sitting in the café the next morning, I'd turned my face up to him ready for more helpful ideas and offers of help, excited about sharing my secret dreams.

'Oh yeah,' he'd said, after looking baffled for a second. 'Doing up the house with stuff we've bought in France? We'll have a lovely time in the antique shops choosing things, but there's no rush, is there? There's nothing wrong with the house as it is.' I'd stared at him, my golden haze disintegrating, while he picked up the final slice of toast and wiping up the grease and bean juice from his plate, obtusely oblivious to the change in my demeanour.

'Come on, Rach, get a move on. I'm meeting the boys in town in twenty minutes, it's the Cup match, remember.'

***

The next morning I have the predictable reply to my email. He insists on seeing me face to face, so that he knows that I am well, and we can talk about the reality of what I'm saying. His patronising tone infuriates me. He will hire a car and meet me at Le Grand Saut the following day. I spend the rest of the morning in the garden ostensibly helping Annie again, but I'm so tense and jumpy that I'm not much use. In the afternoon I am in the kitchen showing Annie, Layla and David how I can turn my Gift off, when Brian walks in as I have it simmered down as low as I can. The others are squealing and clapping at my efforts, Layla clamouring for me to show her how to do it, Brian looks at me uncomprehendingly for a moment, then shakes his head and walks back out of the room. David apologises to me, explaining that Brian has not forgiven himself for what happened between us; he sees it as cheating. He is not letting go of the idea that his Meg could still love him.

That evening Elaine calls me into the kitchen and gives me two bags of blood.

'You need to make sure you are not hungry at all,' she explains. 'You could be around several humans and you will need all your concentration to keep the glamour off without worrying about hunger as well.' I force the thick cold blood down and then go off to bed for a restless night spent thinking about what exactly I will say to James to get him to leave me alone as quickly as possible.

The next day Simon and I set off very early. The Deesse, or Goddess, is a beautiful little cream car that looks both classic and futuristic at the same time, like a flying saucer with wheels. It reminds me of the Jetsons cartoon from my childhood. The car is small inside though, so I need to concentrate on keeping my Glamour dimmed and lean as far away from Simon as possible as we zoom down the almost empty French roads.

I can't help remembering the last time I saw James. I woke in his bed in a lurch of horror. Consciousness crashed in and dread set my heart pounding so it tried to kick its way out of my chest. I sat bolt upright in bed, my head spinning and my stomach roiling with the previous night's alcohol. I peered at him sleeping soundly next to me, and he rasped a nasal snore. Relieved, I kept my eyes on him as I slipped one foot out from under the duvet, and patted around with my toes to check the floor was clear. Once I was sure there's nothing there, I slithered out of bed, legs first, dropping silently to my knees.

He'd rearranged the room since I'd left, switching the bed to the opposite end of the room, and covering up the painted floorboards with plush taupe carpet. I hate carpets anywhere in a house, but I appreciated his when it muffled the sounds of my escape. I crawled around fumbling for my clothes in the faint light that sneaked around the edges of the curtains. I was a bit disorientated from the room being back to front, but eventually, I located my shoes and jeans, blithely scattered across the floor with drunken abandon the night before. I hooked my t-shirt and bra out from under the dressing table, and poked my hand around under the bed and arm chair, but I couldn't find my knickers anywhere. Mortified, I crouched undecided for a moment, contemplating sliding my hand under the duvet to scout around for them, but James snorted and rolled over, so I made the reluctant decision to abandon them and crawled inelegantly out of the room, dragging my clothes and pulling the door closed behind me.

On the landing I staggered upright using the bannister for help, pausing to allow the swimmies to pass, then I tippy toed into the bathroom, grateful again for the luxuriously soft carpet, a small gesture of spite on his part that aided my stealthy exit. Ugh, I averted my eyes from the mirror and plopped down onto the toilet, pleased to find that emptying my bladder relieved a smidgen of my misery. Sitting seemed like a good idea, so I stayed on the loo while I dragged my clothes on. Steadfastly, I refused to meet my own eyes in the mirror above the basin until, finally, I had to stand up to zip my jeans and I couldn't avoid them any longer. That's what I remember best now, taking a good long look at my dishevelled self as I wiped a bit of toothpaste over my teeth with my finger. James had put a toothbrush in the beaker for me, but I left it in its wrapper.

'Rae Reeves, this has got to stop,' I'd promised my swollen, tear-battered, alcohol-raddled reflection.

Despite the horrors that being a vampire entails, and the devastation of never seeing family or friends again, a part of me is so glad that the virus has forced me to keep that promise to myself.

Within a horribly short couple of hours I am perching on a rock in the shade of some trees, trying to resist scratching at the sticky makeup that's balancing on my face, watching James approach me. The weather is in my favour, with very bright sunshine outside the dank spot of shade I've chosen to sit in. I've selected a boulder that puts the waterfall over my left shoulder and the sun over my right, while I am in the valley's shadow. This means I will be hard for his weak human eyes to focus on and James's gaze will be drawn to the water instead. Even while James is quite a distance away, his scent is alluring, and despite my big meal the night before, I feel the hunger raise its evil head and coil through me, like a giant snake that is slippery to hold; I am in danger of losing my grip. I have to keep reminding myself not to pull or chew my lips, my normal tell when I am anxious. I cannot risk James seeing my teeth. I do not stand as he approaches me and just gesture brusquely to a boulder slightly below mine for him to sit on.

'What is all this about?' I've decided that attack is the best form of defence, and that I am going to control the conversation from the outset so he can't talk me down any blind alleys I can't get back out of. 'Why are you here? I told you what I was doing, I left you the house. What more do you want from me?' From behind my sunglasses I can see his eyes flinch off me at my angry words and settle on the beauty of the big waterfall over my shoulder, just like I planned.

'Did you take the drugs the other girls took? Is that why you're behaving so strangely?' he asks quietly. Yikes, I hadn't expected this line of questioning. I do a quick calculation and decide to feign ignorance of what he was talking about.

'What on earth are you on about? Drugs? Why on earth would I take drugs? It doesn't take drugs for me to finally get the strength to leave you, just the love of a good man, who listens to me. Someone who recognises that my friends are women, not girls,' I hiss at him contemptuously.

'I just thought…'

'What? What did you just think?' I snap.

'It's been on the news: some men who were in Tours at the same time as you guys took something and died, and Lizzie is dead, too; they think she took something which gave her a massive heart attack, so I thought, you know, with you experimenting in uni, and you've been behaving so strangely this past year. I thought you might have been having a mid-life crisis, and have taken something, and it's made you go a bit loopy. There was some woman on the T.V whose sister's fiancé was friends with the guys who died, and he's taken off with no explanation too…' James looks at me hopefully.

'What guys, James? I've got no idea what you're talking about.' I heave a big sigh, I am genuinely insulted now, so I don't need to act exasperated, I am fuming at his complete dismissal of all the soul searching I have done over the last year. 'At uni I took a few drags on some joints my friends were smoking. I didn't even like the stuff. I just used to talk about it because I knew it pissed you off,' I snarl, his face drops and for some reason this make me crosser. I struggle to control my temper, God the last thing I need is to get the rage here and start transforming.

'I have never done anything stronger,' I continue icily. 'And I would never do anything stronger. Think about where I worked and what I saw. Not an advertisement for the use of substances really, was it? I have no idea what Lizzie and that stupid cow she brought over with her got up to. Layla and I hated what's her face, Melanie? We didn't sit with them at the party, and we had a big row with them after the others caught their flight back. They blamed us for not waking them up, so Layla and I just went out together, and we met Gerard and Pierre. We only went back to the hotel to get our cases. Within a week of living in France, with French men, we knew this is it, this is what we want; our happy-ever-afters. I'm happy, so just get over it.' I am spitting this diatribe at him, so it will be too uncomfortable for him to look back at me. I'm horribly aware of just how bitterly far from the truth my rant is. But if I could snap my fingers and change everything back, I wouldn't, if it meant going back to James. I know this with all my soul.

'I still love you. You know this. I just want one last chance to sort things out with you, and if you really, really, must live in France, then that's what we'll do. I don't know how, but we'll find a way if that's what you need to be happy.' His voice is quiet and resigned. This isn't going to be as hard as I had feared. He is already feeling defeated. Just trying to manage on his own in France for a few days has convinced him of the futility of this plan. James doesn't speak French and charm only gets you so far. He is looking a little seedy, needing a shave and a haircut and his skin looks greasy and grey, so his charm won't have got him as far as normal, either. He is just going through the motions. He has come up with a speech and is going through it, but his heart isn't in it; he knows he stands

110

no chance. I heave another big elaborate sigh and toss my head.

'Don't be so utterly ludicrous,' I say, my voice dripping with contempt. 'I've told you, I don't love you anymore. I've met someone else, I'm getting on with my life and you need to get on with yours. How you do that is not my business now. I'm not interested. We should never have got married; you are too boring; being with you almost destroyed me. Let me go.' '*Cruel to be kind, cruel to be kind,*' I keep chanting in my own head as I watch his face crumple and his shoulders sag.

'Ok,' he chokes.

'What?' Can it have been this easy?

'Ok. I can see you're over me. You look so different, younger and more carefree. I never meant to destroy you. You won't hear from me again.' He turns his back on me and walks closer to the falls.

'Well, good,' I call after him. 'Well, look after yourself,' I find myself adding despite my best intentions to be cold, but my vampiric hearing means that I can hear his hoarse sobs over the thundering water and for that moment I hate myself completely.

Knowing that I better get going while I can, I cast one last look at the big broad back that I loved so much for so long. I'm grateful for the infection now, because this is when I would crumble, and my instinct to stop his pain would kick in and I would run after him, and smother my own need to be free with the need to stop him hurting. But now my need to protect him from what I have become means I can let James go. I hurry back to the car, fling the door open and slump into my seat. Simon looks at me for confirmation that everything went to plan, and I give him a curt nod.

I spend the journey back to the farm looking out of the window telling myself over and over that I have done the right thing, but I have never done anything cruel to anyone before, and the defeated hunch of his back hurts my heart each time the image flashes before my eyes. If he had been angry with me, I could have hated him back, but that sad acceptance, and his belief that he had done me harm, cuts me to the quick

111

and strangles my breath in my chest so it comes out in hiccoughs and dry little sobs.

As soon as we get back to the farm, I leave Simon to let the others know that everything had gone according to plan. I slip up to my room, grab my MP3 player and then slide back out and away from the farm buildings. I trudge up a hill, and through a dense copse of trees. When I am far enough away from the farm that no one can see me, I flick through my tracks for some suitably angry music, put my headphones in and start to dance. I throw myself into a stamping, whirling angry storm, deliberately contorting my body into ugly angles and stupid shapes, determined not to be beguiling or seductive. I lift my knees and stamp, I thrust my hips and twirl. I dance out my grief for the girl I was, and the boy he was and the dreams we had.

James was a couple of years older than me, and earned enough to take me on a long weekend in Paris for my twenty-third birthday. He was content to trail around the Louvre and the Pompidou Centre with me while I wowed and pointed. On our second evening, in a little restaurant in Montmartre, he took my hand and solemnly gazed at me, his face alight with love.

'You know I love you more than life itself. You are the most amazing person I have ever met. You light up my life. You show me things I would never even notice on my own. The thought of ever losing you is more than I could ever bear,' he told me gravely.

'I'm not going anywhere.' I grinned at him. He'd knocked back several glasses of the house vin rouge, and I thought he was becoming a bit maudlin. Not his usual style, but booze will do that sometimes.

'Hush! No! Listen to what I'm saying.' He raised his hand as if to push back my words, grabbed his glass and took another swig. 'No. What I am trying to say, if you wouldn't keep so rudely interrupting.' He grinned at me to show he was joking, but I was a bit pissed off by now and scowled. 'I am trying to ask you, my love, if you would do me the honour of becoming my wife.' His face had gone a bit green and he looked scared and hopeful.

112

'Oh my God! Yes! Yes! Of course I will,' I squealed, clapping my hands in delight.

He reached into his jacket pocket and pulled out a small navy velvet box and snapped the lid open. As he held it out to me, I saw the pretty little sapphire and diamond cluster. Sapphires may not have been my first choice of stone, and I had actually told him I didn't like clusters when we had looked in a jewellery shop window just before Christmas, but his whole face was alight. As he slid the ring onto my finger, he was full of the story of how he had taken one of my rings out of my jewellery box without me knowing, so he could take it to the jeweller's with him to make sure my engagement ring would fit me perfectly.

'I wanted you to love it as much as I love you.' He glowed at me, holding my left hand to admire the ring on my finger.

'Of course I do.' I leant forward to kiss him, slightly awkward with the table between us, but it was a tiny table, so we just about managed. By now the other diners had realised what had happened and were applauding, and the maître d' was bringing us flutes of sparkling wine to celebrate. It was such a joyful night; I was so happy, I felt like I finally belonged. Here was someone who was promising to love me forever, whatever life threw at us.

The next morning when I woke up in a wash of terror, I reassured myself it was just the normal post-alcohol anxiety I had started to suffer every time I had a drink. I looked over at James - he was already awake and gazing at me adoringly. He pulled me gently towards him and tucked me into his side, under his arm and kissed me resoundingly, not at all bothered by my morning breath. This is real, I told myself, this is love, and I drifted back off to sleep safe and warm in his arms. Layla had sounded stunned when I phoned her with my happy news, but I had found a man who looked at me with adoring eyes, so I leapt at the chance to marry early and settle down.

After I have danced off my remorse, I flick through my MP3 player and find Chris Isaac's 'Wicked Game' and howl along. Until I realise with a start that I'm not singing or dancing about James anymore. I haven't been for a while.

Layla

As a new vampire it is easy to forget how far another vampire can see. When Rae returns with Simon, I know she will be struggling with what she has done, her relief contradicting his pain. I'm stood by the door to my room when she comes up, but she doesn't see me, she goes straight into her room grabs her MP3 off her bed, and then slips back out. I watch her go from my room and see her make her way up the hill, disappearing into the trees for a while. I'm about to turn away from my window when she remerges above in the field at the brow of the hill. At first I'm confused by the odd things she's doing, and think she is having some kind of fit, but then it dawns on me that she's dancing, and trying really hard to make herself ugly, a dance of fury and pain. I can tell by the way she flings herself around that she thinks no one can see her. I let her rage for ten minutes, and then set off after her. My timing is perfect and just as blood tears threaten to spill, I bound through the tree line grinning at her.

Without a word I take her music gadget and skip the song over to Cake's version of 'I Will Survive'. Rae is grinning and hands me a headphone and turns the player up as loud as it will go. Together we shake our deliberately unfunky stuff until we are laughing too much to stand upright. Once I know she will be ok, that she has remembered who we are, I head off back down to the farm. It's getting late and David will be wondering where I am.

Rae

In my room I open my window as wide as it will go to let in summer scents on the fresh breeze. I feel calm now, and gently melancholy. I curl up naked under the duvet, finding some comfort in my soft bed. I lie with my back to the door and put my play music on my laptop on as loud as its tinny little speakers will allow. Scarlet tears slip down my nose and stain my pillow case.

I only realise that Guillaume has come into my room when he sits beside me on my bed. I start, and try to turn towards him, but he spoons in behind, slipping my headphones off my head while he whispers gruffly in my ear not to turn around. I remember what he told me about my glamour no affecting vampires when they are behind me, but I still concentrate on keeping it turned down as low as possible. I feel so lonely and desperate for comfort and my desire for Guillaume has only grown after our conversation in his office on the evening of the fight. The fact he has obviously been avoiding me since has hurt me deeply. I had thought we'd made a connection that evening, and I've been bitterly disappointed when he's gone out of his way to avoid bumping into me since. I've been feeling foolish that I had ever hoped I might mean anything to him, but now here he is, right when I need him most.

There isn't much space in my single bed for both of us, so I am pushed to the far edge while he lies tucked in behind me. He is still whispering to me, telling me I have been brave, and not to take on so. He strokes the back of my neck lightly with one finger, easing the duvet down. I can feel his warm breath on the back of my neck, as his finger moves in widening circles. I hold my breath as I desperately try not to move, not to arch and flip with desire. My heart is pounding as his fingers move lower, pushing the quilt off me, so he can spoon in against my bare skin. The coarse fabric of his trousers tickles my skin and I can feel the hot hardness of him against me.

I do not move as his hand slips around to my breast and he strokes my nipple while his lips, tongue and teeth replace his fingers on my neck and back. The girdle of my womb is molten with wanting him. His fingers trail down the line of my ribs, across my stomach, and then he is tracing the crease of my hip around and down to the melted core of me. Despite myself I cannot help my breath catching and snagging as he touches and strokes, his nibbles on my neck become harder bites on my shoulder as he arches away from me for

115

just long enough to undo his trousers and free himself. I feel his hand guiding his cock into me and I am whole for magnificent moments. My attempts at self-control are forgotten and I rock myself along the length of him as his hot, firm thumb rubs me and his teeth pull my skin. And then we are sobbing in our breaths and trembling rigid, as the tidal wave of bliss engulfs us.

For a second he remains inside me, his hand on my hip, and his head on my shoulder as his breath heaves and shudders. Then he is on his feet doing up his trousers.

'What the fuck was that?' he growls. 'I knew I couldn't trust a Pretty One. You lot always take more than you are given.'

'What..?' I start. I hadn't used the Glamour. I hadn't lost myself like I did with Brian. I had been exquisitely aware of each delicious second.

'You knew I had feelings for you. You made sure of that. Then I come up here and tell you not to glamour me. I only wanted to comfort you, to see if we could be friends without the glamour being a problem, but no, you had to take all of me, what I was offering wasn't enough. Will never be enough.' With that, he turns and stalks out of the room, leaving me lying there with a cold draught down my back where the duvet hasn't been pulled back down.

That night I am miserable and confused. I can't understand why Guillaume reacted like he did. I controlled my Gift to the best of my ability, our loving had not had the impersonal burning of the Need I experienced with Brian. I let Guillaume set the pace and lead the way; I hadn't tried to seduce him, he came into my bed. We both felt the intensity together. Has he never felt passion with a woman before? The heady rush of climax? I think back over what he told me about his earlier life, was he a virgin when he was turned? If so surely he has had sex since Patrice? I long to talk to him, but I'm hurt and angry that he would think such a wicked thing of me. For the first time I start thinking that I am not going to be able to stay with the Pride after all. This is Guillaume's home, and if he thinks so little of me, things are never going to be comfortable here; certainly most of the rest of the Pride wouldn't be sad to see me go.

Chapter 6
Rae

The next day I seek Guillaume out, determined to speak to him and resolve his misunderstanding. I am furious with him still and tempted to wait until he comes to me, but remembering what Patrice did to him has made me feel magnanimous. I find him in his study, speaking to Simon, who is standing by the open door about to leave. I smile tightly at Simon, and tell Guillaume I need to speak with him.

'Whatever it is, Simon will deal with it, I am busy,' he snaps before skirting around me and out of the room. Gobsmacked, I catch Simon's eye, he raises his eyebrows sympathetically, and tilts his head to invite me to speak.

'It doesn't matter,' I stutter, backing away. I am mortified.

I hurry to the kitchen were Layla is chatting with David and Brian. She takes one look at me hoverig in the doorway, wringing my fingers and biting my lip to stop the tears and leaps up, grabs my hand and tows me to one of the hay meadows. I confess all. She laughs when I tell that her I'd thought Guillaume was a Pretty One too, and shakes her head. She tells me that I have always had an odd taste in men. I'm shocked and ask if she finds him attractive too. She wrinkles her nose and tells me his head is too far up his own arse for her taste. I'm amazed. I'd thought all the females found him attractive. Layla laughs out loud, and tells me my head is in the clouds. She points out that this is what I always do when I fall for someone, become convinced everyone must want him, but my taste is so eclectic that that is rarely the case.

'We aren't going to have another Sebastard situation, are we?' she jokes nudging me. I ignore her, pinching my mouth closed. I don't need reminding about the other time I had made a fool of myself over love. Then I sigh. On further consideration, maybe that's exactly what I need. Sebastian, Seb, the one. We got together during my second year at uni. I had been entranced by him from the first moment I saw him during his Fresher's week, at the start of my second year. I was

118

in the student bar, an old hand at university life now, watching the newbies in bemusement. I was well aware I had looked just as overwhelmed on my first week a year earlier, but couldn't resist this rare opportunity to be the assured one.

Seb had swaggered in alone and lit the whole room up. Seb did not display any of the gauche appeal that the other Freshers were wafting in waves, as scared individuals desperately tried to form a new herd. They had flocked to surround him, drawn to an instant leader. He had long red hair that glistened in the subdued, smoky pub light. He wore Levi's when none of the rest of us could afford them, Levi 501s that cupped his peachy arse perfectly, worn low on his neat hips, teamed casually with tight white Gap t-shirts. He was a bit older than me- I learned that he had taken a couple of years out after failing his A levels and had spent some time working- so he had more money than the rest of us. He had taken an alternative route into higher education, and was now studying creative writing and media, but all he spoke about was his love for poetry.

I saw him frequently around campus, but he always seemed tantalisingly out of my reach, surrounded by exciting skinny girls with unwashed hair and pierced noses who wore cropped t-shirts flashing smooth stomachs over long velvet skirts and clumpy boots. Sometimes, I would come upon him in the library, forehead on clenched fist, engrossed in a book, oblivious to the sunlight that cascaded through the window behind him catching his curtain of copper curls, which hung to one side as he concentrated, lighting them into a sheet of strawberry blond bliss that I longed to run my fingers through. I would stumble, entranced, and gaze at him until I realised I was staring with my mouth open, then I'd slip away back into the shelves of books as if I'd never been there.

He was completely oblivious to my existence until after Christmas when Layla was stuck in bed with a cold. I tagged along with some friends to a party at the house of some achingly cool theatre students I didn't know. I was nervous, surrounded by all these beautiful strangers, so I got stupidly drunk on a poisonous cocktail of cheap white spirits and tropical fruit drink. Real juice was too expensive for even these

119

glamorous father-funded students. I ended up falling down the stairs into the basement kitchen where everyone was mingling. I landed in a heap at Seb's feet, and the Fates were smiling on me, because somehow I managed to look up at him appealingly from my tangle of hair and dress and legs.

'I appear to have fallen for you,' I beamed up at him. He was impressed by my apparently blasé reaction to what I was later assured was a quite spectacular fall. It had always been a bit of an issue for me that I never appeared as drunk as I really was, so people weren't prepared for the stupidity that I would then become part of. I blithely scrambled to my feet and offered to replace the drink my errant foot had kicked out of his hand. I can't really remember exactly what happened after that, but apparently I had decided he was mine and I was not to be dissuaded. He was charmed by my persistence. I demanded he walk me home and for some reason I decided we needed a walk in the park. We ended up climbing over the six-foot park gates where I promptly puked in the flower beds until we were chased back out by a security guard in a golf cart.

Seb was also very drunk and thought this was the most fun he'd had since he came to uni. We went back to my room and had such loud sex that none of my housemates would look at me the next day. Apart from Layla who had slept the sleep of the ill; she just pointed at me and laughed. Seb never stayed a whole night with me in all the time we were together, and that first night was no exception despite me imploring him in between spewing in my bin. When I woke up the following day, I hurt everywhere. The fall I had ignored the night before had bruised me from top to toe, I had a hangover from hell, and I was sore from too much rough sex, but I couldn't stop grinning.

Of course Seb thought I was a devil may care party animal, and oh how I wanted to be. I threw caution to the wind and went all out to be exactly the girl he expected. By risking my health and my education, I just about managed to keep him entertained. Until he went home for the Easter holidays of my final year, and never returned. His parents had moved during the previous term, so I didn't have their new address or phone number. He was supposed to ring me to give it to me, so I would be able to ring him every night, like I had for every other term break we had spent apart. I was never invited home with him to meet his parents - we didn't have that sort of relationship - so I had never dared to ask if he would like to meet mine.

I hadn't planned to go home for the break- I rarely did because my parents would be away doing their research somewhere exotic. I was desperately behind on my coursework and my plan was to spend the entire two-week holiday in the library trying to catch up with the essays I needed to hand in, so when he returned, I could be the party girl again. Layla didn't really have anywhere to go- her father was with his new wife and their new puppy, and had no more desire to see her than she did to see him. So she was there to witness my concern the first evening when he didn't phone. She heard the flimsy excuses I made to myself that Seb must have gone straight to the pub with his old mates as soon as he got home, and then forgotten to ring me once he got drunk. She was there to watch me crumble as hours became days, and then the whole Easter holidays.

Layla

Seb disappearing was disastrous in Rae's life. The kind of Richter scale upheaval that sends shockwaves and ripples years into the future. I blame him for her marriage to James the Dull, and actually, it's his fault we are here, in a roundabout kind of a way. If he hadn't left, she wouldn't have been so shattered and scarred, she wouldn't have even looked at James, she wouldn't be so traumatised by leaving James, so we wouldn't have come to France, so we wouldn't have been infected by Mel the Cow. There, see, his fault entirely.

Rae's grief when he left shocked me. I knew Rae loved him in a feet first, all consuming adoration. It pissed me off, to be honest, the way she hung on his every word, the way she took his cruelly casual insults, that she called honesty. The way

121

she contorted her very being to try to please and entertain him. She lit up when she saw him across campus, she glowed when she spoke about him, and when he'd dumped her to shag some theatre lovey, she plummeted into misery until he came back to her, like a roving tom cat returning home after a night time's marauding.

That Easter I tried to drag her to the pub to take her mind off things. I was sure he had met someone pretty on the train, and he'd be back, nonchalantly unapologetic after the break but Rae wouldn't leave the house in case he phoned, or someone else did to tell her that he had been in an accident. The lies she told herself that fortnight infuriated me. I managed to get her to leave the house one afternoon, but she only wanted to check her bank balance to make sure she had enough of her grant left to be able to rush to his bedside. Just as soon as she knew where to rush.

This was in the days before email or mobiles had become common, and we had neither. We counted ourselves as quite sophisticated for students because we had a landline with a payphone attached, so we could receive incoming calls and make outgoing ones. The landlord had set it at an extortionate rate per minute, but at least we didn't have to venture out to find a phone box in all weathers. Rae hardly moved from her stool besides the phone for the entire two weeks, rarely eating, she even brought her duvet down and slept on the tiny two-seater sofa, in case the call came in the middle of the night and she wouldn't hear it from her room.

Seb didn't return after the holidays, and I had to watch my best friend disintegrate before my eyes. She became pale and withdrawn, with an empty haunted look about her eyes. After a couple of weeks, when she wasn't pulling herself back together, I went to grill all of Seb's friends for information, but they were as baffled as Rae. Most thought he'd decided that he was bored of university life, and found himself a job and a girl, or two, and so not bothered returning. I passed this information to Rae, and she looked at me imploringly as tears rolled down her drawn cheeks and asked me why he just hadn't told her, she would be ok if he'd just let her know. I refrained from reminding her of all the other times he had forgotten her and chased off after some other distraction without telling her.

I couldn't understand Rae's misery. With men I was easy come, easy go. I had taken a few knocks over the years, and spent an evening or two weeping into my pillow, but then a pretty new face would catch my eye, and I'd be filled with the possibilities of life, as I chased delightedly after my new fancy. Rae tortured herself, pouring over every conversation they'd ever had. I got tired of her sodden mood, and tried tough love, reminding her that he had never been as committed to the relationship as she was, and they were officially off as often as they were on. But she just sadly told me that she had always felt that honesty was one of his best qualities. He was frequently, searingly, hideously truthful about how attractive he found other girls, or how Rae had annoyed him, but she claimed she found this refreshing. She never had to wonder how he felt, or worry that she didn't know what was going on in his head. She could not understand why he had not simply told her he did not want to see her anymore.

I was tired of always talking about him, and my rage at his dishonesty started to leak out. I took to calling him Sebastard. Since he had indeed been such a bastard, Rae couldn't really disagree, could she? She buried herself in catching up on her coursework, and scratching her way through her final exams. She might have scraped a third, but she was a ghost of herself, haunting her old life. I wished I hadn't got annoyed with her, and tried to get her to talk to me again, but she just smiled gamely, and gazed off into the distance as soon as she thought I wasn't looking. Her lack of recovery started to scare me. We went to France, and on the surface we had fun and high jinks, but she was brittle, and her happiness had an angry, scraping edge to it.

I couldn't really cope with the loss of her. It was like his disappearance had opened some chasm inside her, and all our hopes and plans for the future were spilling into the gulf with each day that passed. When we came back to Cardiff, I tried. For a year I tried, in shitty jobs, and shitty flats, until I felt as empty and hollow as Rae, and I knew I had to get out. I felt so guilty when I told her I had the new job in Swansea. I half hoped she would come with me, and we could start afresh by the sea front. But, if I'm really honest, part of me was glad when she wouldn't come. I could be free from the bewildered sadness that still clung to her like a wispy cobweb cloak.

Sat in the field together now, I lean my shoulder to hers, and we rest our heads together as I reflect on the fear I feel, watching her slide into another infatuation. Eventually, I stand up and pat her on the head, leaving her to stew in her own thoughts. As I walk away, I catch sight of Guillaume in distance, tall, aloof, looking in a different direction. I know Rae, and I know this difficult hero will own her heart. I want to shake her. I want to punch him. Instead, I retreat to David's side, and curl up in the warmth of his approval.

Rae

I'm lounging in the kitchen with Annie, Layla, David and Brian, and we're listening to some of the loud angry thrash metal music that Annie loves. She has been very excited by Spotify on my laptop and begs to use it whenever I'm not browsing the internet. Normally, I make her use my headphones because it isn't usually my thing at all, but I'm finding the wordless screaming suits my mood well this evening. It also removes the need to speak because it's so loud we couldn't chat even if we wanted to. Tonight, I really resent the loss of alcohol.

Suddenly, Georgette comes skidding through the back door and into the kitchen, panting and disarrayed. I turn Annie's music down just enough so she can shout over the top of it. It's the most concession I'll make to her agitation.

'Oh thank God, there you are!' Georgette gasps. 'They've got a woman and child out there. Suzannah brought them back and let them go. The others are hunting them. They let them get so far and then they leap out and chase them in the opposite direction. It's awful. I don't like the killing, but the others laugh at me when I try to Compel them, but now it's

124

a woman and child, and that's just….monstrous.' She's gabbling, gazing at me with horrified eyes.

'We are not falling for that trick again, Georgette. Go and get your jollies somewhere else,' David's reply is dry and unfriendly.

'No! Really!' Georgette looks between us in appeal. 'It's awful. They keep separating them and the child is screaming and screaming. This is too much.' Georgette starts sobbing, blood tears and snot quickly smearing her pale cheeks as she tries to dash them away.

'Ok.' I stand up. I have decided to believe her: if what she is describing is really happening, then it has to be stopped. They have to be stopped. If it is another vicious prank at our expense, well, I am in a dreadful mood, and the opportunity to take it out on some deserving beasts is alarmingly welcome.

Even as I start moving towards the back door, I can feel the transition starting, twisting my shoulders and stretching my neck. As soon as I am outside, I can hear the terrified screams of the child and her mother, and the delighted shrieks of the pursuing vampires. My own agonised screams join theirs as the devastation of my bones lengthening and ripping through my skin tears through me. Layla is quickly besides me, her own body convulsing in spasms as she disfigures. We lengthen our strides and lope through the garden and into the yard.

The other vampires hear us screaming our Rage, and their answering shrieks become more intense, and they sound like a troop of excited chimpanzees' intent on destruction. I run, looking for their prey, and as I turn the corner out into the fields, I see the child crouching hidden behind some pallets leaning against the wall. She's little and chubby, not much past being a toddler, with tousled hair just growing out of baby ringlets.

It is a clear night, with a large full moon, and as I approach her, planning to grab her and take her into the house for safe keeping, she looks up and sees me. I reach out my hands to beckon her towards me, but her little mouth O's in horror at the sight of me, disfigured by the Rage. I try to Compel her calm, but I can't, the Rage is blocking it. Time

125

slows hideously, as I battle to rein in my Rage, to calm myself so I can Compel her, even as she backs out from behind the pallets, away from me, wheeling off into the night, straight into Melanie's waiting arms.

I look up in relief, sure that Melanie will bring her into the house and I gesture her to hurry, checking behind her for the other vampires, but she waits until my gaze meets her one furious eye, and even as I realise her intention and scream at her to stop, she rips out the child's throat. I hear the mother's scream become a gurgle as the others catch her behind one of the barns. They have always known where their prey were, they were just chasing them to and fro for their own sport. Their cruelty incenses me; I cannot bear for it to remain in this world. With the same certainty that I knew I would not kill that man in the barn, I know I am going to kill these monsters tonight.

Howling my hatred, I leap onto Melanie and it doesn't take a heartbeat for me to reach my long bony claws into her chest and rip out her beating heart. No one comes to her aid, but a young male sprints past, snatching up the child's body as Melanie drops it, laughing like a hyena at the game. I am on him in an instant, ripping and tearing at his flesh. He screams and fights back more strongly than Melanie had. The other New Ones, and some of the older Pride vampires who'd joined in the hunt come to his aid, rushing around the side of the barns to engulf us like an evil wave. Patrice and Suzannah leap from the roof where they've been crouched enjoying the spectacle of the chase, screeching their delighted battle cry.

Layla and I are quickly surrounded and overwhelmed. David jumps in, to Layla's defence, using his immense strength to tear at the swarm that encircles us. I catch a quick glimpse of Georgette and Brian stood to one side, faces rictuses of horror before I go down under several furious vampires. I know instinctively that Patrice and her New Ones have been waiting for this opportunity, and they will not stop before I am dead.

The last thing I see before they close out my line of vision is Elaine and Simon hurdling over the back-garden wall towards us, limbs lengthening and jaws extending, then I am lost in a sea of tearing teeth and claws as I gnash and claw right back. I let every ounce of delicious fury and frustration fuel me; I cannot feel any pain, just the delectable contact as my fingers gouge and bore, and my teeth rip and score.

I have no idea how long the massacre continues: it seems to be both eternal and over instantly, but suddenly I am aware there is no more resistance. I stagger to my feet and look around me; Simon is wiping the blade of a large sword on the grass. He catches my eye and raises his eyebrows at me, nodding slightly in his understated, Simon way. There are the beheaded bodies of several vampires lying around and a couple of others that either have their throats ripped out, or holes in their chests where their hearts used to be.

I look around frantically for Layla, and then see her, heart-stoppingly still in David's arms. She is back to her normal, diminutive self, and lies limply in his petrified grip. I try to hurry to her, but find my arms and legs won't work properly anymore. All the pain I haven't felt during the fight is flooding in now, and mixing with the agony of my bones retracting. It takes the breath right out of me and my legs out from under me. Giving up on walking, I crawl over towards her.

Claws grab at me and I look down at the raggedy pile I had assumed was another corpse; it takes me a moment to realise it's Patrice, missing half her skull, but still gnashing her teeth at me. I am filled with hatred, white and pure as light.

'All this is your doing,' I croak. 'All this killing; all this death.'

She laughs a gurgling chuckle.

'But what fun.'

I meet her gaze and hold her eyes as I dig into her chest with my bony, extended claws and pull out her heart. I hold it up in front of her glazing eyes and then throw it down in disgust. As I attempt to crawl forward again, toward Layla, I see that before I'd disturbed Patrice she had been feeding on another vampire. I freeze as I realise it is Guillaume, eyes closed, throat torn. I have no idea if he is alive or dead.

'Oh God, no,' I shriek. 'No. No. No.' I pat his face with my bloodied, muddied fingers. I did not think for one second that he would become involved in the battle. He is too weak, and now she has drunk his very essence. He lets out a tiny gasping groan. I look around, calling wildly for Simon. He runs to my side, and drops to his knees beside me once he realises who I hold in my arms. He lets loose a stream of expletives in French as he reaches for his fallen friend, then he looks at me urgently.

'Go and get the girl, the red-haired one that didn't fight. She's been feeding on humans all week, so she'll be full of their blood. We don't have time to get him any from the hospital; she'll have to let him feed on her. It's his only chance.'

I stumble to my feet and stagger towards the wall where I'd last seen her and Brian when the fight started. It takes me several moments to find Brian, and then Georgette, tucked away behind him. Brian backs away as I approach, looking sickened, and then walks towards the house shaking his head.

'George, Georgette,' I call as I stagger towards her. I don't have time for Brian's finer feelings.

'I'm sorry, I'm sorry, I never meant for that to happen, honest.' She's huddled in a ball in the shadows rocking and whimpering.

'I know,' I gasp. 'I know you didn't. I need your help, please, Georgette. Guillaume will die without you.' I hesitate to touch her, anxious about the effect my touch might have, but I remember that I hadn't been able to glamour the child in my agitated state. Although the worst of my rage has passed, my body is still on high alert, limbs elongated and jaw distended. I don't think there's much risk of accidentally Glamouring Georgette, so I reach out to her and pat her leg. Nothing happens. I heave a sigh of relief. I need to win her trust quickly, and touch will be the easiest way to do that.

'You love Guillaume, don't you?' asks Georgette, overcoming her fear now I've treated her kindly. 'Patrice said so. She was very jealous. She said you didn't stand a chance with him, but I've seen how he looks at you when he thinks no one is looking.'

'How old were you when you were human, Georgette?' I suddenly think to ask. It's almost impossible to tell how old a human had been when they were infected once they were a vampire, but her childish babble gives me pause for thought.

'Fourteen. I ran away from home because my stepdad kept coming into my room in the night, and the second night I was on the streets, I was so scared and cold. I had just decided to try going home and speak to my Mum when this pretty lady approached me. That was Suzannah, and well, you know the rest.'

'Ok lovely,' I soothe her. 'You've been really, really brave. Can you be a little bit braver for me? You're right. I do love Guillaume, but you mustn't tell anyone.' I whisper the last bit so only she can hear me.

'Why not?' she whispers back, mirroring my secretiveness.

'Because he doesn't love me, and it makes people very uncomfortable to be told that someone loves them when they don't love them back.'

'Well, that's stupid. He does love you.'

'He doesn't. He told me. It would also be very embarrassing for me if anyone knew. They would feel sorry for me.'

'Mmm. Ok.' She scrunches her mouth and nods. I wondered how I haven't noticed how young she is sooner. I feel guilty, but there isn't time; I can hear Simon hissing at me to hurry up.

'Guillaume will need to feed from you,' I explain as we crawl towards where he lies. 'And maybe Layla too.'

'Will they hurt me?' she asks breathlessly.

'I don't know, lovely,' I admit. 'They might, but they won't mean to, and you will be saving their lives.'

'Ok, but please will you stay with me?'

'Of course I will.' I pat her hand as we reach Guillaume and Simon.

'About time,' Simon mutters, ungraciously as we arrive.

'She's fourteen and scared witless,' I snap in response. 'How do we do this?' Simon catches hold of Georgette's wrist and holds it over Guillaume's mouth.

'Ok?' he asks her, holding her eye as she nods and he nicks her vein with his hooked thumb nail. She gasps at little as the blood starts to flow.

'You're being so brave,' I tell her, squeezing the fingers of her other hand. 'I have to go to check on Layla; are you ok for two minutes?' She looks up at me with her big trusting eyes and bobs her head in assent, and again I kick myself for not noticing her earlier and offering comfort and a reprieve from the others.

I scoot over to where David is still sat holding Layla in his arms.

'Is she ok?' I ask. He shakes his head, and for one horrible second I fear the worst.

'She's badly hurt, Rae, really bad.'

'Bring her over to Georgette. Simon says that if Layla feeds from her, she'll get the human blood Georgette has been drinking and she will be able to heal. But be gentle with Georgette. She's only fourteen.' David stands up effortlessly with Layla in his arms, and carries her over to where Georgette fed Guillaume. As I kneel down beside them, Simon looks up at me and smiles. I'm shocked; Simon never smiles, especially not at me.

'I think we've got a Healer. I've heard of them, but never seen one before,' he tells me. I look down to where he gestures. Guillaume is already stirring, his eyes fluttering open.

'What?' I ask, astounded.

'Their blood heals vampires who have been mortally wounded, and allows any wounded vampire to heal even faster than they would normally,' Simon explains. 'As well as the Healing, she is immune to all other vampire gifts. She is a valuable asset. Good job you didn't kill her too,' he adds sardonically. I ignore his jibe.

'Ok, sweetheart, can you let Layla have some now?' I ask Georgette. She looks up at me proudly.

'Simon says I'm good at this,' she says happily. 'And it doesn't even really hurt.' I decide in that instant that if

Suzannah wasn't already dead, I would kill her all over again, but slower this time. Thankfully, that monster can never again turn a child so sweet and young, and then inflict on her what this girl has endured these last few weeks.

Guillaume sits groggily upright as Georgette moves to kneel besides Layla, dripping her precious Healer's blood between Layla's lips. My eyes meet his and for a long moment we gaze at each other, but then he looks away and raises his hand so Simon can help him to his feet and support him as they walk away from me towards the house. Neither of them looks back.

I suddenly think of Elaine, and hurriedly look around for her. I find her collapsed in a crumpled heap next to Suzannah's corpse. She holds Suzannah's heart in her fist, but is hardly breathing herself, and I only have to glance at her to see that she is bent in ways she shouldn't be. Carefully, I scoop her up and carry her over to Georgette. Layla is already coming around as I approach. I see instantly what Simon had meant. The vicious gouging down her cheek, which David had patiently held closed for her, is healed and although she still looks woozy, she is already trying to talk. I lay Elaine besides Georgette.

'Last one,' I reassure her.

'No,' she says as she drips the blood into Elaine's mouth. 'You need some too.'

'No, really, I'm fine. You'll exhaust yourself.' My healing is well under way, and although I'm tired to the bone, I am upright and mobile again.

'No, really, you need it,' her laugh tinkles merrily. 'Your lip is hanging off and you're bleeding all over, and just look at your cheek- I can see your teeth! But no need to worry, I can make you all better.' Once she has listed my wounds, they each set up a trill of pain in a bitter symphony. I sit down with a thump, suddenly exhausted. David catches me up with one strong hand, and pulls me upright beside him, so my back is against his side.

'You need the blood,' he tells me sternly. Georgette crouches beside me, and I tilt my head back, open my mouth and allow several delicious drops run into my mouth. For one

131

sweet second I let myself to savour the spicy blood, let the hunger surge up in me threatening to overwhelm my resistance. I feel a growl start to grow in my chest, like a cat with a fresh kill, but I wrench every ounce of strength I have left, and reach up and pinch the little wound on her wrist closed. Within seconds, it seals, scabs, and starts to scar. I look down at Elaine who is slowly opening her eyes and gingerly sitting upright.

'What the hell happened to your face?' she asks me.

We staggered indoors and I go straight to the mirror over the fireplace as the others collapse onto the sofas. While I had concentrated on getting the dangerously injured vampires to Georgette, I had not held my own wounds closed, which means that they have healed by stretching scar tissue across the gashes. I am left with raised bluish white areas down my cheek, and beside my mouth raising one side of my upper lip. They mar the otherworldly perfection of my face. I am delighted.

**

The next morning I get up bright and early. I should feel wracked with guilt, but I don't. I've never killed anyone before, never come anywhere near it before the Mel incident, but I don't feel like a murderer. Those vampires were abominations, and the world is better without them. I'm feeling high-spirited, heroic. I head downstairs humming happily and into the kitchen, to where the other vampires are sitting round the big table, discussing what chores need to be completed on the farm, or at least that's what they are supposed to be discussing, but as I enter the room, they fall silent.

'What?' I demand, looking around at them. Simon is sitting in the corner at the back of the room.

'We've processed the bodies,' he tells me. Despite my delight that Patrice and her New Ones are dead, the clinical phrase makes me judder. Some of the other vampires give a little nod and get up to go out and start their work, but three black-haired females remain in the kitchen looking at me with their gaunt vampire faces, and big black vampire eyes.

'It's not right what happened,' one of them spits at me. 'We don't kill our own.' The other two nod in agreement, and their hard pebble eyes bore into me as they hum and hah, and agree with her. They remind me of three crows sitting on a fence cawing over a lamb corpse. Simon is still standing behind them, at the back of the room. He clears his throat with a polite little cough, and the three flinch and spin around; obviously, they thought he'd left with the others.

'What happened last night started when Patrice broke the Pride rules, and the High Council's rules, by turning one, then she let her turn others, and they turned still more. Then they brought living humans here and hunted for sport, a woman and child. We would have been discovered if they had been allowed to continue. Patrice was given every opportunity to change her ways, and she chose not to. Guillaume may still face the High Council for what she did. We just have to hope they haven't heard of it, but I suspect they will.' It's the most I've ever heard Simon say at one go. His voice is level, almost bored.

'That's as maybe,' mutters the woman, 'but that's still not our way. We should have held a meeting and discussed it and all had a vote. Guillaume had not sanctioned it. She acted without consent.'

'Yes, coz of her and her friends we can't vote now. Nothing but trouble that one.' With her final comment on the situation ringing loud and clear in my head, she and her friends leave the kitchen. Simon raises his hands and gives me a noncommittal, and very French, shrug. My good mood has dissipated.

'How's Guillaume?' I ask, as Simon tries to walk past me and out of the kitchen.

'He's much better. He could really do with more blood. He told me that he's told you about his problem.' Simon shakes his head, making it plain he thinks Guillaume is stupid for sharing his vulnerability with me. It makes me wonder what Simon thinks I'm going to do with the information- take over the Pride? No chance. This bunch of poisonous vipers are welcome to each other as far as I'm concerned. I'm glad I haven't even told Layla about Guillaume's physical troubles, I've guarded that nugget of confidence closely.

133

Georgette and Annie walk into the room chattering happily together. This cheers me up, they are a lovely pair; they could be great friends, and look out for each other. If I am going to leave, and it is looking more and more likely that I will, they will need each other.

'Why can't you bring Georgette some of the pig's blood, she can drink that, and then Guillaume can drink again tonight?' I ask Simon, who is again trying to slip out of the kitchen. Georgette nods happily to show she would be pleased to help again. 'Oh! And maybe Annie could drink from her as well; maybe she could be permanently healed by her Healing?' I'm careful not to allude to Guillaume's longer term need for the Healing. Simon laughs drily.

'It's not that easy. Even a Healer can't work with animal blood. Got to be human.'

'Well, can't Elaine get more from the hospital?' I ask, unperturbed.

'No,' replies Simon. 'Her contact asked too many questions last time, we can't risk that again.' With this bombshell Simon stalks determinedly out of the kitchen.

Later, sitting on my own in the river meadow, with my toes trailing in the silken flow, I mull the situation over. I am not a naïve woman, I have worked for probation for more than fifteen years, and I know the world has a lot of bad people in it. I started work on the frontline, full of optimism and belief in the good that rehabilitation could do. I still feel that way, not as idealistic maybe, certainly a lot more realistic about possible outcomes, but mainly I believe that with the right help and support people can change their ways. Most of the people I've supported have lived up to these beliefs, but there are a few who haven't.

It's these few who have taught me about the darker side of humanity, even as they answered my questions with all the right phrases to gain their release. They looked at me with their cold shark eyes and I knew they were laughing at me, and the system that was releasing them to prey on the innocent again. And I hate these men with a passion; the predators. I've never believed in the death penalty because there is a chance that an innocent person could die.

134

But what if you could be absolutely sure of their guilt? I brew over what Patrice told us about a vampire accessing their victim's memories when they drink from them directly. Guillaume and Annie need human blood to heal. We can't get human blood from the hospital anymore. Some of the other vampires who are left, still wanted to hunt humans. Guillaume has already explained he would not prevent, or even judge them for this, as long as they stick to the rule of hunting those who will not be missed: the transient, the destitute and the unloved. Why should the weakest within society be their prey? I ponder to myself.

I can see a solution; why not hunt those who cause harm? There must be a way I can Compel a person, tie them down, slice an artery with a knife and drink from the arch of blood that fountains out, without making any contact with the open wound. I'll be able to check they're guilty without infecting them with the virus. Once I have drunk and the images I see confirm what they have done, then Georgette could drink them dry. If they aren't guilty and there has been a mistake in the vetting procedure, then I can just Glamour them, so they just have a blurred memory of some really kinky sex, and then I could let them go.

This would supply the blood to Heal these two vampires I've grown to love, and it would provide a morally corrupt supply of humans to the hunters. Guillaume might feel he should not judge, but I can't help myself.

How to find an abuser? There must be an untraceable way. I mull ideas over for several hours until I am sure I have a viable plan, then I go to discuss my idea with David and Layla. Layla is the sounding board for all my ideas, and David was working with computers before he was infected, so I'm sure he'll have good advice.

Layla and David do like my idea. Layla's work in the rape clinic has brought her into contact with enough victims - some male, but mainly female - for her to be keen on an idea of retribution for the abusers, especially when the legal system has failed the victims so often. We are both aware abusers pick their prey carefully, so they often make imperfect witnesses that society doesn't feel the need to save- prostitutes, drug addicts, grubby girls who have told angry lies, so their inconvenient truths are ignored.

David tells me about his niece who'd been groomed by a paedophile online. Luckily, her parents had found out in time to stop him doing physical harm, but the audacity of this man sending his tentacles of abuse into David's brother's family home, and the depth of the psychological damage he inflicted, had shocked David to the core and left him with a taste for revenge. I was hoping that he might be able to hack into paedophile chat rooms and we'd choose a victim that way. I hadn't stopped to think about how he would find a chat room, and then find a paedophile's contact details from an anonymous chat room. They always make that bit look so easy in films.

I have a more complicated plan: we will hunt them on Facebook. We can dress Annie up; it won't be hard to make her look twelve. Even though she is a vampire, the poor start she'd had after her transition, and the permanent pain she is in mean she is a drawn, wan, little thing. With a bit of make-up and some Photoshop we can easily make her look like a human child. We can use an array of disguises and false information to create Facebook profiles. Then we can let the paedophiles find her. We can let them make all the running and then lure them somewhere that suits us. Easy.

Layla

I don't know why she does this. Will she never learn? This is none of her business. Who does she think she is? The Caped Crusader? I can see the appeal in pervert hunting, but actually doing it? It can surely only lead to trouble. Rae is so naïve. She just sees a problem, figures out a solution, and blindly sets about putting things right. But she's completely oblivious to all the subtle nuances of group politics, so she can't see that by doing this, she is forcing a change in the Pride dynamics, and we are unpopular enough as it is.

She's a bit confused about why I won't join in, but she doesn't see herself. She's enjoying the hunt too much; this is the vampire in her. She was always a total pacifist before, to the point where I thought she was too soft, a bit of a mug. Now it's like she's got a taste for the excitement of the kill, and wants more. The annoying thing is that I know that in a few weeks, she'll be all upset and confused when the rest of the Pride turn on her. She just doesn't understand that people don't like being helped most of the time. And guess who'll have to comfort her, and try to help her understand.

I don't want this. I want to curl up with David and escape everything. After the fight he carried me to his bed, and tenderly laid me down, then he gently kissed where each wound had been, murmuring his fear, his relief, his love. I was actually completely healed by then, and felt fine physically, but my soul was sore and his kisses were soothing me, so I lay nestled in his pillows and love and let him nurture me. When he lifted his head from kissing my healed shoulder, his eyes were dilated dark with desire, and I reached for him. Our kisses melted us and we melded into one.

He eased my muddy, bloody clothes off me and then feathered kisses over every inch of me, even stopping at the end of the bed to buss my grubby toes. Then I saw his eyes rove over my nakedness, and his expression intensified, as he paused for a moment to strip his own clothes off in seconds. I saw him in all his flagpole glory for a moment before he knelt between my calves and ran his big strong hands up my legs, softening my hips, and opening me to him.

He licked and kissed his way into the sweetest core of me, then sucked and tugged the nub of me until the dancing flames of pleasure became great roiling waves of ecstasy. I don't know if he is especially skilled, or if being a vampire has changed my clitoris, all I do know is that I have never cum that hard before, it engulfed me entirely, it became me, red roses bloomed and swelled in the blackness behind my eyes, and I sobbed with the bliss. As the final ebbs shook me, I felt his strong fingers part the velvet smoothness of me, and his great, burning, cock filled me. I screamed. David froze, and started to withdraw, but I wrapped my legs around him as tightly as I could, clamping him in, eyes closed, filled with the intensity of hugeness filling every bit of me. Slowly, I ground myself against him, panting with the want of it, until I couldn't contain my want anymore, and dropped my legs, and arched, begging him to fuck me.

Which he did, thoroughly. Afterwards, he confessed that he used to have quite a small cock, but it has grown in delicious proportion with the rest of him, and is now a thing of utter magnificence, so perfect it looks like a dildo in an Anne Summers catalogue. He was initially unsure how to handle his newly engorged member, so when I screamed, he really thought he'd hurt me. My satiated smile soon reassured him this wasn't so; however, we were both quite disconcerted that his semen is now red. It's quite repulsive. Soon after we decided to try how different it would be if I turned my glamour right up, and he submitted to it. It was nice, very sexy, but we both missed the intimate intensity of the first time. Good for a quickie, we agreed, but not every day.

Later still, we disagreed about his love of chunky woollen jumpers, I complained they were itchy and nasty, he insisted they were classic quality. Then we discovered that David is surprisingly ticklish, and I'm not, and we both really enjoy it when I go on top.

Chapter 7
Rae

Baiting the trap is easy, so hideously, deliciously easy. We can order what we need from eBay; the gothy garb are popular products for human teenagers and we can use my account, I'll just change the delivery address. Annie hasn't seen eBay before, and she gets a bit overexcited by everything she could buy from all over the world at the click of a button. I gently remind her that we only need a couple of things, and show her how to set up a Watchlist so she can collect everything she likes in one place and just choose her favourites. I can't blame her, I was the same when I first discovered this magical portal into the worldwide department store.

We create a profile for a troubled teenager called Verity - I can't resist the name - with a couple photos of Annie made up with dark alternative make up, looking sulky, that David Photoshops to include jet black hair with a fringe that flops over her eyes. I add some sad little poems, some pictures of rain drops on windowpanes, and droopy-eyed puppies. I click like on the Facebook pages of some suitably emo bands, leave all the privacy settings on public, and let the friend requests flood in. Within minutes of putting her fake account up Verity is getting messages from grown men. With no encouragement from her at all, several of the conversations quickly turn sexual.

I decide that I will make extra sure the abuser signs his own death warrant: I do not arrange to meet anyone, I just put up posts on Verity's wall that she is feeling down, that nobody understands her. Then I post that she has a favourite secluded place where she likes to sit and think when she needs to be alone: a tiny cove in the little seaside village of Trinity Sur Mer, in Brittany.

I stumbled upon the little seashore, which is surrounded by trees, while I was on holiday with James in nearby Carnac eighteen months ago. It's a long way from the farm, though. I ask Simon about it, explaining that Routeplanner advised that it will take eight hours to get there.

'I take six,' he says contemptuously, curling his lip a little. I check he feels he can do that trip three times in a row, he shrugs and pouffs a little, but nods.

'I am a vampire, my dear. It will not be a struggle, just very boring and a lot of petrol, but that is fine if it is what you need to get Guillaume the blood.'

All I need to do then is post a few comments about watching the reflections of the stars on the waves.

After scouring the area on Google maps to ensure we are completely confident of the lay of the land, and making sure we are all confident of my plan, Simon, Elaine, Annie and I head off to Brittany late in the afternoon. True to his word Simon covers the journey in just over six hours; at nine thirty we park a few miles from the coast and slip through the rural lanes under the cover of the twilight.

I find I can easily run several miles with the vampires with no effort at all; indeed the pleasure of stretching myself to my extremes is a revelation. I try to ignore the stirring hunger within me and the feeling of flattening myself into a hunting lope.

Once we reach the cove, Annie sits on the sand in the moonlight with her knees drawn up to her chest, hands clenched around them, and chin resting on her knees as she gazes forlornly out to sea. She is in clear view of anyone who parks in the little parking spot, and walks up the sandy bank separating the parking area from the beach. She's wearing a knitted hat that hides her blond hair, little black lace gloves to hide her nails and the exaggerated dark make up that at once covers her vampire skin and finishes the emo image she's portraying.

Annie looks tiny, childlike and vulnerable, curled there and I need to remind myself how easily she would be able to protect herself against a human if she needs to. Although it's a balmy night, this isn't a tourist beach, so there's no one else here and she is sat out of the line of sight of the little cottage on the point. The rest of us have merged with the shadows under the trees and we wait, crouched in the shadows. I spend the next forty minutes wrestling with my emotions. On the one hand, I have been adamant that I'm not going to become a killer, and I've always abhorred the idea of even squashing an earwig.

On the other hand, I never knew that vampires existed outside of my nightmares, but I did know about the human monsters that prowled the internet and residential Children's Homes, picking their victims like ripe plums. I hate the predator abusers, with a passion born of supporting so many of their victims, and I know that many of the cold, calculating perpetrators escape justice and run rings around the legal system, which I don't feel can deal with such soulless monsters. To remain fair to ordinary people, there are too many loopholes they can wriggle through. We have set this trap so that no one with innocent intentions will fall into it, and I admit to myself that I don't feel they are any loss to humanity, and my friends need their blood, I am finding that I can be coldly dispassionate about the maths of this equation.

There is another part of me that I can feel stirring, despite my best attempts to quash and ignore it, a part of me that has awoken as I ran to the beach, that I can feel uncoiling and flexing like a newly woken cat, excited at the prospect of stalking, toying, and killing. The scents of humans still linger from the locals who have picnicked on the beach this afternoon. They choose it because it's kept secret from the tourists, so there is somewhere peaceful for the locals to go. Their smells stir the hunger in me and stoke the desire to hunt I am battling.

Eventually, I hear a car crunch over the gravel as it pulls slowly into the carpark. My new vampire limbs mean I'm not at all cramped from stooping in the shadows for so long, and my vampire hearing means it is easy for me to listen as the man leaves his car, quietly clicking his door shut and slowly approaches Annie. He appears to be in his mid-thirties, average height and build with brown hair. He wears a t-shirt featuring one of the older bands we had 'liked' for Verity, and dark jeans. He looks utterly average, utterly nondescript.

'Verity?' Annie turns towards him. 'Verity, I saw your posts. I was worried about you,' he calls softly as he approaches her, crunching slowly through the sand in his Converse. Once he has obliviously passed by my hiding place, intent on his prey, I turn my back on the beach and I turn my mobile on. It is set to Verity's Facebook page. I've had a good look at his face, so I can scroll quickly through the profile pictures on her friend list. He's not on there. Ah, cunning: leaving no trail. The hunter in me wriggles in anticipation. This was not your common or garden pervert; we've hooked ourselves a proper monster. I almost pant in anticipation, and then, horrified, I remind myself that I am not supposed to be enjoying this. No matter who, or what, he is, I am about to be involved in killing a human being. I have to remember to consider what this will make me, who I could become. I must not lose myself in the thrill of the hunt. I must not let myself become a monster too.

'Verity, I saw what you wrote. I couldn't bear the thought of you sat here alone believing no one understood. Verity, I understand you. I read your poems, and I know you are an old soul. Kids your age won't understand you, but don't blame them, they can't help being stupid. You're special. That's why I came to find you, we're the same, you and I,' he croons to her as he squats besides her and takes her hand.

I know where this would lead if she really was a human girl sitting out here on her own at night, with no one at home caring where she was so late and no peer group to protect her. This monster would groom her until she was completely under his control, so he could do whatever he wished, and she would thank him for the privilege, and never, ever, tell. He would undermine all her other relationships, using lies and insinuation to make her doubt everyone she had left. Then, if any of her friends or siblings was tenacious enough to stick around, he would flirt outrageously with them. This would serve three purposes. It would damage her relationship with the unlucky recipient of his attention, because he would swear the flirtation was the other way around; it would chase the friend away because there would be a veiled threat in the flirting that the friend would feel; and it would break Verity's confidence that little bit more, because she's so ugly her friends flirt with him under her nose. She would end up feeling that he was so good to put up with her at all.

142

He is looking at her hand as he traces the pattern of the lace with the tip of his finger, testing, testing, to see what she will allow.

'My name is Thierry,' he tells her. 'I live near here and when I read that you would be here all alone, I couldn't bear it, I had to come to you.' Liar. I don't know how I am so sure, but my gut tells me that he's travelled almost as far as us to get here tonight. For the same reasons. As he speaks, he lifts his head slightly so he can glance at her coyly through his eye lashes, so subtle, no confrontational behaviour, luring her in with his romantic gestures and promises of understanding and care. As his eyes meet Annie's, his head jerks up and he rears back as his instincts scream at him that he's stumbled onto a predator more dangerous than himself. This is my cue; I turn my Glamour up to full blast and then swag out of the shadows.

'Thierry!' I coo. 'Darling, come here.' I cover the distance between us deceptively quickly, keeping my gaze on his as I sway towards him. I see terror on his face, which soon dispels as the waves of my Glamour thicken around him and his pupils dilate. He stands and steps obediently towards me. He is spellbound. There is nothing he can do but comply and come with me as I lead him back towards the others. Over his shoulder Annie grins viciously, even her hunter has been stirred. Before we reach Elaine and Simon, I turn Thierry to face me and look deeply into his eyes. I just want to satisfy myself that right in the very depths of his soul he is still aware and screaming.

I smile broadly at that bit of him, and can't resist a small gnash of my pointed, shiny teeth. Still smiling broadly at him I take the paper and pen that Elaine holds out to me, and take him to his car. I hand him the pen and paper and then in my best pussy-cat purr I dictate his suicide note, citing his guilt over how many lives he has destroyed. We leave the letter on the front seat, and the notepad and pen in the foot-well along with his shoes, socks and wallet.

I know he won't be able to keep up with us on the run back to our car, and I don't want anyone else to carry him, I don't want the Glamour to falter at all and have him start to scream. I tell him to climb onto my back so I can give him a piggy-back. I'm a bit worried that my Glamour wouldn't work while he is on my back, but I link his arms around my neck so his hands are touching the front of me where the Glamor works. Simon starts to say something, but I just gesture at the human on my back and take off towards the car.

The aromatic scent of Thierry is hard to resist so I need to get the process underway as quickly as possible. I hope that once there was some distance between me and the hunt site, my desire to feed will lessen. The whole point of this enterprise has been to get blood into Georgette to heal Annie and Guillaume, I remind myself repeatedly, and using images of Guillaume's smiling face, healthy and pleased to see me, I fight down the urge to just drink Thierry dry now. I think of little Annie as well of course, I just find her hopeful little face doesn't motivate me as much as Guillaume's approving one. I try to ignore the discrepancy; I have enough to worry about without adding guilt to the mix.

Sickeningly, I can feel that my Glamour does not lessen in impact from behind for humans; as soon as he touched me, Thierry has become inflamed, the rigid rod of his arousal pushing and poking into my back as his hands rove my breasts and he slobbers over my neck. There is no risk of me feeling the Need in return, but he is quickly lost in it. I run as fast as I can back to the car, and try to distract myself with other thoughts, but let's just say he is spent by the time I get there. Elaine sniggers as she draws up beside me while I peel him off my back and throw him into the back seat of the car. I climb in beside him, and Annie sits on his other side, while Simon drives and Elaine travels in the passenger seat. Simon openly laughs at me as I hold Thierry at bay with my palm against his forehead, while he babbles and paws at me. Taking pity on me, Elaine finally reminds me how to turn the sexual allure off, enough to allow the trance-inducing Compelling to finally knock him out into a deep slumber.

The journey home takes an unfeasibly long time as I scowl out of the window, cross as a wet cat. In my rush to Glamour him and get him back to the car without eating him, I had completely forgotten I could have just Compelled him and then carried him back to the car in my arms. With my vampire strength, I could have carried him easily. I realise that this is what Simon had been about to tell me before I dashed off, full of my own importance. God I feel like such a knob.

***

When we finally get out of the car at the farm, Annie skips off to fetch Georgette while Elaine, Simon and I make our way to the barn. I make Simon carry Thierry, in all his stickiness. Once we are in the barn, Simon lays him on the row of three bales that have been arranged and covered in new tarpaulins ready for us by Simon's friends, Nicholas and Marcus. I pick up the sharp, slender knife that has been left on the window sill for me. I have done some research on the internet to make sure I don't actually kill him too soon. I just want his blood to reach my mouth, without any cross-contamination from the vampire virus, so I can access his memories and be one hundred percent sure he is guilty.

I've decided to start with a short deep cut into the artery beneath the base of his thumb. I read that this would sever his radial artery, a fairly large artery, and if the cut is straight across and all the way through, the artery will constrict, drawing back into the wound and stopping the bleeding quickly, allowing me just enough time to see some of his most vivid memories. If by some bizarre twist we are completely wrong, this would allow him to live. He could be slipped back into the stupor and returned to his car in Brittany, where Elaine could fudge out whatever memories he had remaining, as well as removing the suicide note. So he'd just wake up in his car with a cut and some fuzzy memories of a very kinky night with two friends.

If, as I suspect, he reveals memories filled with other people's misery and pain, all orchestrated for his perverted pleasure, then we kill him. Georgette drinks her fill, and if Simon or Elaine fancy any, they can have some too. We need his death to look like a suicide so I will cut the artery lengthways in both arms, then when the body's own defence system causes the artery to constrict, the constriction will actually pull the cut open and cause it to bleed more profusely.

Death from exsanguination from the radial arteries

145

wouldn't normally be a quick death, but with the vampires sucking his blood out, the process will be speeded up. First, his heart rate will go up, and he will become pale, lethargic and lightheaded. Then, he will start to become short of breath, unable to inhale a full breath; his blood pressure will start to drop and, finally, he'll have lost so much blood that there won't be enough left to circulate to his organs and he'll die. The femoral arteries in his thighs would have been a quicker death, but wouldn't have made such a convincing suicide.

Annie and Georgette clatter into the barn, giggly and chattering as Annie updated her on everything that has happened while we've been out. I glare at her as she starts to share my ignominious mistake Glamouring Thierry, so she quickly shuts up. We've all stepped back from where Thierry lies on the bales and stand in a wide circle around him so that he can surface from his stupor. We wait until the terror registers on his face and he draws a breath to scream.

'This is for the girls,' I say as I slink forward again. I give him time to register what I mean, see the horror in his shifting eyes as he tries to calculate the lies he'll need to tell to win me over. Then I send a wave of sedating Compelling over him so he quickly returns to being compliant. I kneel besides him and lift his limp wrist up to my face; I use the small sharp knife to slice into his unresisting artery, so the delightful spurt of his blood arcs into my mouth.

My mind is immediately filled with the images of young girls' faces, tear-streaked and desperate. My ears hear his cruel laughter as they paw at him desperate for love. My eyes see bodies, several of them, dead in bath tubs of blood, or with blue lips coated in vomit as their cold fingers clutch empty pill bottles. I am shown how he made sure they knew that a couple of Paracetamol wouldn't kill them. I see how he spent amusing afternoons with them, on suicide websites, claiming he was trying to shock them out of hurting themselves, but in reality he was making sure they knew how to do it properly. Then he would sit and watch as they died, before disappearing. He would never let the girls tell anyone about him, so no one ever knew to even look for him.

146

Just as I feel the rage and hunger entwine and fill me and threaten to overwhelm me, my limbs throbbing with the agony of rage transformation, his artery closes. Without the blood, my mind clears and I stagger back, away from him. I turn towards Georgette and nod, beckoning her forward as I turn back and slash his arteries quickly.

'And don't Compel him,' I croak as I stagger out into the yard.

***

The contrast between the delicious blood and the horrors it caused me to witness has really shaken me up. I'm too hyped to sleep yet, so I go to Layla's room to talk to her about everything I've felt and seen. She isn't there, so I guess she must be in David's room where he has a double bed. David enjoyed setting up the profile, dressing Annie up in different disguises, and editing the photos, but once it was done, neither he nor Layla had expressed any disappointment that they couldn't come to Brittany to hunt a hunter. They are both too wrapped up in each other, experiencing that delicious first honeymoon period with the intensity of their new vampire senses.

I can't blame them. The reason I've been so passionate about the whole idea is that I hope that once Guillaume is completely healed, he will talk to me again. I hope that when he's healed and has the strength and vitality he should've always enjoyed as a vampire, then maybe he will be my friend; if not my lover. I consider leaving Layla and David to sleep until a more reasonable hour; it still isn't quite six o'clock in the morning, but I can't bear the thought of sitting in my sparse little room on my own, unable to sleep. I'll just end up playing game after game of FreeCell and Klondike Patience to distract my whizzing thoughts.

I listen from the end of the corridor to make sure I won't be disturbing them too much, but happily I can't hear the sounds of even the most muffled love making, so I tiptoe down and tap David's door. He murmurs hello, and I whisper that I'm looking for Layla.

147

'Come in,' she chirrups. So I push the door open, and try to ignore the jealousy that briefly flares at the sight of her happy face resting on his big strong chest. His arm is around her shoulders, one finger stroking her cheek. She is keeping her Glamour turned low, but it is love that lights her up like a beacon. I can't resent her, though, she deserves this happiness. I just want it too.

'Oo! Are you back all ready? How did it go?' As Layla wakes up fully, I see her interest rise. Her nostrils flare as she sits up, tucking the sheet tightly around herself; she can smell the sweet spicy scent of the human blood on me. She tucks her feet up so she is sat cross-legged at the top of the bed, leaning back on her pillows and David's arm. She leans over and pulls one of his pillows from under his head, kissing him sweetly as he protests, then she pats the end of their bed for me to sit down and chucks me his pillow to put between the carved footboard and my back before I rest back on the knobbles.

I have my Glamour turned as low as it will go, but still check David's feet are nowhere near me before I sit down. He shares my concern and carefully tucks his feet up so he is sat crossed-legged next to Layla. I offer him his pillow back, but he smiles and shakes his head. David's love for Layla means he is fond of me too, much fonder than Mike ever was, and I have learned that I can be open with Layla in front of David; she trusts him completely, so I do too.

I share my tale of derring-do, and give them the full unedited version. Layla and David start giggling, then belly laughing at my account of running to the car with Thierry humping my back all the way; they howl with mirth when I admit that I'd completely forgotten that I could just send him to sleep, and grudgingly confess that I'd been so full of my own self-importance that I had completely brushed off Simon's attempts to remind me. By the time I'm describing his repulsive panting and groping in the car, while I held him off with a hand in the face, I'm laughing too. Only with Layla can I see past my wounded pride and laugh at myself like this. It still burns, but the laughter soothes, and I can see how silly I must have looked to the others.

All laughter stops though as I describe the memories I'd witnessed when I drank Thierry's blood. I recount all of it, down to the last pictures I'd seen of a girl of about eleven, gauche and awkward when alive, then cold and blue in her bedroom. In the retelling of what I had exposed from Thierry's memories, I become aware that while in the moment of feeding, I may have just seen the succinct flashes of scenarios of the hunt, abuse and kill, now I'm re-examining these foreign memories in more detail. I realise they unfold into a full recollection, with all the nuances of my own memories. I can remember how he'd dumped the eleven-year-old suddenly, and then four days later made her think it was her idea to stay home from school 'sick' while her parents went to work. Her misery and despair at the brutal ending of their relationship meant they had easily believed she had the flu. Once they left, she let her secret ex-lover into her home, allowing him to slip in through the back door so no one would ever know he had been there.

I can remember how she'd begged for another chance, how he had used this power to get her to perform degrading sex acts she normally refused to consider, and then her despair afterwards as he reminded her he'd only come round to talk, not to get back together. I hear him tell her that a man couldn't be held accountable for his actions if a silly little slut threw herself at him. I watch her take the cocktail of tablets she'd harvested from her parents' en-suite bathroom cabinet and wash them down with alcohol, sobbing hysterically while Thierry sat in the pretty wicker chair in her pink child's room, and told her not to take on so, while I can feel his arousal pressing against his fly, as she became more slurred, then quieter, until eventually she was still as she lay curled in a ball under her duvet gazing at him with heartbroken eyes. I can remember his lust as he made sure there was no trace of him in the room- he kept himself cleanly shaven to prevent any body hair shedding, until finally he could photograph her corpse.

Later at home as he looked through his pictures, adding them to his collection, he masturbated over what he had done, finally allowing himself the climax he had not allowed her to give him earlier; although she had choked and

149

gagged and cried in the desperate trying. I cannot regret this man's death. In the retelling I am able to clarify this for myself. All my fears that I will become a monster were well founded: I had loved feeling the hunger, the thrill and pleasure in the chase as I carried out the seduction and caught this killer. And that scares me, I will not be involved in any more kills. But I will not regret this one.

Layla

Blood-bloated and dazed, Elaine comes to find Rae before going to bed to sleep off the post-feeding narcotic lull of memories. It hasn't taken them long to kill him, they've wrapped the body up in the tarpaulins and slung him into the boot of Simon's car. They can't leave until afternoon since they need darkness to slip his body back to the cove. Rae refuses Elaine's offer to go back to Brittany with them later, but runs through the disposal plan one last time with her. Rae's planned this final section of the exercise as carefully as the rest, but still checks through every step in meticulous detail. They are to unwrap him, put his car keys into his pocket and then tow his body as far out to sea as possible. They will take the knife Rae had used to slash his wrists out with him too, wiping any fingerprints off it and pressing his on from his dead fingers. They are to drop it into the sea at the same time as his body, so when someone finds him, if anyone finds him, it would appear as if he had waded out to sea, stopped to cut his wrists and then floated off to die.

I watched their conversation with appalled fascination. The Rae I'd known for over twenty years was sweet, self-depreciating, clumsy and socially awkward. Giving her orders, this Rae is regal, a reluctant heroine, sure and true on her path. The kill had thrilled and excited her, but her repulsion towards her prey had neutralised her guilt. I feel a thrill of fear spark through me. Will I ever have my bumble-bum friend back?

'Shall we put stones in his pockets? Before we take him into the sea?' Elaine suggests. 'To make sure he sinks, no one will find him then.'

'But if they do, a pathologist would not find sea water in his lungs. With stones in his pockets, he would have sunk and drowned before he bled to death,' Rae points out. 'If he is found, his wounds need to add up, along with the note in his abandoned car, to a suitably realistic picture of suicide. If he is found, we need the police to trace him to his home-address.' Rae swallows, nose wrinkled. 'There they will find his computer and camera, which are full of the photos he's taken of his victims. His souvenirs, his trophies. There's no trace of Verity, though.' She looks up at Elaine and holds her gaze. 'By covering his own footsteps, he's covered ours too. I'm pretty confident that if they saw what's there, police interest in his case would fade and any little inconsistencies I've missed will be overlooked.' Elaine, flushed and sleepy-looking, nods and leaves our room to go and sleep off her indulgence.

After Elaine leaves, Rae sinks into a contemplative silence. After what this kill has brought out in her, she has a lot to think about. After staring into space for several minutes, she gets up, mutters something vague about sleep, and stumbles off. David leans forward, hand out, as if to call her back, his brow creased in concern. But I put my hand on his arm and shake my head, then curl into his arms. This is something Rae needs to do alone now.

Rae

Over the next few weeks the rest of the Pride are more than happy to take over the hunt. David keeps creating profiles using the photos of Annie from before the healing blood had made her blossom and bloom. He Photoshops her to sport red, mousy blond, and washed-out purple hair; he adds a pierced nose, multiple earrings, hats and scarves, he lengthens her nose, gives her grey eyes, brown, or blue; he

151

makes her chubbier or skinner, and even manages to make her look younger still. The hunting vampires pose as Rosa, Beth, Maria and post that their favourite places are near the borders with Spain, Belgium, or Switzerland. Places that are in easy reach of the ferries from Britain, and airports from all over the world. They make it easy for the predators to find her. They don't need to drive back to the farm anymore. After the first successful hunt Simon had invested in a campervan, bought off the internet and picked up from a layby late at night so the seller was tired from driving and could hardly see him in the dark.

Now they can park in deserted places within a five-mile radius of the hunt site, leave a lookout in the camper in case anyone approaches, and then bring their prey back to the plastic-draped bed. The slightest threat of discovery and they could instantly call the hunt off, but thanks to Google Earth, they can select their hunt sites carefully, and there is rarely even the slightest risk of being seen, never mind remembered. Sometimes they have to wait several days for prey to show up, but they hide in the camper in the day, driving to different areas each day so they are never seen in the same place twice. Their patience always pays off. The monsters always come eventually.

Sometimes they find nasty little perverts panting and wanking in the undergrowth peering at Annie through the bushes. They don't kill these sad little men; they are too likely to be from the neighbourhood, so they might be missed. The men they are after are the psychopaths who leave no traces. The ones who, when the occasional news story broke about the suicide of a man with a computer full of disgusting images, their bewildered-looking neighbours were always filmed gasping the same comments: how quiet they were, always keeping themselves to themselves.

These sad little Peeping Toms, grunting and tugging in the bushes, would suddenly find Simon and Elaine towering over them asking what the hell he thought he was doing, that was their daughter. All the seedy little shit would remember the next day would be getting caught by the girl's parents, but he would be vaguely aware that this memory would fill him with far more terror than it should. The teams Compel their victims into the sleep state as they approached them, then lug them back to the camper, carry out the final test, and then Georgette and whoever else wants human blood feed, and the bodies are either brought back to the farm and fed to the pigs, or left in staged suicides. With this system in place, Georgette is able to feed Annie and Guillaume every few days.

As Annie becomes stronger and develops a minxier disposition, she starts Compelling the prey herself, she gets a kick out of commanding their actions. To begin with, I worried that Annie wouldn't take the blood from Georgette, knowing that the blood came from a human source, but after she helped setting up the first profile and saw how quickly the vultures had circled, and then attacked, she'd had no qualms about drinking their blood. She's even keener now she's realised that Georgette thrives on helping her; she can see Georgette feels like healing goes some way towards making up for her actions when she was first turned.

Annie's pointed out to me how it has bonded the other vampires. Those who hadn't wanted to drink human blood were usually permanently a bit tetchy, like smokers in the first week off cigarettes. Now they feel that they are doing a moral good taking these sharks out of the world, and the human blood cheers their cranky dispositions. Those who have always fed on humans find they enjoy feeling like they were no longer at a moral disadvantage to the others, and join the hunts enthusiastically, abandoning their vagrant and street worker prey.

The mood around the farm is relaxed and jovial. The hunters get their kicks from toying with their victims on Facebook, like cats playing with rats before the final kill. They never pick more than one victim per profile to kill, but that doesn't stop them bating other men on other profiles for sport. They always keep the profile going for a while after a kill, but with new privacy settings, so it looks as though a parent has discovered their open Pages and changed the settings, and the child has lost interest.

I don't get involved. Sometimes I read a profile over someone's shoulder, and think of something they could add, but resist mentioning it, and I often welcome Annie and Georgette home, buzzing and fizzing with the tales of their adventures, smelling deliciously sweet and pungent. Georgette offers to feed me, but I always refuse; I am back on the pig blood. Thick and disgusting it may be, but I don't have to kill for it.

Annie can Compel the animals into the same kind of stupor as human victims, and then a quick nick on the big artery in the neck and I can fill a glass and then pinch the cut closed while the artery contracts and the flow stops. The pig can be sent back to doing happy little pig things after a quick spray of antiseptic to make sure that no infection will set in. After watching her a few times, I asked Annie to show me how to calm the pigs, and soon I didn't need her help anymore.

Layla, David, Brian and I feed from the pigs while the main group are out hunting. After listening to my description of the lust for the kill, David and Layla have decided to stick to the animal blood rather than risk becoming the bloodlust-driven fiends we fear we could easily become. And Brian just always does what the rest of us do. I tried suggesting that feeding from Georgette might heal his depression, but he just looked at me with even more disgust than usual, and walked away from me.

I haven't told the others that I think the memories themselves can become addictive. I badly miss dreaming, and I can see I could slide into the escape that other people's memories offer, even evil ones. Nightmares are better than no dreams at all. It is different for the rest of the Pride; they are older and surer of themselves. Feeding on humans does not seem to present them with the same temptations, or maybe they just don't care.

Since feeding on the human blood I've noticed that I find it a lot easier to control my Glamour. It's dawned on me slowly since the hunt that I can keep simmering low most of the time, and I actually have to think about turning it up if I want to check I still have it in the mirror. With my scars, with my Glamour simmering low, I think I look pretty bland now.

I've received gratitude and enthusiasm from Annie and Georgette, and even several of the other vampires who hadn't bothered speaking to me before, for my plan to get human blood for healing and sport. Guillaume hasn't spoken to me at all. He stays in his study a lot, and if I ever do see him out on the farm, he is always studiously facing in the opposite direction from where I am. It is as if he has developed a sixth sense for where I am going to be, so he can make absolutely sure he isn't there at the same time. He never asks for me and I am never invited into his study when Georgette goes in to treat him.

One morning I turn out of the kitchen door and stride towards the yard just as he swings through the gateway from the yard into the garden. We are only feet apart, and I am transfixed. Now that he is well he is absolutely magnificent. Like a male lion in his prime; like a Sun God. Most of the vampires are very pale, like classic white marble, but he looks like he is made from creamy marble that has veins of gold running through it. His bronze curls are swept back from his high forehead and tumble down to his collar, tipped with gold. His shocking green eyes seem all the more dazzling with his improved health. His gaze seems to brush over me and then he calls to Marcus, over my shoulder in the garden, and hurries past me without even acknowledging I am there. I deflate, devastated and stand for a second blinking and gasping as I wait for the pain to subside, before stumbling through into the yard and burying myself in the heavy work of mucking out the stable block.

Affecting nonchalance later that evening, I sidle up to Elaine as she sorts through a pile of fresh clean laundry, carefully folding it and putting each vampire's clothing into their own pile. I pick up some socks and started pairing them off, but quickly realise I don't know whose they are, so I put them back down again.

'Elaine, I was just wondering how come Guillaume is darker than other vampires, more um, eh, golden even?' I look at her from the corner of my eye to see her reaction to my question, while I pretend to be fixated on finding the partner to a pink stripy sock in my hand. I know whose this one is, I was there when Annie squealed with glee at the idea of having feet that looked like bonbons and ordered them from eBay. I can see Elaine is swallowing a smirk as she replies.

'Quite a few of the vampires are darker if you look at them. Those who had the colouring of Asians, or Africans while they were human, are much lighter now, but they are darker than those of us who were Caucasian. Have you not noticed Philippe and Maya, and Matthew?' No, I haven't. I've always been pretty colour blind as a human, far more interested in who a person is than the colour of their skin, but this is pushing it even for me. I feel ashamed that my obsession with Guillaume is distracting me from even seeing other vampires as I go about my day, and even worse that my fixation has led me to asking Elaine such a stupid question. I feel the flush of my Glamour rise as it always does when I'm embarrassed.

'Guillaume's family on his mother's side is Spanish, of Moorish descent, and his father was French Algerian,' Elaine explains, but I'm absorbed by the thought that I can't even really remember what I've done from one day to the next, who I've spoken to, what I have seen. All I do know is that it wasn't him. Everything has just blurred into one while I push myself as hard as I can to keep my mind busy and try to make sure I am tired enough to sleep at night. I stand still thinking about this, then come to my senses and smile sheepishly at a bemused Elaine, mutter Goodnight and go up to my room early to sit watching mindless films on You Tube. There isn't any point trying to watch anything good; I couldn't follow the plot.

Chapter 8
Rae

Two days later, while most of the Pride are off hunting, Layla, David, Brian and I are in the lounge; we've connected a laptop to the television because we're sick of French quiz shows. Now we'd managed to order the cable we needed through the internet, we are happily squabbling over which to watch on catch-up TV first: 'Silent Witness' or the newest episode of 'A Place In The Sun'. Suddenly two strange figures are standing in the lounge doorway, they've appeared silently, and we aren't entirely sure how long they've been there. I feel instantly wrong-footed as they smirk at us.

'Your security is not very good.' The male vampire speaks English with a strong Spanish accent. 'We could just walk in. We could have been anyone. Where is Guillaume?' he demands.

You *are* anyone, I think to myself crossly. I'm reassured that he's mentioned Guillaume, at least he knows whose Pride this is. I am frantically calculating how at fault I am, if we New Ones are in the wrong. Do the rest of the Pride keep the doors locked of an evening when they are here? I don't think so, certainly we haven't been left with any instructions to do so, as the others departed to hunt, and Guillaume, Marcus, and Robert are still here. Guillaume never hunts and always keeps at least two of his closest allies near him at all times.

'I'll go and get Guillaume for you now,' I offer, now I'm sure this isn't my mistake. 'Who shall I say is here?' David has closed the laptop, so the opening theme tune to 'Silent Witness' has been silenced.

'I am Agata, and this is Darius. We are old friends of Guillaume and Patrice,' the female replies smoothly, her English is almost accent-less. I hop up to my feet and trot through to Guillaume's study. Ok, I admit it, I am delighted to have an excuse to knock on his study door, although my blood did boil when she had spoken of him and Patrice as if they were still a couple.

157

'Come in,' Guillaume calls as I knock firmly. He is sat at his desk working as I open the door. He glances up briefly, sees it's me and looks straight back at his computer screen.

'Darius and Agata are in the lounge. They're asking for you,' I snap. Guillaume leaps to his feet, and turns to the window with his hand over his mouth. After a second or two of thought, he walks past me and out of his office.

'Go and find Marcus and Robert, I think they are up with the pigs, tell them to ring Simon and Elaine and get everyone back here, now!' he says quietly from the doorway, before he strides down the corridor towards the lounge greeting his guests loudly with bonhomie. I've picked up his caution, though, his palpable fear and when I find Marcus and Robert, there is no mistaking their tension at my news. Marcus immediately does a quick scan of the path I've come up to reach them and only once he is sure it is clear does he nod to Robert who has his mobile phone out of his pocket ready. I can't overhear the hurried hissed conversation he has, because he walks away from us and Marcus stands firmly between us so I can't move closer to listen, without pushing past him. Robert seems calmer when he hangs up.

'They had a good hunt. They are already on their way back. They'll be here by morning,' he tells Marcus.

Once we are back in the farm house, I yawn widely while catching Layla's eye.

'Well, I'm off to bed, lots to do in the morning, there's so much to do while the others are away,' I say, rubbing my eyes. For a second I think Brian is going to argue, but Layla's caught my eye signal and kicks his foot as she passes him, so he obediently scrambles to his feet and follows as we slip away upstairs.

'I don't know exactly what's going on,' I whisper to the others when we are all in my room at the top of the house for a conference. 'But Guillaume is totally freaked out. He sent me to get Robert and Marcus to phone the others, and get them to come straight back here.'

'Really?' Layla's eyes go huge. 'He was all friendly when he came in the lounge, all handshakes and long-time no see. Oo! I wonder what's going on?' Layla loves a bit of intrigue, whereas I've seen how shaken up the other vampires are, so I can't share her delight in my gossip. We agree to keep our eyes and ears open and our mouths shut, and to avoid the visiting vampires at all costs.

'Most of all don't let them know what your gifts are,' I whisper. It's a gut reaction to the fear I saw in Guillaume. These visitors are dangerous and we need to be careful.

***

I go downstairs and straight out of the back door to do my chores the next morning, being as quiet as possible. I'm hoping that I can avoid the visitors before the rest of the Pride returns, but as I bring the cows into the parlour to be milked, Agata appears at my shoulder.

'So, have you lived here long?' Her opening question seems innocent enough, as she picks up one of the milking attachments, but I am on guard. I take it off her and fit it onto the nearest cow's udder. She is a dramatic-looking female, with thick black hair, golden skin, and deep brown eyes. She has a wide sensual mouth, and should be beautiful, but there is something cold about her despite her warm colouring.

'No, no, not long,' I eventually respond nonchalantly. I bustle around noisily getting the milking underway. I make much more of a song and dance of it than I needed to, dropping things and clattering around, asking Agata to help out with complicated tasks which need long explanations. While she seems friendly and helpful enough, my guard is up. I really don't want to stick my foot in it and I have no idea what the official story will be about how my friends and I have come to be living on the farm, or what the explanation will be for why Patrice isn't here anymore; they never met the other New Ones, so I don't have to worry about them noticing that Suzannah or any of the others are gone. I'm confident of vampire law around the killing of one's own kind, and I've broken it according to the three bitches, the collective name I've granted the three vampires who had a go at me in the kitchen and continue to bitch and gripe whenever I'm in earshot, even though they've benefited from my hunting idea.

Just as I'm running out of things to distract her with, Nicholas strolls into the milking shed. I can tell his relaxed attitude is affected, and hope Agata won't pick up on it too.

'Ah, there you are. We are back, and Guillaume was wondering if you want to join us in the hall? Everyone is looking forward to seeing you.' He smiles at her charmingly. As they leave the parlour, he chivalrously gestures her to go through the doorway first, so he can look back at me with raised brows. I give the tiniest shake of my head and I'm rewarded with a small tight smile.

'Thanks for the help with the milking,' I call after her, raising my hand in farewell. She looks back at me over her shoulder and her eyes flash with amusement, I'm left feeling sure she knew what I'd been up to, and sure she is confident she will find out exactly what is going on.

I gather Layla, Georgette, Brian and David and keep us busy for the rest of the day, finding chores to do as far from the house as possible. In the afternoon I look up from the section of fencing I'm fixing and see Elaine coming towards me.

'Thank you for keeping out of the way,' she says. 'This is very awkward and exactly what we were hoping would not happen.' I look at her patiently, waiting for her to explain. She keeps glancing over her shoulder back the way she's come and is speaking in a hurried rush. 'Darius and Agata lived here for a while when it was just them and Patrice and Guillaume, before Simon, Marcus and I arrived. Things were very different here then.'

'When we were summoned to the High Council to explain ourselves, they did not confess and were stubbornly defiant, insisting they had not broken any rules. Simon, Marcus, and I had to give evidence against them. Officially, all has been forgiven. The High Council would only let us all go if we agreed to get along, but they have never settled since; they move from Pride to Pride, spending time here, time there. The rumour is that the High Council only allowed them to live on the secret understanding that they would spy for them. Whatever the truth of the matter is, they are never popular

160

guests in any Pride, they always stir up trouble, and this is the worst possible timing.'

Elaine rubs her nose, and glances over her shoulder again. Seeing the normally unruffled Elaine so flustered is horrible. With all that has happened since I've known her, to see her displaying so much anxiety over these visitors scares me. The rest of my group are gathered around us by now, subdued and listening closely to what is being said.

'They are going to try and get to speak to you New Ones on your own. If they do, it is imperative that we all give the same story. You were infected by a rogue nomad in Tours, you've no idea who bit you. It was dark, you were walking back to your hotel together and you never saw who bit you. Luckily, Simon and I were up there on a hunt and stumbled across the aftermath, and cleared up the mess. We didn't know who had done it so there was no point alerting the High Council. Patrice was angry and jealous of New Ones arriving and left, we don't know where.' Elaine looks around at us, waiting for our agreement.

'Is all that clear? Guillaume has decided that this is what we will say, and we must all stick to the same story. Everyone is being told what to say.'

'Why on earth doesn't he just tell the truth?' I ask. I hate telling lies. It never leads anywhere good in my experience. 'Patrice disobeyed the Pride rules, and the High Council's rules, she and her New Ones were dealt with. Sorted.'

'Guillaume should have reported her and asked for assistance when she first turned Suzannah. Since he didn't, he stands to be punished as harshly as they would have punished her,' Elaine explains.

'Well, why didn't he?' I ask. I still don't understand this point. I'm feeling utterly baffled by all this extra information that Elaine has just given me. What exactly had gone on that made Guillaume so ashamed he couldn't admit the full truth to me even, when he had appeared to be telling me his history? He hadn't even mentioned Darius and Agata.

'He is loyal, he and Patrice had their history, and he did not wish her to be condemned to death for what he had

161

hoped was a mistake on her part. He thought he could cover for her one aberration since we had been pardoned by; and then it slid so quickly out of control that within hours we all stood to face the death penalty if the High Council ever heard about what happened, all of you New Ones, Guillaume, Simon and I. He should have killed you all at that meeting. He should have handed you over once you killed the other vampires, the list goes on. He could only cross his fingers and hope news of it would not leak out. Even this story he has concocted leaves him open to punishment, but it should protect the rest of us.'

'Why don't we Glamour them?' I ask, delighted by my sudden inspiration. They aren't part of our Pride, so no rules would be broken. 'Layla and I can seduce them and you can wipe their minds. We can send them on their way with warm fuzzy feelings, but no clear memories.' Layla gives me the eloquent eyebrow at this suggestion, but doesn't actually argue. David frowns, but doesn't object.

'If only we could. Agata has the same gift of forgetting as me, so I could not wipe her mind, and there is no point wiping one without the other. That was why she and Patrice were so formidable together: those two gifts in two such morally corrupted beings…' She shudders, unwilling to finish her sentence. 'All we can do is be consistent with what we tell them, and do not let yourselves be separated off. All of you need to stick together in a group. 'What about Darius?' I ask. 'What's his gift?'

'He's psychic.' Elaine sounds defeated as she answers me. Everyone's faces register the horror this knowledge provokes. 'He needs to get you on your own, and then he stares into your eyes and reads your thoughts. If he thinks he can get away with it, he'll drink some of your blood too. All vampires can read each other's memories in their blood if they feed directly from them, and he is known to be addicted to the dream state the memories induce. Agata would wipe away the memory that you'd even seen him, so be very alert, and try not to be alone at any time.'

'Psychic?' I ask. 'Hang on, I thought we weren't supernatural. I thought the virus just made us highly evolved?'

'The human heart acts like a radio and receiver, it sends out messages of emotion and receives them from others. It's why they will suddenly feel an unexplainable dislike towards someone. His vampireness has increased this skill to clarity, so he can read your thoughts quite clearly from your emotions.' I gape at her in horror, I know she's telling the truth, I've read articles about the heart and wondered how human language ability interacted with this, and whether this is why some people can cold read others so well. Apparently, I had been right.

Layla

For the next two days there's a subtle game of cat and mouse. Darius and Agata appear to be casually mingling with the established Pride members, while we newer ones work long and hard as far away from them as possible. If I'm ever in the same room as Darius, Rae has advised that I sing Kylie's 'I just can't get you out of my head' as loudly and jauntily as I can in my head. It is the most annoying song we know so I hope it will put him off prying in my brain if he tries to take a sneaky poke around. Elaine organises a Pride hunt and makes a big show of insisting that Darius and Agata join them. She used our new hunting plan as a way of distracting the visitors, but they are genuinely interested in our scheme, asking hundreds of questions about the slightest detail. I keep my mouth shut and my head down.

It seems like we've got away with it. On the third night Simon comes up to my room where all of us newer ones are gathered together. Oozing relief, he tells us that Agata had just announced they will be leaving the next day. He flashes us a rare smile before disappearing back downstairs. We all heave a big sigh of relief and sleep better that night than we have since the Spanish vampires arrived.

Rae

The next morning I am a bit later getting up than I have been the rest of the week; I'd fallen into a deep sleep and slept in. Once I'm dressed, I check and see that Layla and Georgette's room is empty, as is the one Brian and David are sharing. Since the visitors arrived, we have been sleeping in each other's rooms, changing which rooms we left empty, but last night I'd wanted to sleep alone. I never sleep very well when there are others in my room and I was exhausted and needed to sleep properly.

I slip silently through the house, pausing to listen as I reach the bottom of the stairs, but the only sounds I hear are coming from Guillaume's office. Relaxing a bit, I ease open the back door, check both ways and then set out towards the hayfields. Halfway down the field closest to the house, I realise I will need some sacks. We have fixed every tiny snag in all the fences, and are resorting to pulling any ragwort, thistles or bracken we could find out in the far grazing and hayfields. I double back up the field and jump lithely over the fence into the grassed-over area at the rear of the barns which encircle the yard. This means I'm approaching the back of the tractor shed, where the hessian sacks are kept folded on the shelves around walls along with all the other tools, while the central space is kept clear for the farm's old tractor. The farm specialises in organic produce so Guillaume hasn't changed to mass production, with the huge machinery that so many other producers use.

I am engrossed in my own thoughts, my mind predictably returning to toss the Guillaume situation over and over in my head, as I walk up the side of the shed. Oblivious to everything around me, I barge through the shed door and scream as I stumble across the three bitches huddled together with Darius and Agata.

'Oh my God!' I gasp. 'You gave me such a fright! Oh! I was in a world of my own.' My eyes quickly scan the group, Darius didn't seem to be gazing at any of the bitches particularly intensely.

164

'Wow!' Agata laughs. 'You're like a cat! We didn't hear you coming at all. The ladies are just showing us how everything works on the farm. We are thinking we might buy some land and do something similar in Espania, so we have been making lists of what we will need.' This all seems feasible. I look hastily around all of them again and everyone smiles innocently back at me.

'Did you need something? Are we in your way?' Darius seems very solicitous. I look at him suspiciously. 'I wanted to speak to you about the hunting method you devised. It is very clever. Elaine explained everything to us when we went out, and it was so smooth. Would you mind if we used it too, once we are settled in Spain?'

The three bitches start laughing.

'What's it got to do with her?' The ring leader jeers. 'It's our system. She only eats pig.'

'It is polite to ask.' Darius laughs. I reach past him and grab a hand full of sacks.

'Still working in the fields?' he asks. 'You will be glad when we're gone and you can come back to the house.'

'What?' I look at him sharply. Is he going to end the polite game and ask about our avoidance of him and Agata? My heart starts to pound.

'I said you'll be glad when you're done and can come back to the house. For a rest, you know. Farm life is hard, even for a vampire. But it is good to be safe in a Pride like this, especially for a New One. You are lucky they found you and let you stay. That nomad will have to be found. The High Council won't allow someone to just go around turning people. But that's their problem, no?' He smiles a big smile at me, and I want to believe him. I want to believe the visit has been an innocent trip to see old friends and get their advice on how to set up a similar Pride. As they walk away, Agata starts to whistle 'I just can't get you out of my head'.

***

I keep my own council about what I had stumbled upon in the tractor shed because I don't want to scare the others unnecessarily. Once Darius and Agata leave in the

165

afternoon, my friends go to relax in the river field for the rest of the sunlit hours. There really isn't anything else left to do around the farm. I make an excuse about needing something from my room and nip back up to the house. I tap quietly on Guillaume's office door. There is no reply. I find him with Simon, Marcus, Nicholas, and Elaine laughing in the kitchen. His face closes as he sees me, and I am loathe to further ruin their relief that the Spanish have left with no apparent harm done.

'I saw the three bitches talking to Darius and Agata in the tractor shed this morning,' I stutter, feeling a bit foolish. It doesn't seem very important when I say it out loud.

'Who?' Nicholas asks.

'Um, the three females who think us new ones should be punished for killing Patrice and the others,' I mutter. In my anxiety to explain what I've seen, I had forgotten my nickname was less than complimentary to three of the established Pride members. 'Simon knows who they are,' I finish lamely. Nicholas swallows a smile.

'And what were they talking about?' Elaine looks concerned.

'They said they were looking at the tools. I just had a feeling they were buttering me up to distract me from what they were saying when I came in.'

'What were they saying when you went in?' Marcus looks worried too.

'I don't know,' I admit reluctantly. 'I was in a world of my own.' I can't help flashing a look at Guillaume and I'm pretty sure Elaine catches my glance from the slight flick of her eyebrows. I feel my Glamour start to glow, and try my best to swallow it back down. Guillaume is looking steadfastly out of the window, his magnificent profile tense, his jaw clenching. 'I screamed when I went in because they startled me. They weren't talking at all normally, that's why I had such a fright.' I look at Marcus and Elaine for confirmation that this was suspicious. Elaine nods for me to continue.

'What was said?' Marcus asks.

'They laughed at me for getting such a fright, told me about looking at the tools to make a list of what they'd need and then started on about how clever I'd been to come up with the hunting idea. Darius said about asking me if they could use the same scheme in Spain, and then the three bi.., the other three started going on about how it had nothing to do with me anyhow because I only drink pig blood. Then as they walked away, Agata started whistling the song I've been singing in my head whenever Darius was near to cover my thoughts.'

'What, hmmm mmm mmm mm mmm mmm mm?' Elaine hums the tune of the Kylie song. I nod, bewildered. 'You've been humming and whistling that all week- you've infected everyone with it.'

'Have I?' Now I really feel stupid.

'Did Darius seem to be staring into anyone's eyes?' Guillaume asks, still turned away from me.

'No.' I confess, I'm starting to feel like a tattletale. 'Not that I saw, but with those three I don't think they'd need to use their gifts. They hate us new ones. They were friends with Patrice.'

'Are you saying that members of this Pride would happily sign the death warrants of myself, Elaine, and Simon, just to get back at you?' Guillaume murmurs. It isn't my imagination, he really is treating me like a bitchy school girl trying to get someone else in trouble. I feel itchy with frustration.

'Were they involved in the fight?' I ask. 'I don't remember if they were there or not.'

'There were a group of three females who were involved in the hunt of the woman and child, and the initial attack of you new ones, but when they saw Simon, Elaine and me, they left and went to the house. They have been spoken to; they were caught up in the excitement of the chase. I can only assume they are the same group?' Guillaume's voice is dismissive. It is plain I am causing trouble he didn't want. I am shocked by the image of me he has. He sees me as a trouble-making little snitch, who can't play nicely with others. No wonder he can't bear to look at me. Despair at the unfairness of it all wells in my stomach and I feel acid tears bite the back of my eyes.

'I'll speak to them,' Elaine says. 'Simon already told me about your argument with them the morning after the fight, so I know who they are. Have you said anything about this to the others?' I shake my head, glad I'd trusted my gut and not told my friends about my suspicions. 'Good. Don't. We don't want any more rifts within the Pride,' Elaine states. Guillaume nods, and I know I am dismissed.

***

The next three weeks pass calmly enough. The three bitches have not changed their attitude; indeed Elaine's questioning about the conversation in the tractor shed seems to make them worse if anything. They continue to hiss and whisper whenever I walk past. I shouldn't let it bother me, but it's a safe outlet for my feelings of devastation that Guillaume is still avoiding me, something to get safely cross about. It is hard to admit, even to myself, just how much I had been hoping that being healed and then seeing me around with my turned-down glamour and scarred face would have changed things between us. I had thought that when he was strong enough, he would come and try to speak to me again. Maybe kiss me again. Oh ok, make love to me again.

I wanted him to experience our love making as a healthy male so he could see that some loss of control and strong emotions were normal. He would be able to see for himself how much more in control of my gift I am, even within the short time since I had been changed. I wanted him to see that he inspired every bit as much of a loss of control in me as I inspired in him, and there was still so much more for us to explore together if he would just allow it to happen. I wanted him to see my scarred and flawed face so I could see if this imperfection would free him from his obsessive admiration and allow him to love me for the emotional connection between us.

His attitude towards me when I told him about the three bitches, and his continued avoidance of me has made it utterly clear how he feels about me, but three weeks has taken the sting out of my humiliation, and lack of consequences has shown that Guillaume was right to discount my overreaction.

Despite myself, desire has nursed hope back to life, and the two stubborn flames burn stubbornly on, no matter how often I try to quash them with common sense.

One morning after working in the garden for a few hours in the hope of distracting myself from my doldrums, the three bitches walk past me giggling and snickering as they kick over the tub of raspberries I've just carefully picked. I look up at them in an immediate fury and see Guillaume standing a few metres behind them, looking straight at me. I freeze, my heart pounding. This is going to be it. He is finally going to speak to me. He has seen the bitches being bitches, and seen that the trouble does not start with me. His eyes brush my face. I am sure they hover on my scars for a second. I wait for some gesture of affection, or even friendship, but there is none; his eyes skim me as if I am a stranger he has no interest in getting to know. His handsome face is completely impassive. Instead he points to something behind me and confers with Simon about it.

I am devastated, utterly winded and deflated. I can't bear it. I can feel my eyes brimming with tears. I am so distressed that I have a sudden terror of the Rage ripping through me. I need to get away, now, but I feel hideously glued to the spot, convinced everyone is watching my double humiliation. I haven't realised that Layla is standing just behind me until she hooks her arm through mine.

'Rae, I need your help over here,' she states loudly, marching me through the garden. 'Keep it in. Keep it in. Head up. Smile!' she mutters as we walk past the others. 'Morning Guillaume,' she calls.

'Oh, morning ladies,' he is forced to reply.

'Morning,' I sing out at a sharp nudge in the ribs from Layla as I smile, smile, smile until we are out through the gate and heading down towards the river field. Once there is nobody around to see, I bend double as the pain takes all my air away. This is why she is my friend you see, because she is always there when I need her most and she always knows just what to do when I am floundering.

'He is such a fucking shit!' she hisses.

'What do you mean? He doesn't know how I feel about him. I've only told you. And Georgette.' She shoots me a look with a raised eyebrow when I say that. I can't do that, raise just one brow, which isn't fair; it always leaves me feeling at a sartorial disadvantage when she can so eloquently express so much with one flick. I wave a dismissive hand, that doesn't matter. 'She wouldn't tell anyone, she promised not to, and you haven't, have you?'

'Sweetheart, I hate to be the one to point this out to you, but everyone knows exactly how you feel about him, because it's written all over your face whenever he walks into a room, and has been since the first time you met him.' I am mortified. I have nothing to say to this; I would like to be able to argue that she is wrong, but it makes sense of Elaine and Simon's bemused expressions whenever I've asked them how he was. I feel like such a stupid child. They must have been laughing at me for weeks, protecting Guillaume from his puppy-dog stalker. I have to leave. I cannot bear this a day longer.

'Layla, I have to go. I can't bear this anymore. Every time he looks straight through me, I die inside. I know I should know better. I know I should be able to comprehend that he doesn't want anything to do with me. He's made that abundantly clear. But love is stubborn, and conspires with hope, so when I don't see him, I somehow manage to convince myself it will be different next time he sees me, but it never is, no matter what I do to try to appeal to him, and I can't live like this. Leaving will feel like dying, but if I stay, I will go mad.' Layla looks at me sadly and nods.

'What are you going to do?' she asks. 'Where on earth will you go? With what money?'

I explain to her that I don't know; it is what has stopped me from leaving sooner, but I don't care anymore. I am going to leave, and worry about everything else later. Layla persuades me to go up to my room and pack, but not to leave until she has spoken to Elaine to see if she knows of another Pride we can join. Layla is gone a long time. I am packed and sat on my bed playing FreeCell on my laptop when it dawns on me that she had said where we could go. That cheers me up.

170

She is going to come with me. She will bring David, but that is ok, he is a good man, and maybe he can find some freelance computer work to pay the rent. He, of course, will insist on bringing Brian, the drip, with him. I could do without his moping, I am too caught up in my own heartbreak, and misery does not love company, contrary to popular belief. I am doing my own head in, without his help. But I am cheered to have the luxury of being able to contemplate rejecting company, when I've been assuming I will be completely alone. I doze off, only starting awake when Layla wakes me, returning to my room.

Layla

'Don't worry, Elaine is on the case,' I tell Rae. 'It'll take a few days to sort out, but it's in hand.' I can see her heart sink a little, I know she really wants to leave immediately, but there's nothing that can be done in her timescale. How like her to leave it until crisis point before she does anything. Elaine had been really quite cross with us. She poured scorn on the idea of another Pride taking us, pointing out that very few Prides make any provision for animal feeders, and given how much difficulty we've had fitting in here, she'd understandably demanded that I tell her what would be different elsewhere.

I'd started to point out the obvious differences- no Patrice, no Suzannah, no Mel, and no Guillaume, but I'd realised from Elaine's scowl it had been meant as a rhetorical question. When I considered her meaning, I understood. There would be difficult vampires wherever we went. Vampires by their nature are difficult, old age and extreme power does not make them mellow and sweet-natured apparently, rather it creates vicious power hungry despots. Elaine rolled her eyes and huffed a lot, and told me to tell Rae to suck it up for a while longer. She would look online for a small, cheap, isolated property that would suit us to set up our own satellite Pride. She pointed out that France is full of such houses, hovels for the English, she sneered shrugging, as baffled as the rest of the French over why Brits liked their isolated ruins.

I pointed out that we don't have any money to buy such a house, no matter how cheap it is. She cocked an arrogant eyebrow; I don't like it when people do that back to me, it feels rude. She pointed out that Guillaume could buy the property through the farm, and we could pay him back slowly. I grimaced, that was not going to be easy to persuade Rae to accept, any more than waiting as long as it takes to buy a house in France, an interminable process.

As I sit on her bed now, and tell her the plan I can see her shoulders droop. I am about to point out all that she's suffered already, and reason that a month or two more won't actually make that much difference. She can just stay in her room, or down by the river and avoid seeing anyone, but she looks up at me with her big soulful eyes.

'But you are coming with me?' she whispers while twisting her fingers in her sheet, her bottom lip and chin doing that collapsing thing that makes babies so irresistible. A blood tear runs down her nose and plops onto her sheet. All my exasperation at her melts, and I reach out to hold her crumpled fingers. How can my silly little friend think for one second I wouldn't be coming with her?

'Of course we're coming, you dope. If you'll have us?' Her face lights up, and we laugh and cry, and hug a while. Once she knows she won't be alone, Rae shakes back her hair, and we make whispered plans into the night. One thing we agree immediately is that once we've left this Pride, we will never, ever come back here, and we will never ever see any of these vampires again. There has to be ways we can make a living online, we are bright and hard-working, and we won't need much. We sit in her room as the light fades outside and try to tussle the jigsaw pieces of our future into a coherent picture.

Rae

The next day, I feel hollowed out and exhausted. I do as Layla and I had planned, and stay in my room, sleeping and worrying. I have to change my pillow cases twice, as they become clotted with blood tears and snot. I'm not happy to find that if you cry hard enough, for long enough as a vampire, you produce dark clotty blood from your nose. It's disgusting. Layla brings me a glass of pig's blood in the late afternoon, and plonks herself onto my bed for a gossip. I show her some of the plans I've typed up on my laptop.

'Have you spoken to David about all this yet?' I wave my hand vaguely at the laptop to encompass all of the mess I'm in and our plans for our future. 'Will he come too?' I don't doubt for one second that he would walk to the ends of the earth if Layla asked him to, but I want her to see that I welcome him along into our new life. Just because I'm not to be loved by the man I adore, doesn't mean I expect her to suffer. Her face glows at the mention of his name and she happily chatters away about some of the ideas he's had about how we can cope on our own. I nod sagely, and add the best ideas to my list. Layla squeezes my foot and looks at me sincerely.

'David sends you his love. He wanted to come and see you, but I told him to wait until you feel better.' I nod gratefully, love David as I do, I can't bear the thought of any company other than Layla's at the moment. I'm too close to tears all the time, and putting a brave face on for company feels like an unobtainable achievement today.

'Thanks. Maybe tomorrow...' I peter out, not wanting to make promises I can't keep.

'No rush. He just wanted me to pass on a message, though,' she grins mischievously. 'He said to tell you that Guillaume is a stupid fucker who does not deserve you. In fact, he deserves to sit on his pompous arse in his stupid office being utterly self-important, all on his own, until the end of time.' I ignore the clench of pity I feel at this awful image of Guillaume alone for eternity, and nod in agreement. I have to admit that sad as that thought is, the thought of him being in love with someone else is much, much worse.

'Tell David that Guillarse is actually a stupid fucking arsehole fuckity fuck fuck face,' I reply.

'Guillarse?' she hums. 'Yes, that'll do'. With another impish grin, Layla collects my empty glass and trots out of the room, happy to see a spark of resilience in me.

It's much later, just as the last blush of light fades from the evening sky that there is a knock on my bedroom door. I expect it to be Layla come to say goodnight, and call for her to come in. However, it's Simon who sticks his head around the door. I'm mortified that he should see me in such a state, with blood crusting my nostrils and lower eyelashes, and blood-soaked tissues stacked on my bedside table, and strewn over the floor. He doesn't take any notice, though, and just gestures with a jerk of his head that I am to follow him downstairs. He looks even more solemn than usual.

I change quickly into an unstained dress, and shake my fingers through my hair. Then I follow behind him to the Big Hall, picking the dried blood off my face on the way. In the Hall, Layla, David, Brian, Georgette, and Elaine are already sitting around the banqueting table that has been pushed into the centre of the room. My friends look bewildered, and Simon and Elaine look horribly solemn. I sit in the empty chair next to Georgette, opposite Layla, and Simon sits near us at one end of the big rectangular table. My heart is pounding, and I can feel the Glamour flushing through me, as it is Layla. I'm about to ask what's happening, worried that this is yet another problem I've caused with my request to leave when Guillaume enters the room and sits heavily at the head of the table. He drops his head into his hands for a moment, then vigorously rubs his face while exhaling loudly. I'm horrified at the sight of him looking so discombobulated.

'We have been summoned by the High Council,' he announces. He looks around the table at us all; after his initial display of stress, he is quiet and calm, but I know him well enough now to recognise the tiny tells of anxiety that leak around his mask of control: the tiny twitch in his jaw, the slight fidget of his fingers before he remembers himself and clasps his hands. 'We have to go there and account for ourselves; despite our best attempts, they have heard rumours and want us to explain. I received a telephone call half an hour ago telling me to bring all of those involved, including all the New Ones, to their headquarters in Germany.' He takes a deep breath and looks directly at me.

'I'm sorry, Rae, I should have listened when you tried to warn us.'

His apology is short but heartfelt. There is no glory in it for me, no revelling in being right. We are all in danger of losing our lives. It is very likely that some, if not all of us, will never return.

'We will need to leave first thing in the morning. You New Ones will travel with Elaine in the camper van. Simon, you and I will go in your Renault. They expect us to be there tomorrow evening, no excuses,' he finishes bleakly.

Chapter 9
Rae

No one sleeps well and we are all quiet and sombre as we climb into the camper in the early dawn light. Nicholas hugs and kisses Elaine at the door, but she shoos him back inside, and avoids our sympathetic gazes, busying herself with loading us into the camper. I'm surprised, I didn't know they were together, but when I think about it, it makes sense, they suit each other. As Simon holds the passenger door open for Guillaume, Marcus runs from the house and throws his arms around him, clutching Simon tightly. Simon clasps him back for a moment and then gently pushes him away.

Marcus wipes blood tears from his cheeks, his eyes only on Simon as he lifts his hand in farewell before stumbling back indoors. Simon stands with his hand on the door of the car for a moment longer, then closes it firmly and walks around to the driver's side. His face is as pale and impassive as ever. I'd had no idea that he and Marcus are a couple either. I like him more for this flash of his tender side, which he normally keeps completely hidden.

I ignore Guillaume's snub in our travel arrangements and I refuse to even glance at him as I climb into the back of the camper with Layla and Georgette, while David and Brian sit in the front with Elaine. We head into the countryside, up past Dijon to the border with Germany and cross the border in the countryside outside Roppeviller. Layla and I laugh when we first see the sign posts for Bitche, suggesting Elaine should look for a house for us there. She ignores us and the joke soon wears thin and we settle back into a tense silence, broken every now and again by Georgette asking what we think will happen. We patiently take it in turns to remind her that we know as little about what is going to happen as she does.

It takes us almost twelve hours to drive right across Germany and reach the forested area between Berlin and Frankfurt Oder. Eventually, we stop outside a nondescript, isolated house set back amongst the trees. Once both vehicles are parked, we all climb out and huddle together for a few moments before the front door is opened, and an incredibly ugly vampire gestures for us to come in. He speaks heavily accented French, and would have made Melanie look positively pretty in comparison. We enter the house and follow the vampire down the internal corridors and then upstairs; we pass several large rooms with their doors wide open. A quick glance into each room reveals large groups of vampires within. Some of the groups are working at computers, others are sat around playing cards or watching television, all of them without exception stop what they are doing to watch us pass. None of them smile.

I notice that a lot of them are big and ugly, with large plates of bone in their foreheads. Their almost non-existent necks mean that their lumpy earlobes scrape their huge shoulders. I wonder what gifts these vampires possess. Part of me is terrified, there is no doubt that we will not leave this house unless they want us to, but part of me is intrigued too. What could I learn about my new existence here? I have so many questions still that Guillaume and the others have not been able to answer, and have even seemed annoyed at me for asking. As a human I asked too many questions, and apparently I've carried that trait over to being a vampire too.

As we follow the vampire through the multitude of corridors and stairways, Georgette slips her hand into mine, and Layla slips hers into David's. Even arrogant Elaine is quiet and sticks close to the rest of us. Only Guillaume stalks forward with his head held high. I begin to suspect that we are actually being led in circles to disorient us, the house does not look this big from the outside. At that moment we stop outside a set of grand double doors. Our escort knocks firmly and waits for a response.

'Enter,' a rich voice calls after a few seconds. Our massive guide opens the door and sweeps his arm inwards, gesturing for us to enter. The Hall is magnificent, decorated in reds and purples, with swathes of silk and velvet and huge, heavily carved pieces of dark furniture. Five vampires dressed in white robes sit looking at us from behind a huge ornate table. It takes me a few seconds to realise that there are no windows in the room; the only way in or out is through the double doors. As the doors bang closed behind us, and a key turns in the lock, I look back in horror and see a line of six huge and revoltingly hideous vampires stepping into place across the doors. The vampire who brought us up to the Hall makes a show of dropping the key into his inside breast pocket and patting it, then takes his place with the other six.

The five vampires waiting at the table look at us impassively. They are all finely featured, androgynous and pale blond, so pale they almost look albino. It is hard to tell which are male and which are female.

'Guillaume, Simon, Elaine. What a shame to see you here again. Of course you all know us, but allow us to introduce ourselves to your new friends,' says the central councillor. 'I am Adelfried. I am the head of the Council. I am seven hundred years old. As far as anyone knows, I am the oldest existing vampire. This is Ludwig, and this is Jürgen,' he gestures to the two vampires on his right. I only realise they are male when each of them says hello in deep Teutonic tones. 'This is Ula, and this is Chloris,' he announces, gesturing to the two vampires on his right, who say hello in bell-like feminine tones. 'They are all many hundreds of years old too. Between us we have great wisdom, and it falls on us to set and maintain the rules we vampires need to live by to prevent humans becoming aware of our reality.'

'By necessity, the breaking of some of our rules is punishable by death. Between you, you seem to have broken most of them.' He raises his eyebrows at us, a bemused grandfather discussing sending us to bed without supper because we have been naughty. 'Now, Guillaume, please introduce your New Ones.' Guillaume does so courteously and everyone in the council nods their head and says hello politely at each new introduction. It is quickly apparent that the Council know everything about us. Guillaume introduces Brian first, then Georgette.

'Ah, the healer,' comments Adelfried looking at her closely. Then David.

'The strong one.' Adelfried is not so interested.

'Layla,' Guillaume continues.

'And Rae,' says Adelfried, looking straight at me. 'The Pretty Ones. Well, let's see then.' He gazes at us expectantly.

I step forward, as does Layla, so we can make sure there is a wide berth between us and our friends. Behind us, there is no risk to them succumbing to our Glamour. We are now stood in line with Guillaume and I look at him with my eyebrows raised until he catches my meaning and steps back. Then I let myself shine.

'Go on, my dears, all the way. We can take it,' says the one I think is called Jürgen, in a faintly licentious way. Adelfried and the two females glare at him, but gesture for us to proceed. I stand as tall as possible, smile my best smile and sway slowly towards them using every ounce of Glamour I can muster. Layla sashays beside me.

'Oh, very good.' Jürgen claps. 'They really are quite lovely. So shiny and new.' His words are enthusiastic, but his voice and eyes are cold. 'And I hear you have the Rage?' As he asks the question two of the big vampires at the back of the room move quickly to stand behind Layla and grab her hair and throat. She is completely vulnerable to them and shrieks as she sees the curved blade one of them holds. I stare at them, unable to believe my eyes. Only five seconds ago, Jürgen had been clapping in delight and now the end is upon us. I know it is futile to fight back, but I also know that if we have to go, I want it to be quick; they are not going to get any fun torturing us.

Layla screams again as one of the big males slices the blade across her stomach so blood cascades down her front. I feel the Rage surge and my limbs twist and thrust as my bones tear my flesh, my jaws and teeth lengthen and I grow in stature. Behind me I just about hear Guillaume command the others to stay in a deep, sonorous voice I have not heard him use before, but my ears are flooded with the frantic pounding of my heart as the adrenaline rips through me. I turn on the nearest male and claw at his eyes. He lowers his head so my nails rake down the big plate of bone protecting them, and then he punches me in the stomach with his immense fist. The force of it winds me, but the Rage prevents me from crumpling. Instead, the pain intensifies the Rage and spurs me on as I slash and rake at him.

Layla is transformed now too and is gouging at her attacker, even as the blood pours down her into a pool on the floor.

'Stop!' The command rings out, and we all freeze. Ula stands with her arms raised. No one has any choice but to cease all movement at the force of her words. I feel the Rage leave me as quickly as it had arrived, leaving me shaking and queasy. 'Healer, heal them.' She beckons Georgette forward. Georgette is quaking, but quickly drops to her knees besides Layla, where she has fallen in the pool of her own blood, as soon as the Rage had been stopped. Georgette neatly slices her own left wrist with her right thumb nail and drips her blood into Layla's mouth. Having learned my lesson at the fight, I lift Layla's t-shirt and hold the two sides of the wound together as they quickly bond, leaving Layla smooth and perfect again within minutes of being sliced.

'And now the guards,' barks Ula. Georgette looks at me for confirmation. I nod. I have no desire to antagonise our hosts further. Ula sees the hesitation and narrows her eyes. Once the guards are healed and return to their position at the back of the room, Adelfried rises to his feet.

'We have seen what you can do. We need to consult. You will be shown to a room where you will wait until you are brought to us to explain what happened, in full, and let me just say now - do not even consider any more lies, and do not think that any detail is too small to concern us.'

We are led away by the guard I had clawed. He glares at me spitefully, and I snarl right back. He started it; I don't care if he was following orders. Once we are settled in a large room filled with couches, but without windows again, Guillaume perches on one sofa with his head in his hands for a few moments before he speaks.

'I am so sorry it has come to this. You must all speak the truth and look after yourselves. If they offer you any way out, take it; you do not owe anything to anyone else, and if anyone can survive this, they should. Don't bother trying to use any of your gifts on them. They collect vampires with every different gift, so whichever one of you is in the room, if your gift could be used to influence their decisions in anyway, they will have someone else in there with the same gift so they can

180

warn them if you try to use yours.' He rubs his hands over his face, then looks up at Simon. 'Simon, if you would not mind, I think it may be nice if you shared your gift with us all now.' He leans back in his seat and closes his eyes.

***

At first I think that Simon is not obliging him, but slowly I notice that I'm feeling deliciously serene. I try reminding myself that I am in mortal danger, but find I don't care, and it dawns on me slowly that Simon's gift is working like opium on the brain. My thoughts drift blearily back to the car journey straight after we transitioned. I've always wondered why we accepted what Guillaume was telling us so calmly. Now I know. I remain in the calming haze as one after the other the rest of my group are called away. Eventually, it dawns on me that no one is being returned to the room, and I find I can't care enough to even sit upright, but then Simon is taken from the room, and there is only me left.

Within minutes the soporific effect of Simon's gift has faded and I'm left, heart pounding, hands clenched as I realise I have dozed through all my friends' deaths. The clock on the wall tells me that it is now two o'clock in the morning; I have been up for almost twenty-four hours, running on adrenaline. Despite my rest while Simon's been here, I feel hollow and exhausted. Blood tears run down my cheeks, and clots of red snot clog my nose. I wish I could slide back into the delicious fog Simon had created. A smart rap on the door has me hastily wiping me face on my cardigan, which I scrunch up and tuck under the sofa cushion.

'Come in,' I croak. A different guard puts his head around the door and gestures for me to follow him.

'Are they all dead?' I whisper. He looks at me as if I was mad.

'No, they just take everyone who's spoken to the council to a different room so there can be no conferring over what has been said with those still to speak. They want the truth. We aren't monsters,' he exclaims indignantly. I raise my eyebrows as I think about the previous evening's events.

181

He leads me to a small side room, not the Great hall. When I enter, I see that only Chloris is in there, along with a digital camcorder set up on a tripod pointed at my seat. There is a window behind her, and the sight of it warms me. She doesn't feel that I might want to escape this next bit, it seems.

'Hello Rae. Take a seat please,' Chloris says pleasantly. 'Firstly, I shall explain the process. I will ask you to recount exactly what happened when you were turned, and since then with the Pride at Guillaume's farm. I am particularly interested in how Patrice and the other New Ones died. I will ask questions throughout if I need any extra information. Please include every detail; nothing is too small to be important to us. All the interviews are being filmed. The Council share the accounts together later when we discuss the outcome of our investigation.' She smiles at me serenely. 'Then they will be kept in our archives for reference.'

Everything feels surreal; she is speaking as if she is carrying out an investigation into missing funds and deciding whether someone will be sacked from their job, rather than whether or not we would all be killed.

'Why were Layla and I attacked in the hall last night?' I demand. I do not like the way she is being so calm, behaving like it is perfectly reasonable to treat us the way they have.

'We wanted to see exactly who we were dealing with. We had received information that you both have the Rage; that you distort far more than most vampires when you are threatened. We had been informed that you were in the grips of this rage when you killed Patrice and the others. We were told you became animalistic and uncontrollable at the slightest provocation. We wanted to see how much strain we needed to put you under before the Rage showed, and how much in control of yourself you remained. It was a very informative little experiment we carried out,' she explains blithely.

I narrow my eyes at her. I want to be crosser, but I can see the sense in what she's saying. In their situation I would probably have done the same thing. You can be guaranteed that the report they received, which had originated with the three bitches, would not have been flattering, and the test had provided a clear guide to how much in control of ourselves we are.

'Please tell me everything that has happened to result in you being sat in this room,' Chloris requests again. I recount everything, from the party in Tours, to Melanie attacking Layla and me, to Guillaume coming to get us and taking us to the farm. I leave out the bit about finding out about the Need with Brian, and jump straight to the homeless man in the barn, the fight in the hall, Guillaume's decision to let us all live.

I describe the night the mother and child were hunted by Patrice, and Georgette enlisting our help in attempt to save them. I recount the fight, the healing and the spite afterwards from the three bitches. I retell our discovery that the vampires who had only had animal blood could be healed by Georgette permanently, and the decision to hunt evil humans for the blood to do this. I finish off my explanation by detailing the visit from Darius and Agata. Chloris asks questions to clarify precise details, and I take pains to be as accurate as I can. I do not discuss my feelings for Guillaume, though; I feel too foolish and they don't really impact anything else. After I have concluded my tale, she thanks me for my co-operation.

I think I am being dismissed and get up to leave. However, she gestures for me to be seated again.

'Do you know much about our history?' she asks. I shake my head. 'Would you like to?' I nod eagerly. She folds her hands neatly together and leans further back in her seat.

'We don't know when the first vampire came, or how. All we know is that it was long ago when humans still believed in monsters, and we were the monsters they believed in. Because they believed in us, they were able to kill us. This is all I know of this time. While Adelfried was still a young vampire, he realised that if the humans did not believe in us, they would not hunt us, and we would be able to survive with them harmoniously. They will always kill far more of each other than a small population of vampires would ever wish to. He set about finding other vampires who could share his vision of peace, and so over the centuries he has created the High Council. Throughout history, those who have chosen not to live by our rules have ended up being killed by humans.

'This has meant that over time a sort of natural selection has prevailed amongst vampires too. And so the true vampire has faded from human memory. We have encouraged the silly legends about garlic and crosses, and other such nonsense, for as long as all mention of us is tied up in such silly stories no human will look behind them. Humans have always been selfish and dangerous, but now with the technological developments they have made, it is more important than ever that they do not find out that we are real. Now they would not just annihilate us, they would test us, and cure us, or use our virus to create super soldiers and wreak chaos upon the world. And so we have no choice but to monitor compliance with our rules very closely. If humans find out about us, it won't just be vampires that are wiped out; they would destroy themselves and probably the entire planet with them.

'This is why we were concerned and needed you New Ones investigated. We were hearing such strange tales: drugs, a nomad, seeking husbands and grieving fiancées. We needed the truth, and when that was not forthcoming to Darius and Agata, we needed to see you all in person. If we'd had a clearer picture of what had happened, we would never have sent Darius and Agata. Of course Guillaume would never tell them anything, but we recognised Patrice all over this and thought she may brag to them. When we were told that she had been sent away from the pride, we were very anxious, but then we were told she was dead. We had to know for sure whether we had a marauding nomad and an angry Patrice on the loose or not,' Chloris explains in her cool Teutonic tones.

'I knew Guillaume should have just been honest to you in first place,' I exclaim happily.

'Well, yes, that would have made our lives so much easier,' Chloris agrees. 'I can understand why he didn't: you have all broken so many of the Council's rules, and he and Simon and Elaine were already on a final warning. He has left us with very little option,' she continues in her calm, quiet voice, with a sigh. 'It gets slightly more complicated around you New Ones that killed. The boy Brian and the healer, they should be ok, but the rest of you have broken the basic commandments. I shall meet with the others and we shall discuss all of your accounts, and all of the rules you have broken, and see what can be done. We do not like putting vampires to death, but there have to be rules, and they have to be abided by.' She rises and ushers me from the room in front of her.

I'm dumbstruck and stumble to do her bidding, my mind spinning. First, I thought we'd be killed in the Hall, but we weren't, we were healed, then I thought my friends had already been killed, but I was sneered at for this. Now I understand that the High Council sets great store in our trial. They will be utterly fair, but also utterly rigid to the rules. I am shown into another big, windowless room full of couches where my friends are curled up under Simon's protective influence. I meet his eyes briefly, desolately, before succumbing to his narcotic mists.

***

I don't know how long I sleep, but suddenly there is a strange vampire in the room with us.

'They wish to speak to you all in the hall,' he tells us. Within seconds the fogginess Simon has induced clears and we are all on our feet. Georgette grabs my hand again and clings on as we all follow the guard back to the Grand Hall.

'Don't worry,' I whisper. 'You'll be fine'. I feel surer of this now, after my conversation with Chloris, although I can't tell her why; I don't want to raise her hopes in case I am wrong. I squeeze her hand and she clutches mine even tighter.

When we enter the Hall, the vampires are set out as before, with the High Council sat at the table and the guards lined up behind us.

'We are having difficulty agreeing on our conclusion,' Adelfried cuts straight to the point without any preamble. 'There are no doubts that each of you, apart from Brian and Georgette, have broken enough rules to have the death sentence applied, most of you several times over. However, there are motivational impulses that have clouded the issue. Those of you who remain seem to have a strong moral code, and this presents us with a dilemma. We feel we have no choice but to request that each of you allows each of us to feed on you, to see if this makes our pathway forward any clearer.

You may, of course, refuse this request. However, this would affect our ability to construct arguments about your motivations outweighing the rules you have broken.' Adelfried smiles ghoulishly and I get a horrible feeling that this whole process has been leading to this for him.

'This procedure will take several days, and you will need to feed well each night to ensure you can withstand our investigations. We understand that you all prefer pig blood if you can't hunt the human predators? We will make sure you are brought fresh pig's blood. We will give you a schedule so you know when we will wish to see you; while you are not with us, you may come and go as you please. Feel free to explore the beauty of the surrounding areas. Do make sure you return for your appointments, though.' He bows his head solemnly at us, and the other four follow suit before filing out from behind the table and parading majestically out through the hall.

We make our way back to the room we were in earlier, and I notice my cardigan, freshly laundered, and folded on the back of a sofa. I pick it up nonchalantly, hoping nobody will notice me, I'm embarrassed about the amount I cried; no one else is covered in crusty fecks of dried blood. I sit down clasping it in my lap, looking at the three older vampires for guidance. The mood in the room is one of relief that we aren't going to be put to death immediately, but consternation about the twist the investigation has taken. Everyone knows that by agreeing to let them feed from us, we will allow them to burrow in the deepest recesses of our souls. I can't shake the feeling that for Adelfried at least this access to our feelings and memories is what he wanted and I suspect Jürgen has a similar motivation. I ask Guillaume if he noticed anything and he nods sadly to express he knows what I am talking about.

'They will comply with the rules perfectly. They will be utterly fair, but if they are able to pleasure themselves in the process, they will. They live very restrained lives, and have done for centuries. Their opportunities for gratification are few and far between. This has had a slightly corrupting influence.' I look at Guillaume with my eyebrows up in bemusement, waiting for him to recognise the irony in his interpretation of their behaviour, it is similar to my concerns about his monkish existence. He ignores me.

Layla

'Why don't we just run away now they'll let us out?' I ask.

'Where to?' Guillaume replies. 'If you made a single withdrawal from your bank, ever went online for anything, were ever seen by any other vampire, they would find you, and there would not be any further trial. Your fate would be sealed. If you think you could happily live in the wild, feeding from animals, never reading another book, never watching another film, for eternity, then you may run, but please don't tell me if you are going to choose this life. For me this is no sort of life. I would rather die quickly and cleanly than to live like an animal looking over my shoulder all the time. What would you do with all that time?'

I calculate how happy David and I could be together living such a wild life. I can imagine turning my Glamour up high so the Need enthrals us both completely, and then we won't care where we sleep as long as we are together. Trust Guillaume not to even consider this option. I look my question at Rae, who shakes her head.

'You two go if you want,' she whispers. 'You know me, can't break the rules.'

'Apart from the really important ones? Like when you're ripping a fellow vampire's heart out?' I laugh sardonically. Only bloody Rae.

'Well, yes,' she concedes. 'But that's different. I wanted to save that little girl, and then they attacked us. It makes sense to me anyway. Rules are there, and shouldn't be broken, unless there is a really good reason.'

I shake my head in resigned bewilderment, the stupid cow means it. I look up at David, and know when he holds my gaze that he will come if we need to.

187

Rae

One of the guards knocks at the door and holds up the sheet of paper with the schedule printed on it to show us why he is here, then pins it onto the back of the door. They want to see me, Guillaume, Elaine, Simon and Layla immediately. This afternoon they will see David, Georgette and Brian. I am surprised Brian's name is on the list. I'd thought from Adelfried's pronouncement earlier that Brian is in the clear because he hadn't been involved in either fight or any of the hunts, but it seems that the Council want to get as much information as possible, from every viewpoint. Or access as many memories as they can, I consider cynically.

I'm led back to the small room where Ludwig is sat in a big leather winged-back chair waiting for me. There is a strikingly handsome male vampire at the back of the room. He completely ignores me as I enter the room. I realise he is another Pretty One, sent to make sure I do not Glamour the Councillor. I think about what this tells me about Chloris, who had confidently interviewed me alone. Ludwig smiles at me and gestures for me to be seated. I perch opposite him and hold out my wrist. Ludwig grabs my arm with his icy grip and without preamble or social niceties, neatly slashes down to the artery with his thumb nail. He leans forward and I feel the sucking at the wound, a low tugging through my arm, which is repulsive and compelling at the same time. His feeding feels immediate and eternal. I swallow down the Rage as I feel his mind flick through my memories, like a clerk through a filing cabinet, looking for an interesting file. The desire to Glamour him and flee this place is almost overpowering. The best way out is through, I remind myself.

His suckling is stopped when the wound heals. I see the temptation to cut me again cross his face, but he restrains himself and leans back in his seat, his eyes rolling back in his head and the reptilian tip of his tongue seeking the last drops of my blood from the corner of his mouth. He makes a leisurely gesture of dismissal.

Each day is the same. Each vampire feeds from me, one each morning and each day my antipathy towards them grows. I hate them knowing all my secrets, but there isn't much I can do about it, although I have learned that if I show a flash of an erotic memory, they will chase after that like a rabbit tail down a burrow, which allows me to distract them from my most intimate parts. It turns out that they can't access any memories from Georgette, a Healer's thoughts are hidden. I'd noticed this when she Healed me, but hadn't really registered it. I envy her the sanctity of her secrets, but the council all enjoy the revitalising effect of her blood and feed from her in turn, just a little so there will be enough for the others.

In the afternoons, after I've been investigated, I go out with Layla into the grounds of the High Council headquarters. There is a degree of comfort in creating our own routine, but still we are low and dispirited, and there doesn't seem any point in ranging further afield. Layla tells me that she and David have decided to stay with the rest of us. Although it is tempting to run from the danger, when they stopped and thought about what that would mean in reality, they had to acknowledge that Guillaume was right; it is no kind of life hiding for forever. They have decided to just hope that the Council will show mercy. They only fought back against those who had attacked them first.

'I'd miss you too much,' Layla confides, patting my hand.

The final day of the feeding dawns. As those of us who are seen in the mornings leave our room, Guillaume steps in behind me.

'I need to speak to you,' he says quietly. I jump out of my skin. I'd known he was behind me, I always know where he is, but I did not expect him to speak to me. He has behaved as if I don't exist most of the time this week, only speaking to me when I asked him a question, and even then hardly glancing in my direction. To be fair, he has hardly spoken to anyone; he is very withdrawn, and seems eaten up with guilt. I want to shake him and scream at him that it isn't his fault, he's done his best.

'Ok,' I agree softly. I have no idea if this is a good thing or not. My heart pounds and I try to stop my imagination galloping off into a torrid fantasy of a last goodbye, Guillaume allowing himself to be lost in me. I am aware of my Glamour thrumming as my arousal rises at the idea. I swallow it down quickly, glad Guillaume is behind me and hasn't witnessed this loss of control. As a human I'd cursed my easy blushes, but this is so much more of a giveaway, and a thousand times more embarrassing.

'Wait for me by the car after you've been seen. We'll go somewhere private,' he says gruffly. Oh God, now what am I supposed to make of that? I quickly swallow the Glamour back down and try to look calm and unflustered as Elaine looks back at us. Her gaze flickers to Guillaume and her eyebrows twitch inquisitively.

***

After the feeding, I wait by the car for him. I've told Layla what he'd said, and she begged me not to get my hopes up. I remind myself of her advice now as I see him coming towards me. I feel my face light up as I smile at him. He looks down and refuses to meet my eyes. Too much, too much, be calm.

'They want to see us at ten tomorrow morning to give their final decision,' he tells me, and then lapses into silence. He drives us out to a huge lake called Helenesee. As he drives, he explains he visited the lake last time the High Council had summoned him. Now there is a campsite where he explored, so he drives us to a wooded area on the other far shore, where there are no other cars. We climb out of the car and walk further into the forest, still in silence. I am obediently following his lead, waiting for him to tell me why he has brought me out there. I long for him to grab me, kiss me, slide his cock inside me. Finally, we reach a secluded clearing. Guillaume stops walking, but keeps his back to me, shoulders thrumming with tension.

'Elaine has told me I am being cruel. She says I should explain to you why I can't love you,' Guillaume speaks quietly, but I hear every word as clearly as a tolling bell. 'I cannot bear to speak aloud what you need to understand, but those malignant gluttons have ferreted through all my secrets, all my shame so you may as well know too. You will feed from me and then you will see.' He turns around and finally looks deep into my eyes. All I can see is his aching sadness, I long to kiss him happy again, but he's just told me he doesn't love me, can't love me. He would not be soothed by my kisses, only repulsed.

'You don't have to,' I say sadly. 'If we survive this, I'll be leaving. Elaine is looking for somewhere else for us to live.'

'I know. I'm sorry. The girls will miss you.'

But not you. I don't say it out loud. I don't need to, it rings in the silence between us.

'Please accept my blood. I wish for you to know what the others know, so you can understand my decision.' Decision? I long to be able to make the decision not to love him. I've had enough; I don't want to argue with him about it any further. I just want to be alone so I can cry without embarrassing myself any further.

Guillaume sits against a tree and pats the earth beside him, my chin rises and I start to turn away from him. I'll walk back to the Council building. He sighs and calls my name with such melancholy that I look back at him. He looks so exhausted and lost that I melt. He pats the ground again, and I see once more the tenderness that I'd witnessed flashes of before we had sex. I give in and sit next to him, carefully not touching him. I cross my legs under me so I can face him, he slits the artery in his right wrist deftly with his left thumb nail and holds his bleeding wrist out to me.

Reluctantly, I drink and I'm immediately swept away in a swirl of images and emotions. It is far more intense than feeding from a human. His blood seems more concentrated, and he has a hundred years of memories surging into me. Twenty as an earnest, hopeful human, and eighty as a vampire. The images flash past too quickly for me to catch more than a passing impression. His early years with Patrice explode into my brain in a decadent orgy of seduction and destruction. Elaine flashes in, concerned and sisterly, followed by the years of self-hatred and guilt and continual gnawing pain from his stunted transformation.

Then I burst on the scene, seductive and delicious as a tropical flower in an arid landscape, but his memories of me

191

are not how I remember myself. In his mind I am permanently coquettish, flashing alluring looks at him, always trying to take more than he is willing to give. Our love making is fraught with his fear of losing himself again. Guillaume wrenches his wrist away from me, and I realise I've grabbed it and have been sucking greedily. I loll back against the tree, his memories blossoming and blooming in my head, like a massive firework display.

I concentrate on his early years with Patrice; they are alluring and addictive, bright with new vampire senses and first love. I watch them work as a team to seduce whole Chateaus of people, plying them with drugs and alcohol, and Compulsion, as they fed and fed in a wanton gluttony. I see sumptuous settings, men and women in velvet and silks, and starker environments with men in uniforms, a whole section of the Nazis army one day, Allied soldiers the next, innocent boys wickedly lured to their willing deaths. I am reluctant to give up the memories: the physical desires for blood, and sex, and the hunt they've roused in me are compelling. It is dark when I finally come back to myself. Guillaume is sat silently beside me, his legs triangled in front of him, his arms resting on his knees, and his chin sunk onto his arms. All his boundaries are up.

'You see?' he asks as I come round.

'I would never make you do those things,' I protest.

'But you could,' he replies simply. 'And I promised myself, and the High Council, that I would never, ever, put myself in that position again.'

'You have a very low opinion of me,' I say sadly as I drag myself up the tree until I'm upright, my head is still woozy with memories, but I am loathe to put Guillaume into a position where he has to offer me assistance out of chivalry.

'Would you feed from me, so you can see I would never do those things to you?' I ask hopefully, holding my wrist towards him. He recoils in horror shaking his head, and strides off in front of me, out of the forest.

It is an uncomfortable journey back to the High Council. My head is filled with his memories, and I know he will be aware of that. It feels horribly intimate, like leaking the sperm of a man who has just dumped you. Once we get back, I can't bear to go indoors and sit in the shared room with everyone else, so without a word to him, I bumble off and I find myself a quiet corner of the garden to hide in.

My heart is breaking into a thousand razor sharp pieces. I know there was no point arguing with him, because I know that if the roles were reversed, I wouldn't be able to take the risk either. To open your heart to someone who could turn you into a monster like that would be impossible. It wouldn't matter if they promised not to, you would be completely reliant on them not to go against their word, and that wasn't a risk I would take, so how could I expect anyone else to? I remember my fears when I was first changed and how I thought that I would kill myself rather than slaughter innocents.

Guillaume has to live every day knowing he had killed in voracious numbers, in orgies of death and depraved sex. I have experienced his memories as a young human, full of hope and plans for his future. He had never experienced love as a human. At twenty he was still a virgin when he was turned, uncomfortable even in touching himself in those severe times. Since his time with Patrice, he had refused all sexual advances. Patrice had frequently made herself available to him, but although the temptation had boiled in him, he had turned her down each time.

It was after the final time he said no to her that she turned Suzannah. She had flaunted her new toy in front of him, enticingly sexual, enticingly fragrant with human blood from their hunts. They would recount their stories within his earshot. It had taken every drop of his self-control to refuse them. I was the first vampire he had made love to in over sixty years, so it is no wonder she hated me.

Sitting in a blood-induced stupor in the garden, I allow myself to unfurl the memories I had not been able to bear witnessing in front of him. I see myself through his eyes, a nondescript human nuisance first of all, who was in the wrong place at the wrong time, an extra problem for him to sort out. Then I feel his horror as we awoke and he realised we were pretty ones. I relive his disgust and entrancement; his fear and lust when I turned my enchanting eyes upon him. In his memory I seemed to spend every moment we were in each

193

other's company being deliberately seductive. Times when I was sure I had been playing it cool, ignoring him as best I could and only shooting the quickest glances his way through my eyelashes, he remembers me as lash battingly, hip swayingly provocative. He felt hunted, terrified he would succumb to my charms and fall as deeply under my control as he had been under Patrice's.

Heartbreakingly, the time I was furious about the other New Ones killing the homeless man in the barn, he had seen me as magnificent, my arrogant beauty heightened in its irresistibility by the desire for the chase, and the scent of warm fresh blood. But my refusal to feed despite the temptation won his admiration. My Rage in defence of my friends in the Great Hall with Patrice and her vicious kits had warmed him towards me further. The night I had danced out my pain after seeing James I had had no idea that Guillaume's vampire eyes would be able to see me from his bedroom.

He'd caught sight of me storming up the hill, and then sat on the end of his bed to watch. At first, he had been confused by the strange contortions I was flinging myself into, but as he watched, became amused as he realised I was dancing with such gusto and abandon. When Layla appeared from the tree line and I tenderly put the headphone into her ear and checked she was comfortable before we launched into our comedy routines, which were made more effortless and attractive by our vampire grace, but were none the less silly and funny to watch, he'd laughed out loud.

His distrust of me thawed and he had come to my room despite himself. Telling himself he just wanted to check I was ok, denying his swollen, throbbing cock, which had engorged as soon as he gave in and allowed himself to decide to visit me. As he entered my bedroom and saw my naked back as I lay in bed with my blankets around my hips, it was rigid against his stomach, but still he told himself that he could just sit on the side of my bed and soothe me. When I did as he asked, and remained on my side he was unable to resist, and found himself doing what he had promised himself he wouldn't do. As I writhed and sobbed my climax under his fingers, he was unable to resist sliding into the warm damp depths of me and when he came with an all-engulfing intensity within seconds of my rocking myself against him, he blamed my Glamour, convinced I had bewitched him, and abused his offering of friendship in an attempt to control him.

After the array of memories and emotions I've witnessed, I concede that there is nothing I could ever do or say to dissuade him. I cry for him that night. I cry for the lost boy he had been. I cry for his years of pain and guilt; and I cry for myself, for the distorted memories he has of me, for the stupid hopes I've harboured right up to the end. I owe Elaine a debt of gratitude for releasing me from the futility of that hope. She's known all along how pointless my feelings have been and has been decent enough to put me out of my misery. The process was brutal, but it is the only way I would stop hoping. I can't stop loving him. That would take time, if I have any left, if I ever can stop loving him; but at least I wouldn't be hindered by hope anymore.

Layla

Rae's beautiful face is as enigmatic as ever as she joins the rest of us in the ante-chamber next to the Hall. I know her, though, and when she won't meet my eyes, and her fingers rub convulsively at the hem of her cuff, I know there is something very wrong. This is beyond just turning Glamour down, and she isn't scared. I realise with horror that she is utterly resigned. What the hell has Guillaume told her? What does she know?

I clutch David's hand tighter, suddenly wishing with every ounce of my being that we had run while we had the chance. It's all very well being noble and standing alongside the others, but I don't want to die. I didn't even really do anything wrong, no one would have cared about my tiny part in the battle. David hardly did anything at all, I mean he pulled a couple of heads off, but they attacked him, it was self-defence.

I look around, but there are no windows in this room, and one of the huge guards is by the door. I calculate if David and I could take him between us, I think we can. But then we'd have to get out of the building without being caught, and I don't think we could do that. Rae has plastered on a smile and is behaving cheerfully with the other vampires.

I tug David's arm and tow him over to stand beside Rae. I need to know what she knows, I've suddenly decided that dying fighting, at least trying to break free is better than a vicious slash from behind like last time. Rae starts babbling about the beauty of the lake she saw with Guillaume. I look at her in disbelief; who does she think I am? She sees my glare and tells me that Guillaume has asked me to look after Annie and Georgette if anything happens to him. I am about to demand to know what else she isn't telling me when we are called through to the hall. Terror rips through me, it's too late to run.

Rae

I no longer really care what they tell us. I know I should care for the sake of the others, but I am so deflated and miserable I can't find the energy to. The High Council are in their usual seats as we are led into the hall, and the six beasts line the back wall.

'This has been a complicated case,' Adelfried says without preamble, once we are assembled. 'We have had to weigh up the rules that were broken against the motives for breaking them, and the morals and behaviour of those who were killed. We have decided that given the extent of your co-operation, we will waive all punishment in this situation. But be warned all of you: there can be no excuse for this behaviour again. If anything happens, at all outside the norm, you will contact us and discuss the appropriate response.' The other vampires sag with relief as he smiles benignly upon them. I can only stare down the bleak infinity of my future in despair.

'You are dismissed,' laughs Adelfried. 'Except Rae. We wish to speak to you further.' There's a collective intake of breath, and my head shoots up and I look quickly at Guillaume, I can't help it; I still turn to him for guidance and comfort instinctively. His eyes meet mine for once, and I see fear there.

'The rest of you may leave. I'm sure Rae will be capable of driving herself back, if she wishes. We can lend her a car,' Adelfried continues. I frown, what on earth is he talking about?

'I'll wait,' Simon says. 'The others can go in the camper. If Rae is coming back, I'll drive her; if not, I'll drive alone.' He speaks quietly, but firmly, and it brooks no argument. I am stunned; of all the vampires to stick up for me, I would never have expected it to be Simon who fought my corner.

Once the rest of the Pride has left the hall, the five Council members lead me into one of the lounges and gesture for me to sit down, then arrange themselves around me on the sofas. Simon is left waiting on a hard chair in the hallway.

'We wanted to speak to you, Rae,' Ula tinkles. 'We know from all that we have seen that you cannot remain with the rest of the Pride. We have seen that you have a wisdom and moral code we appreciate. You have the recognition of the role that rules need to take within a society that only exists in a small percentage of the population. You are also a natural leader.' I shake my head fiercely at this suggestion. 'Yes, you are. A true leader leads not because they desire power, but because they cannot bear what will happen if they don't. People follow them not because they must but because they wish to. Even here, when Georgette was commanded to heal the guard, your enemy in that moment, she looked to you first before complying.'

'You are a New One, and have only lived at the farm for a few months, but within that time you have dealt with the vicious vampires Guillaume never had the strength to tackle, you organised and implemented a hunting process that protects not only the Pride but also the vulnerable humans you still care about. You have arranged for the sickly vampires of

197

the pride to be healed and ensured that Georgette has a role that allows her to forgive herself for what she did when she was first turned. It was you who distrusted the Spanish visitors, and the three bitches, as you have so eloquently named them, and it was you who presented evidence of your concerns, which was ignored. Your instinct throughout was to tell the truth and deal with the consequences honestly, rather than try to lie your way out of trouble.'

'That's a very simplified version of events,' I protest.

'That's as maybe, but we wish to offer you a place within our headquarters, and then with time and training, maybe you could join our select group of reserves, and ultimately one day you could actually be a member of the High Council itself,' Ula smiles her Poseidon smile and I stare at her in amazement; this is very much unexpected.

'We know you have asked Elaine to help you and your friends find somewhere else to live. I think you need to consider how difficult it would be for another Pride to even consider taking you. You are a large group. You and Layla are Pretty Ones. No one trusts Pretty Ones. You have killed your maker and others. You have been brought before the Council within months of being made. Your reputation is not going to make you popular. I don't think anyone will take you.'

I think about staying here and never having to return to the farm, even temporarily. Not having to see Guillaume's shoulders sag with disappointment as I climb out of Simon's car with him or worry about finding somewhere else to live. To know that Layla will be safe with the other New Ones in Guillaume's Pride. I am the only problem. This offer would solve so many problems.

I think about staying here, contemplating the rooms and rooms of bored-looking vampires, who never once approached us, and didn't speak to any of us, who followed their orders to the letter even when it meant hurting and being hurt. I remember how greedily the council found an excuse to gorge on our memories. I think about why I'd always chosen to work on the frontline in Probation, never following up offers to train for a management position. I am good at doing the stuff that made a good manager, but I hate it.

I think about staying here, and my stomach clenches and I know I can't do it. Becoming a vagabond and living in the wild so I don't cause any more trouble for my friends is better than taking up the High Council's offer. They have over-simplified what had happened at the farm to flatter me, and they have over-simplified my choices.

'No, thank you,' I say politely, smiling broadly. I might not want to accept their offer, but it's still nice to be wanted.

'Oh! Really?' Chloris and the others look shocked at my decision. 'You don't have to decide straight away.'

'No, it's ok. I'm sure.'

'Well, if you change your mind, at any time. You know where we are. Where we always are.' Ludwig seems almost maudlin that I'm not staying. I don't want to think about why.

I turn to leave while the leaving is still good. They are offering the hand of friendship to me, but I still do not trust the Council vampires, or their intentions.

'Rae, be aware of the chameleon,' Chloris calls after me.

'Yes,' I think to myself as I slip through the door. I'll be keeping a close eye on the three bitches, they can pretend to be part of the Pride as much as they want, trying to merge in, but I'll be aware all right. Simon looks up and smiles as I swing in into the hallway where he is waiting.

'Come on then,' I chirrup.

Chapter 10
Rae

Two days after my return to the farm, Elaine calls Layla and me into the lounge where she explains to us that Guillaume is buying a remote cottage in Brittany with his business which we can then buy off him, paying him back slowly, as if it was a normal mortgage. Buying with the business hides our identities and allows everything to be done online. Elaine has found us the perfect place, which is for sale furnished and very cheap. It will take several weeks for the paperwork to go through, but it is empty, so the owners are happy to rent it until the sale goes through. There is even a little Renault included in the sale price. Elaine explains that the cottage had belonged to some Brits who'd bought it without researching the area. They have done a lovely renovation and furnished it beautifully, but it is too far from anything to attract tourists, so their gite dream has failed. They are delighted to find a quick sale and walk away without actually making a loss, so they are more than happy to help as much as possible to ensure a smooth sale.

I am a bit annoyed that we haven't been given any choice at all in the property, but Layla points out that there aren't going to be many properties as perfect as this one: available right when we need it, at a very low price, in a safe location. Layla reminds me that Elaine had been a vampire for much longer than us and knows what to be aware of. She also knows the French property system, and can negotiate for us in a way we couldn't with our vague grasp of how the French buying process works. I can't really argue with these points, and so the next time I see Elaine, I thank her graciously for her help, her help with Guillaume implicit by unspoken. He has hidden from me the entire time we've been back at the farm, but at least I know enough this time to have hoped for anything different.

Hideously early in the morning two days later, Simon loads everyone into his car, along with our bags and we leave with little fuss. Most of the Pride are still asleep, we said our goodbyes last night. Initially, Annie and Georgette had wanted to come with us, but I gently pointed out that there isn't really space, and we don't know how we are going to pay our own way yet, never mind look after two more. I love both girls dearly, but I am in no fit state to be responsible for teenagers, even vampire teenagers. I need a rest. They are the only ones who had seemed sad to see us go, but they have each other, so they were quickly distracted from their disappointment with an invite to come to stay and David creating them a Facebook profile each- their first genuine ones, with us as their first friends.

We sat in the kitchen with Elaine yesterday afternoon and made sure everything was in place so that Guillaume's money would arrive into his account by standing order every month. Elaine spoke of it as the farm's money, but we all knew it was his. It was also implicit that although there was a high level of trust involved in the arrangement, there would be no glitches on either side; there would be no need to speak about the agreement again. We'd kept our British bank accounts as it was far too difficult now to open new ones. It would cost us a bit extra to make the transfer with my FairFX account, but it would be better than making an individual payment each month through PayPal, and having to think of him. We had transferred all the bills for the cottage into my name and set up the direct debits so all the bills would be paid without anyone ever coming near the house; we even arranged for online bills.

Right up until we left, I couldn't help but hope that Guillaume would come out and say goodbye, but he doesn't. Furiously reminding myself of his memories and the logic behind his decision worked for a few minutes, convincing me he wouldn't, couldn't, say goodbye in person, but then I would find hope sneaking back in again, especially if I let myself think of the fear in his eyes when the Council had asked me to stay behind. Despite myself, my heart pounds in my chest as we drive away, and I feel like I can't breathe for the first half an hour of the journey. My thoughts whirl with loss around my head, like little birds trapped in a room without windows. Sitting in the front passenger seat of the car, I turn my face away from the others, and rest my forehead on the cold glass, staring out of the side window as I struggle to centre myself, until eventually, I can laugh bitterly at my own stupidity, and breathe again.

No one speaks to me throughout the journey, and I am grateful for their mercy, as I remind myself over and over that with the exception of Annie and Georgette, I will never have to see any of the Pride again. It takes us almost ten hours to reach the cottage. Although the journey feels like every mile is ripping my heart out further, I am glad of the distance between us and the other vampires. I know that distance and time are my only hope of recovery, and let's be honest, one thing I have plenty of now, is time. By the time we reach our new home, I am starting to feel cautiously optimistic, in a battered, fragile, sort of way.

I'm surprised and delighted by the little house as we finally drive down the private lane, and park in front of the low stone longere. I hadn't bothered looking at any of the photographs online before we came; when I wasn't offered any choice in the selection of my new home, there hadn't seemed much point. I can see now how churlish I've been. Elaine has shown a softer side choosing this little home for us; maybe she is fonder of us than I thought.

It nestles snuggly in its pretty garden, soaking up the early evening sun, its little cobalt blue shutters like sleepy eyelids. It is utterly charming, with tumbling roses around the door, and a honeysuckle and jasmine hedge bordering the front garden from the lane. I climb out of the car, and stretch for the pleasure of feeling my limbs flex, and suck in a lungful of the fresh country air: high top notes of floral perfumes, with musky base notes of cow shit, and somewhere quite nearby, a stinky cheese maker. Opening my chest wide, I inhale and exhale great invigorating yoga breaths, and fling back my head. I am swept away by the colours, and the space, as the warm breeze plays over my skin, and just like that, I fall in love with our new home.

'Tell Elaine I love it. Absolutely love it.' I open my eyes and look at Simon, smiling broadly and holding eye contact so he can see I'm genuinely delighted. I see his eyes start to glaze and quickly catch myself, turning my Glamour back off full beam. Simon looks a bit sheepish, but nods brusquely and unloads our bags from the boot. We offer him a rest before he heads back, but he refuses and quickly drives away with a final wave from the driver's window as he turns up the lane. So here we are, all by ourselves. I feel my shoulders drop, and hope bloom in my heart as I grin at Layla.

After a frozen moment as we look at each other in anticipation, we rush in to investigate our little cottage. It is unexpectedly spacious, and the rooms are golden with sunlight dappling through the windows. The renovation has been beautifully done, keeping all the traditional charm and just adding mod cons. The rooms are all painted warm cream to pick up the warmth from the light, and the furniture is an eclectic mix of chunky old farmhouse pine and some finer pieces of mahogany and rosewood. The kitchen is a delicious Wedgewood blue with good oak cupboards and a wood-burning range. I am filled with delight until it dawns on me that we won't actually use this room. No more cooking for me. Oh well - it can become an office I decide. The big farmhouse table with elm benches will be prefect for our computers.

After a brief squabble, we manage to share out the bedrooms relatively fairly: I get the slightly larger room at the front of the cottage that floods with sunshine in the afternoons because the others want the rooms at the back of the house that look over the big wraparound garden and little river. The cottage sits in the middle of an acre of land, with an orchard, a Beatrix Potter vegetable patch, and a sweeping lawn which slopes gently down to the stream with weeping willow lined banks. It doesn't take long to move our sparse belongings in. Most of what we brought to France doesn't fit us anymore, and nobody really wanted to bring the other vampires' cast-offs we had been lent at the farm. I left mine freshly laundered and folded on the bed in the room I used during my stay.

We don't need much, though, everything necessary for the house is included in the sale, even bedding and curtains. We've bought a couple of outfits each on eBay, when we could get Annie to let us near a computer. Until we have a better idea of where our income will be coming from, we can't risk spending any more money. I am determined we will never miss a repayment to Guillaume and his Pride.

Once we are unpacked, we go outside to explore. In front of the house is a flat area, the section closest to the house is fenced in with a low white picket fence that runs the length of the house and there are slabs of creamy limestone set in golden pebbles, with scented herbs in the pots and window boxes. There are two white cast-benches under each picture-book window. In front of this is the paved area we stopped the car in earlier and beyond that a lawn that slopes gently upwards to the boundary fence, with another larger bench set on a concrete plateau half way up. This huge front garden is separated from our lane by the scented hedge, and the wide white cast iron gate we closed behind Simon as he drove off.

Beside the house, connected to it, is a tiny barn with the laundry facilities, and next to that, at a right angle is a larger open-sided black corrugated iron hangar, where we discover our little bottle green Renault Clio with the keys trustingly left in the ignition. Through the hangar and out the other side we meander, and find the access to the rest of the garden as it wraps around the cottage and rolls gently down to the stream. There are no other houses to be seen: the nearest neighbour is almost a mile away, and the village is almost three miles away, which is perfect for us. We are nestled in a dip, surrounded with fields of cows, so we know that slipping out at night to feed won't be a problem. The blood will be bitter, but no one will be killed on our behalf, and no one will see us leaving or returning.

Layla

A week later, when are settled in and we feel thoroughly at home, Rae and I finally open our emails. We are pleased to see that our fabricated arguments with our university friends have worked. Neither of us has a single email from any of them. They're safe. Rae replies to her parents and sister. She doesn't write much, just tells them about a few places we've looked up on Trip Advisor and pretend we'd visited. Mainly, we both just put lots of cheery posts on Facebook for everyone to see with lots of pictures of local wild life and pretty sunsets. David helps me to Photoshop some pictures of myself from the journey down to Tours into some of the pictures of local settings, and Rae even manages to persuade Brian to let him edit some old pictures of him so his hair colour is different, and he looks less sporty, so everyone can see the great new man she had run away from James for. I do the same with pictures of myself and David. I don't have to worry about anyone missing me particularly, I have Rae with me, but some convincing pictures on Facebook are good to deflect nosey colleagues.

I open a couple of emails from my friends asking how I am getting on, I send cheery replies, mentioning the posts I've put on Facebook, claiming the internet service is bad in our new home, so not to panic if they can't get hold of me. I reassure them that Rae and I are having the time of our lives. I don't let myself think about what will happen when Rae's family want to visit, it doesn't happen often at the best of times, and we will be able to deflect them a few times, but eventually it will hit crunch time. Rae is too distracted with relief that there were no emails from James, to consider this, and I'm not going to be the one to point it out to her. We'll cross that bridge once we get to it.

The good news is that I found an email from my boss. She has stopped sulking and is missing my organisation skills, so she is offering me freelance admin work. There isn't a huge amount of it, and it doesn't pay terribly well. Rae proposed a similar idea to her old boss, her dislike of asking for special consideration outweighed by the anxiety that there would be no other way to make the monthly repayments. She has been offered bits and pieces, so between us we can cover the monthly repayment to Guillaume. David had more difficulty getting some work because the wife he had seemingly just abandoned out of the blue works in the same office as he had. Most of his old team's loyalty, understandably, lay with her. Finally, after some dubious explanations about midlife crisis, and seeing the light, his male boss allowed some bits and bobs to filter through to him. He is too good for them to lose. It pays a lot better than our work, so when we pool all our income together, we are fine.

With our finances sorted, we quickly settle into a routine. We can buy everything we need over the internet, and the postman delivers it into our post-box at the end of our lane, which twists off the slightly larger lane leading out from the village and off into the countryside. Our bins need to be taken into the village and put into communal wheelie bins and recycling bins - common practise in rural Brittany. We don't really have much other than the packaging from what we buy online, so we decide we had better make some to avoid arousing suspicion.

We order some self-adhesive mirrored panels for the car windows, and Brian sticks them into the Clio. They end up bubbled and flawed, but at least no one can see into the car. Every now and again I cover up well, turn the glamour down as low as I can, and whizz around the local supermarket just before lunch time closing to buy the cleaning products we need, and food we don't. I adopt a floaty, arty look, with lots of scarves and draping to flick and flap and hide behind. I wear a pungent perfume of Sandalwood and Neroli so the stench keeps people away, and the combination of crazy clothes and heavy scent adds to the overall impression we give of being crazy English. We have made no attempt to have any contact with the neighbours and rudely refuse all their initial friendly approaches. They eventually decided we are impolite English, living in very dubious sexual circumstances, and ignore us.

The day after my shopping trips I add whatever David and I have harvested from our garden to the shopping bags, wait until late afternoon and then drive into the nearby city of Pontivy and drop the food off at the Emmaus homeless charity crisis centre. It is easy to get all the information I need online, so I could contact them before my first visit and tell them I have a disability and can't get out of my car easily. They are too grateful for the donations to ask questions about why a do-gooder drops off a box of groceries every couple of weeks. Soon it becomes routine. I phone them just before I leave home, then as I pull up outside, I toot the horn and pop the boot so the staff can take the boxes and bags without seeing any more than the back of my head, and my gloved hand as I wave away their thanks.

Rae

Shortly after we move into the cottage, I am adopted by a slender little silver cat that I call Babette. She is dainty and sweet-natured, and she enthrals me. Her little paw is only the size of the pad of my thumb and she meows like a little bell. I expect someone to come looking for her, and fearfully ask Layla to check the notices at the front of the supermarket where people offer babysitting and firewood, but she is never mentioned on there, so I relax and love her. She looks at me with her earnest little face while she paws my lap and I drop my face down so she can biff me with the side of her face, utterly trusting.

I go online, and buy her treats but Babette and I quickly discover that what we like to do best is hunt together. Sometimes I share what we catch with her, I don't like rabbit, their vegetarian diet makes their blood as tart as sheep and cows', but I find that omnivorous rat's blood tastes better and these are clean country rats, in plentiful supply. I decide I like them so much that I go online and arrange for a bag of rabbit food to be delivered each month with the cat food, and I use it to lure them into the little barn besides the house, and I leave bits of meat around so their blood will be sweeter. Of an evening Babette and I settle down quietly to await our prey, happily spending dusky hours together selecting our prey and thrilling at the hunt. The others think I'm bonkers, and Layla accuses me of taking my ambition to grow up to be a crazy old cat lady too far, but she is laughing while she says it and I'm enjoying myself, so I don't care. They can enjoy their cow blood, I'll hunt for rats.

As we settle in, we each find our roles within our tender new Pride. I do the paperwork side of things, and my admin work. Layla and David are doing their paid work too, then they spend their afternoons in the garden, having found a passion for growing in the fertile ground. Layla enjoys her forays into the outside world on her supermarket and charity trips, she comes back pink and shining with the adrenaline of the adventure, the risk of being seen. Brian does some bits of DIY, walks up to collect the post every morning, and takes the bins into town one evening a week, but most of the time he mopes around feeling sorry for himself. I often stumble over the tools he's bought over the internet to do some little job, which he'll start, and then wander off from, midway through. I find my irritation with him growing.

This little cottage was perfect when we moved in, and now in an attempt to find himself something to do, Brian is tinkering, and starting lots of little things which looked fine to me before he started meddling. As soon as any job he starts gets a bit tricky, or even if it just takes longer than he expects, he gets bored and mopes off, leaving the tools he's used nearby. Whenever I ask why nothing is finished, there is always an excuse- he has to wait for this to arrive, or that to set, but still nothing is ever finished.

The final straw comes when I finish a particularly long and boring piece of data entry and decide to recover with a nice scented bath only to find my bedroom door minus its door handle, and stripped of paint, a clutter of scrappers and screwdrivers littering my threshold, along with the curls of stripped paint and the screws from my door handle, one of which I'd just trodden on.

'What the hell are you playing at?' I yell when I finally find him, out in the orchard stroking Babette. 'How dare you do that to my door without asking? What the fuck do you think you're playing at? Every time I turn around, you've destroyed something else and left a mess for the rest of us to clear up after you!' Babette scampers off as soon as I raise my voice. 'You are absolutely doing my head in.' As I shout at him, to my amazement, Brian seems to shrink and merge in with the grass he's sitting on and tree he's leaning against. 'Brian? What the fuck, you're disappearing!'

Layla and David arrive, drawn by my raised voice from the front garden, where they had been watering the flower beds for the evening; they gawp in amazement as I appear to be shouting at a tree. As my voice registers anxiety instead of anger, Brian slowly slips back into focus.

I think back to the time we had fought with the other new ones, how it had taken me several minutes to find Brian and Georgette and then they had suddenly been where I had expected them to be. At the time I had thought it was the twilight, shadows and high anxiety that had stopped me seeing them immediately. I remember the number of times I have gone into the kitchen to make myself a coffee - I can't drink it but I still find comfort in cradling the warm mug in my hands and smelling the fragrant brew - and then I'll turn from pouring it and leap out of my skin when I see that Brian has been sat at the table, on his laptop the whole time.

'Oh my God, Brian, you're like a chameleon!' I gasp, staring at him in shock, as Chloris's message when I left the High Council suddenly makes more sense. 'Be aware of the chameleon!'

'Jesus, mate,' David breathes next to me. 'That's one hell of a gift. Did you know you could do it?' Brian is blinking owlishly and looking baffled.

'No, I thought people were annoyed with me because I couldn't get any work. I thought everyone was ignoring me, only speaking to me when it would be outright rude not to. That's why I kept trying to find things to do to be useful.' He looks so sad and anxious when he explains himself that my heart goes out to him.

'Bri, we just couldn't see you, mate.' Layla giggles. 'Why didn't you say something? You've got your jobs to do, which make you part of the household, but if you want more, just say and we'll give them to you; but please, stop fixing things!'

We all head back to the house laughing, and Brian makes us a firm promise that he will go round and finish all the jobs he has started, starting with my door. He agrees he will tidy up after himself and always put his tools away when he's finished for the day, even if he needs to get them back out the next day. We ask him what else he would like to do and it is agreed he will take over the laundry and housework while the rest of us did our paid work. Everyone is happy with our arrangement, and Brian seems relieved to have talked to us about his worries.

The next day before starting my admin work, I seize the moment and spend an hour with Brian pointing out that holding himself responsible for what we did in the river meadow when we were first changed is unreasonable. He was completely out of control of his faculties at that time and had had no idea that a friendly kiss on the cheek would have that outcome. Neither of us had had any idea that would happen. And, I point out, since we have known, we have steadfastly avoided any chance of physical contact at all.

Brian cheers up a bit once he can accept it wasn't his fault, and I've reassured him he is still welcome within our Pride. From then on, he is slightly less morose, although he still spends a lot of time on Facebook. His fiancée hasn't blocked him, and although he assures us he never posts anything on her page or sends her any messages, he admits that he monitors her statuses closely for any mention of how she is and what she is doing. He lives in hope, and dread, of reading that she is over him and has met someone else.

David and Layla are still slightly sickening; newly in love and totally engrossed in each other, trailing round the gardens together trowels in hand, giggling, spraying each other with the hoses, throwing the windblown apples at each other. I can't blame her though, I have never seen her as happy as when she is sat curled up in his lap with his big strong arms around her, while she chatters on about this or that. He will meet my gaze over her head and smile at me with all his love for her in his face. I smile back at them and leave them in peace. She has finally found someone good enough for her.

I have a lot of free time. The admin work doesn't take me long, and my needs are few now I don't eat and can't dream. I spend a lot of time languidly scrolling through pages on the net, sniffing my coffee, or lounging in a hot bath scented with the tiniest drop of pure flower essence. The essences are breathtakingly expensive, but I only need such a small amount thanks to my vampire senses that I treat myself. Synthetic bubble baths sting my nose and leave an acrid chemical scent on my hair which I hate, but with the natural oils I get delicious wafts of rose, honeysuckle or jasmine when the breeze lifts my locks.

As winter folds us into earlier evenings, I settle into this slow, sweet routine, getting up when I wake, going for a walk or a swim depending on my mood, since the cold doesn't hurt me, and just offers a new range of sensations. I come back to do whatever admin work needs doing. In the afternoons I read or watch TV, sometimes we play card games, or Scrabble. In the later evenings I might hunt, or curl up with Babette and a good book on the eReader I ordered off the internet. Unlike the first time Layla and I stayed in France two decades ago when I was desperate for books in English, the eReader means I can access books from all around the world. My quick vampire mind means that with a little effort I can learn other languages and enjoy literature in its first language so the subtle cultural nuances aren't lost in translation. I have discovered that although I can't dream anymore, I can still enjoy reading, it is like escaping into the dreams of others.

I have a rule, I can only think of Guillaume for an allotted time of an evening. Any time my mind slides towards him during the day I remind myself I can only think of him then. It's a technique I learned to survive Seb leaving. I refuse to let thoughts of him take over my life. I know that if I let myself, I will persuade myself there could still be hope, and then I will allow anticipation to swell each time I check my emails. It takes time, it's hard work, but eventually I am able to reduce the time I need to think of him by a few minutes each week, until I can manage on just a few minutes each evening. I still need to set an alarm, and step into an ice cold shower immediately to startle myself out of the churning trough my brain sinks into. Then I turn the shower to warm, drop some of my essences onto the sponge, and self soothe with delicious strokes.

We moved into our little home in late summer, and spent autumn settling in and finding our routine. We spend a short, comfortable winter round the roaring log fire in the lounge, and we rejoice as spring arrives quickly in comparison to the long wet Welsh winters we were used to; bringing with it the lambs and calves, and baby birds; and buds and butterflies and the scent of new growth and moist soil.

One day I am seated in the garden, leaning my back on a cushion propped against a fallen tree trunk in the orchard. I am completely engrossed in a new Barbara Kingsolver novel on my eReader, with Babette asleep and purring on my lap, a warm trusting weight in the hammock of my skirt. The early spring sun warms my shoulders and the back of my head. I look up from my reading, and slide my gaze over the blossoming and blooming garden, it dawns on me that I am happy. This self-contained life has made me truly content.

Layla

'Oh my God. I am so bloody bored,' I groan to David. 'We never do anything, or go anywhere.'

'I could take us to see everyone at the farm if you like?' he answers uncertainly. I stare at him in bewilderment.

'That's not fun,' I exclaim. 'It has never been a week in my life without going out before. Even when I was ill, I'd get to the chemists.'

'You go to the shops and the hostel every week.'

'But I don't get to speak to anyone,' I say. 'And no one ever bats an eyelid; I don't know what Rae is so paranoid about. We could go clubbing, it'd be dark, everyone would be drunk, no one would notice that we're different. Oh come on, we'd have so much fun.'

'You know we can't. You know the rules.'

'But I want to dance with you,' I wriggle against him, turning my glamour up just a smidge. Even as he shakes his head, I see his eyes soften as his cock stiffens and presses against me. 'No one would ever know.'

'We can dance right here,' he growls nibbling my neck.

This time we will, I concede silently as I cleave to him, but there's always next time.

Author Bio

Chloe Hammond is an Aquarius, very Aquarius. Born in Liverpool in 1975, she grew up in West Wales, but now lives in Barry in South Wales, with her husband and rescue cats and dogs. She always wanted to write, but life got in the way. Last year she was diagnosed with extreme anxiety and depression, which caused nightmares and sleepless nights. In her typically contrary way she used this to her advantage and the nightmares became this novel, and the sleepless nights were when she found time to write it.

She has a lovely sea view from her desk, which she gazes at to still her mind so her characters can burst forth and have their say. This is her first novel, but Rae and Layla are demanding book two and three in the trilogy are written as soon as possible, they have adventures to live.

Hi,

Did you enjoy Darkly Dreaming? If so I would be very grateful if you could leave review on Amazon, Goodreads or Mineeye for me. The best chance an author has of encouraging new readers to give them a chance is from the reviews other readers leave them.

If you would like to find out more about me, and my writing you can contact me, or follow my writing progress at any of the social media links below:

Links:

Website:- www.chloehammondauthor.com
Email address:- books@chloehammondauthor.com

Facebook:-
www.facebook.com/chloehammondauthor
www.facebook.com/pages/Darkly-Dreaming/750124258345038
Tumblr:-
https://www.tumblr.com/blog/chloehammondauthor
Twitter:- @chloehammond111
Linkedin:-
www.linkedin.com/pub/chloe-hammond/91/8b6/b50

I look forward to hearing from you,

Thanks,

Chloe

Made in the USA
Charleston, SC
22 February 2016